300 NEW YEAR'S EVES

K.C. CARMICHAEL

This book is a work of fiction. Any references to historical events, real people, or real places are used fictitiously. Other names, characters, places, and events are products of the author's imagination, and any resemblance to actual events, places, names, or persons, is entirely coincidental.

Text copyright © 2025 by K.C. Carmichael

All rights reserved. For information regarding reproduction in total or in part, contact Rising Action Publishing Co. at http://www.risingactionpublishingco.com

Cover Illustration © Cover Ever After
Distributed by Simon & Schuster

ISBN: 978-1-998672-06-6
Ebook: 978-1-998672-07-3

FIC027190   FICTION / Romance / LGBTQ+ / Gay
FIC027650   FICTION / Romance / Second Chances
FIC027090   FICTION / Romance / Time Travel

#300NYES #300NewYearsEves

Follow Rising Action on our socials!
Twitter: @RAPubCollective
Instagram: @risingactionpublishingco
Tiktok: @risingactionpublishingco

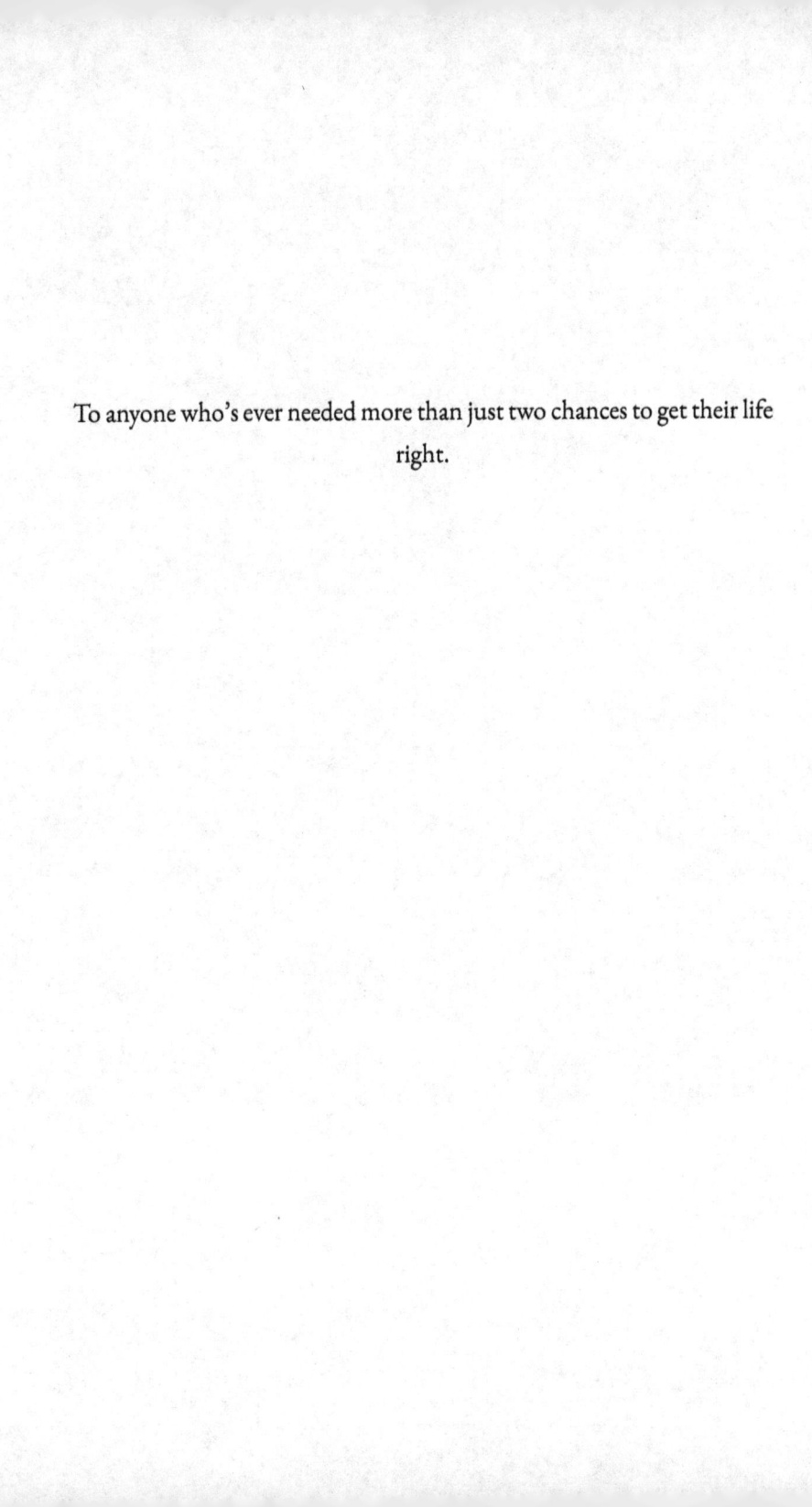

To anyone who's ever needed more than just two chances to get their life right.

300 NEW YEAR'S EVES

Chapter One

Through the lens of a camera, Sergio focuses on a tall, spindly, young brunette with legs for days. She's dressed in a red Dior gown that hangs off her collarbones, cascades to the floor, and trails behind her. Beside her hovers a man dressed in a sharp black suit. He's as tall as she is in her heels, but not nearly as willowy. He's narrow, with an angular body and face. His eyes, distant and unbothered, contrast with the brightness and hope in hers. They're new to the fashion world, and Sergio Durand, the man behind the camera, loves fresh meat.

He can't wait to wrap up this shoot and get either of their legs, perhaps even both, wrapped around his torso later. In his mind, it's one of the perks of being a sought-after photographer. There's always a new and pretty face around, eager to hang off his arm wherever he goes. And being a New Yorker, he goes everywhere and is always in need of someone new to keep him company. His dates, like these Dior ensembles currently being photographed, lose their relevance after one night out on the town.

An audible exasperated sigh comes from behind Sergio, followed by the impatient tapping of a foot wearing Italian leather loafers. He doesn't need to turn around to know that not only is his younger brother, Adrien, who functions as Sergio's assistant, doing the tapping, but that he's also compulsively checking his watch.

"Do I need to remind you how tight a schedule we're on?"

Without looking at his brother, Sergio waves him off with his free hand, causing Adrien to let out a groan of annoyance. He pulls the camera away from his eye and looks at the two models.

"Ignore him," he says, eyeing the models up and down. He lets his gaze linger on the young woman's bare legs peeking out of the dress's slits, then moves to check out the way the young man's ass looks. High and tight. "I have all the time in the world for you two."

"No, you don't," Adrien mutters loud enough for only Sergio to hear.

It's December thirtieth, the last day of work for the year, and these photos, which will be used for Dior's upcoming Valentine's Day campaign, need to be forwarded on through the promotional chain for approval before the close of the business day—inconveniently cut shorter by the fact that the Durand brothers have a chartered flight to catch in two hours. Unbothered by the time deadline, Sergio flirts incorrigibly with the two models who are barely old enough to get a drink to ring in the New Year.

"Alright," Sergio says, holding the camera out to his side for Adrien to take from him. He checks that his dark brown hair is still perfectly in place and then focuses his deep green eyes hungrily on his subjects. "I think we've got what we need. You all can take it from here." By 'you all,' he means Adrien, who is in charge of everything from forwarding the pictures, handling the equipment, coordinating the staff on set, and making sure Sergio has a bottle of Johnny Walker Blue available to him for a post-shoot celebratory toast with the model of his choosing.

Instead of choosing a model, Sergio grabs the aforementioned bottle of booze and opts for both as he wraps an arm around each of them and leads them giggling and blushing off the set.

"You're so talented," the woman says, batting her eyelashes and giggling. "I've seen all your shoots, and I have your book!"

"Stunning, isn't it?" Sergio agrees while moving them right along to the wardrobe closet. He brushes off the wardrobe mistress without even bothering to assure her that the red dress and the black suit will make it onto their hangers to avoid wrinkling.

The moment the door closes, he yanks on the young man's tie, pulling him in for a kiss. His other hand lingers at the shoulder strap of the woman's dress, as both models fumble to loosen his belt. They act in haste, as if this delicious moment of designer-clad debauchery could be interrupted at any moment.

And interrupted it is, the moment the male model drops to his knees before Sergio and the female presses her lips to Sergio's mouth while his hand finds its way up the hem of her dress.

"Oh, for fuck's sake, Sergio!" Adrien exclaims, bursting into the room. "We have a plane to catch! You can get your rocks off in Lake Placid."

Four hours later, Sergio is woken by Adrien kicking his seat as he walks by with his luggage in hand. "Wake up, asshole. We're here."

Sergio blinks at him, confused, trying to piece together where he is. The last he remembers, he was having a post-photoshoot celebratory scotch with his brother once they got settled into their seats pre-takeoff. He vaguely remembers brushing off his brother's attempt to talk business before falling asleep, exhausted from a hard day's work. Forget the fact he didn't arrive on set until noon and was off set with his hand up a model's skirt and his cock in another model's mouth by two.

It's far more likely his exhaustion is from being up until dawn with the Instagram influencer whose name he's already forgotten. Was she a travel blogger? No, definitely one of those yoga girls who posts near-naked pictures of herself doing handstands in exotic places.

"What's got your briefs in a bunch?" Sergio quips at Adrien as he rises from his seat. "You're not the one who got rudely interrupted mid-blowjob."

Adrien rolls his eyes. "As if you're not going to find a way to rectify that before night's end."

"Here? In Lake Flaccid? I don't think so."

"It's Lake Placid, and you've never had a problem getting laid any other year we've come up here for New Year's."

"Do I detect a little jealousy in your voice? Is that what your problem's been lately?"

"Jealous?" Adrien stops in his tracks at the plane's exit and looks over his shoulder at Sergio. "Of you? Hardly."

Sergio shrugs as he throws his Louis Vuitton duffle over his shoulder. "Well, you're certainly acting like you are."

Adrien rolls his eyes again, this time bringing his head into the roll, and steps off the plane, yelling as he does, "Trust me, I'm not!"

But Sergio isn't even listening. He catches the eye of a handsome steward cleaning up their used glasses at the plane's minibar. The young man blushes under Sergio's gaze.

"Here," Sergio says, pulling one of his business cards out of his pocket. He hands it over to the steward—his name tag reads Charlie—and gives him a wink that makes the other man visibly swallow. Sergio watches the rise and fall of his Adam's apple. "Call me if you're staying in Lake Placid for the night."

Adrien glares at him when he steps off the warm plane out into the chilly mountain air. Sergio flips his hands up at his brother. "What?"

"Nothing," Adrien says with a shake of his head. "You are nothing if not predictable."

"Predictably foul," chimes in Holden Haring, Sergio and Adrien's childhood best friend. His arrival breaks the tension between the two brothers, who turn towards him. He is all smiles as he walks up to them, his hands holding onto the sturdy calves of his five-year-old son, Henry, who is sitting on his shoulders.

"Sergio!" the boy calls. Henry is the spitting image of his father: bronze skin and warm brown hair with sun-created golden streaks. The only difference between the two is the eyes—Holden's are a deep friendly brown, while Henry has the striking ice blue eyes of his mother, Rose.

"What is this? Pick-on-Sergio day?" Sergio asks as he wraps Holden in a brotherly hug. He thumps him twice on his back before lifting Henry off his shoulders, squeezing the kid, and then placing him to sit on his shoulders instead.

Henry laughs gleefully the entire way and is quick to curl his chubby fingers into Sergio's hair, messing it up as he kicks his heels into Sergio's chest. And for all of Sergio's faults, as vapid and self-centered as he can be, something about Henry gets through to him.

"Telling the truth is hardly picking on you." Adrien laughs.

"If not the truth from us, then who?" Holden asks, then nudges Adrien's shoulder with his own. "Lemme guess, he joined the mile-high club somewhere over Albany?"

"He wishes." Adrien snickers.

"Pfft, amateurs," Sergio says and begins walking away from them. "I'm already a member." He picks up his speed, going as fast as he can with a child and a duffel bag strapped to his back. Henry squeals the whole time as Sergio makes his way to Holden's parked Range Rover.

Sergio opts to sit in the back seat with Henry. Once everyone is buckled up, they head toward Holden's mountainside home.

"So, where's Red?" Sergio asks, referring to Holden's wife, Rose, known for her bright red ponytail. It made her a standout on the ice during her years as an Olympic figure skater. No one could miss her even if they wanted to. And everyone wanted to, as during her time as a competitor, she was near impossible to beat.

"Red," Holden laughs, "is at the barn, working with her skater."

"She cute?" Sergio asks.

"Oh, yes. Very," Holden says. "Rose is as beautiful as ever." He winks at Sergio through the rearview mirror.

"I meant the skater," Sergio says, while reaching into his coat pocket and pulling out a toy race car that he hands to Henry with a "shh." The child beams at him and plays at zooming the car across his legs, strapped into his safety seat.

"Sergio, could you give it a rest?" Adrien asks.

"He can't," Holden answers before Sergio can. "It's like he has a strange form of horny Tourette's."

"It's called a healthy sex drive." Sergio smirks.

"And this is called a conversation we shouldn't be having in front of a five-year-old," Adrien says. "Let's save this talk until later."

"You hear that, Henry? I think you got me in trouble."

"You got yourself in trouble," Holden points out.

"Nah. It's gotta be the kid," Sergio says and pokes at Henry's side, eliciting a high-pitched laugh from him.

"Uncle Sergio! No tickles," Henry shouts and continues to giggle, happy as can be.

Sergio puts his hands up.

"No, keep going!" Henry demands. Sergio dives back in again, grinning at Henry's unbridled joy.

"How about you, Adrien. How's the book coming?"

"Backburnered until I have more time." Adrien sighs.

Holden nods his head. "Too busy keeping your brother's career afloat, huh?"

"Exactly." Adrien laughs in agreement.

"Hey!" Sergio exclaims.

"Oh, come on," Holden says. "We can all agree Adrien is the most responsible of the three of us."

"Only because he's the most boring." He looks at Henry and tips his head towards the front seat as if to say, 'Can you believe these two?'

Henry smiles broadly at him while still zooming his new car around the confines of his seat.

"And what about Daphne? How's she doing?"

Sergio strains to listen in from the back seat. Last he'd heard, much to Sergio's relief, Daphne and Adrien were on the rocks.

"Oh, she's fine," Adrien says, a hint of sadness in his voice. "She's been spending the holidays back home in Paris with her family."

"I'm a little surprised you're not in Paris with her," Holden says. "I know this is tradition and all for us to be together for New Year's, but ... you're not obligated, you know."

"Sure he is," Sergio says, stopping his tickling of Henry to reach over the back seat to jostle Adrien's and Holden's hair simultaneously. "What would New Year's be without my brothers?"

Brothers who somehow manage to balance each other when they are all together. Holden works as a bit of a salve that keeps Sergio's and Adrien's rougher edges from slicing through one another. It's been like this for ages. The three of them are born and raised New Yorkers who grew up together in the same building, on the same top two floors, in two adjacent penthouses. All of them are wildly rich, talented in their own ways, and genetic lottery winners.

The three are brothers in everything but blood.

"I trust you boys can find your rooms," Holden says, leading them into his well-lit and warm log cabin-style mountain home. He beelines through the house's wide-open floor plan, heading straight for the kitchen.

"Is that damn cat still alive?" Sergio asks.

"Yes," Holden says. As if summoned, a white and black cat jumps onto one of the stools lining the kitchen island and glares at Sergio, his tail lazily flicking behind him. "Gus is still alive, and he's taken to sleeping under *your* bed. So play nice."

Holden pulls three beers from the fridge, twists one open, and then places the other two bottles on the counter. He gently strokes between Gus's ears, causing the cat to purr in Holden's direction before hissing at Sergio. "I'm gonna take Henry down to the barn to get Rose if either of you wants to come with me."

Sergio flips off the cat, then grabs one of the bottles. He twists the top off and takes a sip. A broad smile lifts his lips. "Yeah, I'll join you," he says, then looks at Adrien. "Could you take my bag to my room?"

"Absolutely not," Adrien says. He takes the last beer, then makes a swift turn and struts away from them towards the stairs with his suitcase in hand and his head held high. Gus follows him, walking behind just as proudly.

"Rude," Sergio calls out to his brother.

"Come on, man." Holden claps Sergio on the shoulder. "He's on vacation. Let's not treat him like your errand boy all week."

"I wasn't."

"You kind of were." Holden squeezes his shoulder, then jostles him slightly before he begins to lead him out the back door. "Come on, Henry," he calls out, and the kid immediately comes running after them, his feet skidding on the large-planked hardwood floor.

"So what's the deal with the new skater? Is Rose trying to keep her a secret or something?"

"Nah." Holden brushes off the question and gestures towards a barn twice the size of their house, nestled between the tall fir trees. "It's more

9

that everyone involved likes the privacy of the barn over the public rink in town. Besides, this gave me an excuse to buy a proper Zamboni."

Sergio bursts into laughter. His eyes spark with mischief. "Do you get to drive that thing?"

"All the time!" Holden's face lights up with glee and a crooked smile. He takes a sip of his beer. "What a rush."

"A rush?" Sergio laughs some more. "What does it go, five, maybe ten miles an hour?"

"I can get it up to a good twelve if I really hit the gas," Holden says, nodding his head in continued excitement as he opens the barn's side door. It's warmer inside the barn than it is outside, despite it being an ice rink. Now that the sun has gone down, the crisp winter cold has settled in between the tall aspen trees. "I'll let you take it for a spin if you like."

Sergio sips his beer and grins around the mouth of the bottle. "I would definitely like."

"You will definitely not," Rose says, narrowing her ice-blue eyes at Sergio and sliding in between the two of them to give him a loose, welcoming hug. "I will not have this menace destroy my dream home ice rink." She lets go of Sergio, picks up Henry and places him on her hip, then turns to look at Holden. She points at him. "You're lucky I let you drive the thing."

She turns back to Sergio, but he ignores her and moves on. His attention is now focused on the ice. Or rather, who's on the ice. He's staring at two people. One is a tiny woman with rich brown skin and a head of dark, tight, corkscrew-curly hair piled high atop her head. Any loose wisps and curls are held in place by a silk scarf tied around her hairline. She's stunning and perfectly put together despite the fact that it's nearing seven p.m. and she's likely been on the ice since eight this morning.

Working with her is an average-sized man with creamy skin, slightly disheveled, warm, light brown hair, and a smackable ass Sergio immediately recognizes as that of Jeremy Owens. They'd carried on a mild flirtation that went nowhere at the last Olympic Games (where both Holden and Rose won gold. Holden technically won two golds that year, but who's counting?). Jeremy had seemed interested but ultimately brushed Sergio's advances aside, claiming he needed to focus on the competition and that maybe they could go out for dinner after the games were done. But Sergio had never heard from Jeremy again.

Had he not been so busy chasing other athletes around the Olympic Village after his rejection from Jeremy, he might have known why. Jeremy's dramatic exit from the games was the biggest tear-filled news story on the world's stage at the time.

"So, what do you think?" Rose asks him, breaking him from his stupor of staring at Jeremy.

He rakes his eyes back over to the young woman Jeremy is working with. "She looks good. Promising."

Rose rolls her eyes. "I meant the rink. Pretty awesome, right?"

"Oh, yeah. Definitely ..." Sergio says, his voice trailing off as he continues to watch the two skaters on the ice. He's now giving them equal attention while his libido argues over which one he should try to pull into his bed tonight. The way the woman moves is mesmerizing. She practically floats across the surface, as if her blades aren't carving deep edges into the frozen water. Jeremy, however, looks less sure-footed as he skates slowly beside her, giving her choreographic directions to lead her through a series of flourishes of the arms as well as careful loops, turns, and crossovers of the feet that she mimics in time to the classical music softly playing through the barn's speakers.

"Allison. Jeremy. Let's wrap it up!" Rose calls as she skates onto the ice with Henry in her arms. Eventually, she lets him down onto the surface. He slips and slides on the soles of his shoes, his little voice calling Jeremy's name the entire way.

"Careful, buddy. Remember what we talked about," Rose says.

"I know, Mom!" Henry yells back. "Be careful around Jeremy on the ice."

"Yeah, Henry!" Holden says beside Sergio. "If you want to knock someone over, your uncle Sergio is a much better target."

Sergio mocks being offended by placing a hand over his heart. "How dare you turn my godson against me?"

Holden smiles and laughs, his eyebrows lifting in a playful challenge. "It's not like we all haven't wanted to knock you over from time to time."

"And again, it's back to pick-on-Sergio day," Sergio says with a light-hearted laugh, but he wonders what's with all the cutting remarks leveled at him at first by Adrien and now Holden. He supposes it must be brotherly teasing, and he goes back to watching the skaters.

Allison gracefully makes her way to the low step on the side of the rink and takes a seat. She grabs a sip of water out of a nearby bottle. She looks up at Rose. "That new sequence leading into the triple flip feels more natural. It's an easier flow."

"You hear that, Jeremy?" Rose says. "You were right about changing up that footwork pattern."

"I'm glad that worked. If we need to tweak it some more, we can," Jeremy says as he carefully skates to meet Henry where he's fallen yet again. A big, dimple-filled grin lights up Henry's face when Jeremy gets to him. He grabs Henry's hand and attempts to hold him steady. "Easy now, Henry. Remember what I taught you."

"So what's with this guy?" Sergio asks Holden, jutting his chin forward.

"Jeremy?"

"No, the other guy on the ice."

"You've met him before."

"I know that." Sergio takes a sip of his beer. "I meant, why is he here?"

"Oh, right. Well, he's working with Rose now. She's hired him on as her assistant coach and choreographer." Holden pauses and points up towards the rafters of the barn. To the far side is a closed-off area with a set of windows that look down upon the ice. There's a staircase right to the side of where Allison is sitting and now unlacing her skates that leads up to it. "And he's living up there. We set him up with a nice little studio."

"You're joking, right?"

"Why would I joke about that?"

"Why would a grown man need to live in your ice rink disguised as a barn?" Holden downs what's left of his beer in a final swig, then turns to look at Sergio. "You really only pay attention to what's happening to yourself, don't you?"

Sergio, determined to prove Holden's assertion wrong, makes an extra effort for the rest of the evening to pay thorough attention to everyone else. It starts in the easiest place possible for him, with Henry. He sits on the floor with the kid and lets him chew his ear off all throughout their pizza dinner. He listens to him share his imagination and regale Sergio with his adventures on the ski slopes with his dad, on the ice with his mom, and quiet moments of reading and coloring with Jeremy Owens. It's those last details that have Sergio's hackles slightly raised.

"You spend a lot of time with Jeremy, huh?" he asks, keeping his voice light and cheerful even though he's silently seething at the idea that this other man, this interloper in Holden's and Rose's and Henry's world, living in their barn, could possibly be stealing some of Henry's affection. Sergio has always prided himself on being Henry's favorite. He does not enjoy the idea of someone else shoehorning themselves into his territory.

He looks over his shoulder to where Jeremy is sitting on the large leather sofa across from Rose, his back against the armrest. His knees are pulled towards his chest, and his plate of pizza rests on them. He and Rose appear to be having a very lively conversation, probably reminiscing about their glory days of old. They only pause in talking when Holden comes by and refills Rose's glass of wine, then comes by Sergio and does the same. He takes a seat back down with Adrien and dumps what's left of the bottle into their glasses. Everyone seems happy and content. Even Adrien has a smile on his face as he banters with Holden and idly pets Gus sitting beside him from ear to tail.

Gus catches Sergio looking and hisses at him again.

"Uncle Sergio, are you listening to me?"

Sergio glares at the cat, then pivots his attention back to Henry. "Of course!" he says, exaggerating his words. "You are my favorite person to pay attention to."

"After figure skaters in short dresses, that is," Adrien says under his breath.

Holden laughs and holds his hand out for Adrien to give him a high five.

Sergio shrugs and says, "What can I say, I like what I like."

"And you will not be liking Allison," Rose scolds from across the room. "With Nationals and the Olympics coming up, I don't need you fucking up her focus."

Henry laughs beside him. "Mom said 'the eff word.'"

"Can you believe it?" Sergio asks him, his eyebrows raising and his mouth dropping open wide. Henry laughs some more.

"I mean it, Sergio," Rose scolds again. "I will ban you from my ice rink during your stay here if I have to."

Sergio holds his hands up in defense. "Ye of little faith in this house. I'll be on my best behavior."

"*Your* best behavior isn't good enough," Rose says, pointing a finger at him. Sergio can't help but notice the way Jeremy tries to hide his laughter behind a slightly shaky hand. "I need you to be on Adrien's best behavior."

Adrien reaches over and slaps her a high five from where he is sitting.

"Well, that's boring," Sergio says, with indignation. "Adrien doesn't know the meaning of the word fun."

"I think I'm a lot of fun," Adrien says with a shrug of his shoulders.

"So do I," Rose agrees.

"Yeah, me too," Holden says, then looks at Sergio. "In a different way than you are, of course."

"Thanks, that's really reassuring."

"I think you're fun!" Henry says.

"And I think you're my favorite," Sergio says, pulling Henry into his lap.

"And I think it's getting late," Jeremy says. He places his empty plate onto the nearby coffee table. "It's time for me to head back to the barn to lie down."

"I'll walk with you." Rose places her own plate down.

"You don't need to do that," Jeremy assures her and rises to his feet, his hand holding onto the couch's arm as he does. He stands still for a moment, almost like he's trying to catch his balance, which is strange to Sergio as Jeremy is supposed to be a world-class athlete, the pinnacle of grace and strength, and yet here he appears to struggle on his feet. "I'm sure I'll see you all tomorrow."

"Yes, come by for breakfast," Holden says. "I'm making a huge spread before we hit the slopes."

"Alright." Jeremy nods and takes a step away from the couch. On his third, he stumbles, knocking into the coffee table. Holden is quick to his feet and catches him before he hits the floor, then rights him back onto his feet.

"Have a little too much to drink there, Jeremy?" Sergio teases. "Maybe you should take that escort home after all."

Deafening silence meets him. He looks around the room, waiting for anyone else to join in on the joke. Instead, Adrien hides his head behind his hand, Holden sucks on his teeth, and Rose glares at him like he sacrificed her cat on her living room floor.

Henry breaks the silence. "Not cool, Uncle Sergio," he says and jumps off his lap, then runs over to where Jeremy and Holden are standing. Henry wraps his arms around Jeremy's thigh.

"What?" Sergio exclaims, still trying to catch what he's missed.

Rose rises to her feet and walks towards Jeremy, her face flushed with anger. "He's not drunk, you asshole. He has MS." She gently places a hand on Jeremy's shoulder. "Come on," she says. "I want to talk to you about your ideas for Allison's choreography, anyway. We can have some tea at your place."

"Can I come?" Henry asks.

Jeremy looks at Rose and nods yes.

"Okay," she says. "But you have to be good and quiet, alright?"

"Alright," Henry agrees, and they walk out the door, leaving Sergio, Holden, and Adrien in uncomfortable silence. Even Gus takes off running from the room and up the large open stairs.

Sergio finally speaks. "How the fuck was I supposed to know that?"

"How the fuck did you not?" Adrien asks. "It was only the biggest news story in sports four years ago. Jeremy Owens, men's figure skating Olympic gold medal favorite, is out of the games after collapsing on the ice. Cause later determined to be MS."

"I mean, it's not like I follow figure skating religiously."

"Dude," Holden says. "You were trying to get into his pants at those games."

"Yeah, and he turned me down."

"And that's a reason not to care about someone?" Adrien asks.

"I was surrounded by gorgeous athletes! I had pictures to take and fun and games to have. It's not my fault this news hadn't made it to me."

Adrien lets out a sigh as Holden looks at Sergio. "Look, man, it's fine. Just apologize in the morning or something."

"Why should I have to apologize?"

"Because you fucked up," Adrien says. "Royally."

"It was a minor faux pas."

"Oh yeah, then how does your foot taste?" Holden teases.

"My guess is like Italian suede," Adrien says.

"It tastes like nothing because it's not in my mouth. I did nothing wrong." A cool rush flows through his system at his words that he shakes off.

"Eh, you kind of did," Holden says.

"Whatever." Sergio sighs and rises from the floor. "I'm calling it a night."

Chapter Two

Sergio always sleeps like the dead. Sleepless nights are for people who know shame. A concept Sergio isn't familiar with. It's how he's missed countless phone calls, roaring storms, and a robbery happening in his Paris hotel room. It's no wonder he doesn't hear the fast-approaching footsteps and subsequent leap of a five-year-old mere seconds before said five-year-old lands on the bed, kneeing him directly in the balls.

"Uncle Sergio! Wake up!"

"Oof ..." Sergio's stomach lurches from the impact, causing him to cough. "Morning, buddy," he wheezes out as he tries to catch his breath from the worst wake-up of his life. Gus hisses underneath the bed and then goes careening out of the room. On the bright side, it would appear from Henry's enthusiastic entrance that he's no longer upset with Sergio for last night's minor incident with Jeremy Owens.

"Dad said to come get you. Breakfast is almost ready."

"Did your dad tell you to jump on the bed as well?" Sergio asks, figuring there's a high probability that he did.

"No." Henry giggles and looks away with flushed cheeks.

"Are both your mom and dad downstairs?"

"Yes." Henry starts pulling on Sergio's arm, trying, struggling, and failing to get him to sit up.

Sergio uses his strength and leverage to yank Henry down and into his hold, cuddling him close to his chest. "What about Jeremy? Is he here?"

"No," Henry says. "You should go tell him you're sorry."

"Oh really? Is that what you think?"

"Yes."

"Why's that?"

"Because Mom and Dad always tell me to say sorry when I do something bad."

"Do you do bad things often?"

"No."

"Me neither," Sergio says and ignores the niggling sense in the back of his head that's telling him maybe Henry's right. Besides, no one wants to take advice from someone who can't tie their own shoelaces. Especially when the advice is regarding a mishap that will eventually blow over. This insignificant blip will be irrelevant in a matter of days, maybe even hours. He gives Henry a firm squeeze. "Did you wake up your Uncle Adrien yet?"

"No." Henry laughs as Sergio tickles his sides.

"Do you want to?"

"Yes." More laughing.

"Good." Sergio lets go of him and finally sits up in bed, rubbing his face. "Go get him and make sure you wake him up the same way you did me, okay?"

"Okay!" Henry yells as he jumps off the bed, throws two enthusiastic thumbs up into the air over his head, and goes thundering out the door and down the hall.

Sergio waits until he hears the telltale *oof* of Adrien being woken up in Henry's special manner before he rises and exits the room, smiling and laughing to himself, clad in the sweatpants and T-shirt he fell asleep in.

Once downstairs, the reception Sergio gets from Rose is best described as chilly. She moves around, refusing to look in his direction.

Holden, however, is his usual jovial self with his bright smile and exuberant greeting. "Good morning, shithead!"

Rose brushes past him to open a cabinet without a word, and he's pretty sure Gus is trying to trip him by getting underfoot. He smiles and turns on his charm, an attribute of his personality that has never failed him.

"Lemme get that," he says, sidling up to Rose and taking the plates she pulled from the cabinet out of her hands. "Sit. Get comfortable. I'll set the table."

"Thanks," she says, her tone crisp. She avoids making eye contact, then spins around and whips him across the chin with her full red ponytail. It smells like orange blossoms.

Sergio looks to Holden for help. All he gets is a subtle, apologetic shrug that feels more like an indictment of Sergio than an apology for Rose's well-aimed strike. *Alright, she's still pissed,* Sergio figures, so he tries a new tactic.

"Where's Jeremy?" he asks, purposely lifting his voice to exaggerate curiosity.

Rose, looking at him for the first time, glares. "Avoiding you, obviously."

Sergio turns his back to her and winces, then takes a breath and tries to break through her defenses again. Taking a seat and leaving the dishes she handed him on the counter, he asks, "So your new skater, she's really promising, huh?"

Rose looks across the table at him with her eyes narrowed and her lips pursed. "Do you actually care?"

"Yeah," Sergio says, stung. After all, Rose is family. Of course, he's interested in what she's doing. Same as he assumes she's interested in what he has going on in his career. Which, speaking of ... "I could take some promotional pictures of her while I'm here if you'd like. Free of charge, of course."

Rose tilts her head in thought. Her eyes are penetrating as she stares at him, and she appears to be at war with herself as she weighs her options as to what to do with Sergio's offer. Finally, her gaze softens slightly, and her head shifts upright. "That actually would be nice. Since we've moved to the barn, we haven't had the same press coverage or candid shots that we normally would. Thanks, Sergio. We'll figure something out for later in the week."

"Yeah, no problem," he says, smiling as Holden drops off the dishes Sergio hadn't bothered to bring over, along with a pot of coffee. Sergio pours himself a cup.

"But don't think this means you can openly flirt with Allison while you shoot," Rose says. She reaches and takes the cup of coffee Sergio poured for himself and enjoys a pointed sip. Her eyes focus intensely on him over the brim of the mug.

Without flinching under her intense, warning stare, he pours another cup. "I'll be strictly professional," he promises her.

"A strictly professional pain in the butt," Adrien says as he enters the kitchen with Henry dangling upside down from his shoulders, laughing gleefully. "Did he volunteer us for work?"

"Only himself," Rose assures and takes the second cup of coffee Sergio poured for himself and holds it out to Adrien as he places Henry back down on the ground.

"Thanks," Adrien says as he takes it.

Sergio pours yet another cup.

"Breakfast is served!" Holden says, delivering plates of pancakes and bacon and sliced fresh fruit. Rose takes Sergio's latest mug of coffee and places it in front of where Holden takes a seat. Sergio furrows his brow in frustration. He looks up at her, and she's ignoring him again, pretending she hasn't stolen three cups of coffee from him while she helps Henry pour syrup all over his food.

"Eat up! We're gonna need all the calories we can get for the slopes today," Holden says.

"Can't wait!" Sergio says, shaking off Rose's trick and pouring himself one more cup of coffee from the dregs of the pot. He senses her reaching for it before he gets a chance to take a sip and pulls it from her grasp. "Oh no. Not this time."

"'Not this time' what?" She smiles, feigning innocence, as the rest of the table begins to eat their breakfast.

On the slopes, Sergio is back in his groove. He's enjoying himself, loving every run he makes down the mountain, breathing in the cool, fresh air laced with the soft flavor of the sugar pines. It's fun, even without Holden—who's busy teaching Henry how to glide down the trails on the bunny hills—while Sergio and Adrien make the larger runs together.

For what feels like the first time in ages, there's a lightness between the brothers as they chase each other and carve fresh lines through the powdery snow. They challenge each other to races and toss snowballs at one another in the mountain basin before climbing aboard another chairlift. Sometimes they slowly glide and meander down, taking wide arcs and turns to take in the sights while Sergio snaps pictures and brief video clips with his GoPro along the way, documenting the levity of their traditional New Year's Eve activities. Up here, in Lake Placid, it's easy to reconnect.

Riding the chairlift for their last run before they're set to meet Holden, Rose, and Henry for lunch and a warm-up by the local lodge's fireplace, Sergio pulls his GoPro out again and snaps a few shots from high above the slopes. It's not one of his professional cameras, but it is good for capturing candid moments and action shots while on the go without the fear of destroying it with excessive goofing around. He turns the lens towards Adrien, who flashes him a peace sign and sticks his tongue out.

"Is that the look you want people to see on your dating profile?" Sergio asks.

Adrien glares at Sergio. "In case you forgot, I'm in a relationship. I don't have any dating profiles."

"Yeah, but like, Daphne ditched you for New Year's. I think we should put you back out there."

"She didn't ditch me," Adrien corrects. "She opted to spend the holiday with her family. Which is her right, by the way."

"Still kind of seems like she ditched you."

"Well, that's your wrong opinion."

Sergio shrugs and snaps another photo of his brother. "But I mean, if she was as serious about you as you are about her, don't you think she'd want to be here with you?"

Adrien lets out a heavy sigh and turns his gaze to look wistfully over the tree line in the other direction. Sergio cranes around, the safety bar digging into his midsection, so he can snap a shot of Adrien's contemplative profile.

"It's not that she didn't want to spend the holidays with *me*, Sergio."

"That's what it seems like."

"Well, it's not. Can we drop this, please?"

"Sure," Sergio says and leans in closer to Adrien, holding the camera so he can capture them together. "It's just, you know, I think Daphne is nice—"

"Pfft," Adrien cuts him off. "Sure you do."

"But you're my younger brother, and I think you deserve better."

"Better than an heiress to the largest name in millinery?"

"I'm not sure a lifetime's supply of one-of-a-kind women's hats is worth the effort or the heartache."

"Daphne doesn't cause me any heartache."

"Then why are you suddenly so glum on this lift?" Sergio knocks his shoulder against his brother's.

"I'm not glum," Adrien defends. "And I asked you to drop it."

Sergio holds his hands up as if he's ready to dodge a hit. "Okay, I'll drop it. I only want what's best for you."

Adrien lets out a bitter laugh. "You've never wanted what was best for me. It's always been about what's best for you."

"That's not true! I have always looked out for you, and you have always been ungrateful."

"Ungrateful?" This time, Adrien lets out a genuine laugh. "Full offense, Sergio, but you're the ungrateful one!"

"Me?"

"Yeah, you!" Adrien looks ahead and adjusts himself for their approaching drop-off. "You walk around this world like it was made for you and you alone and completely take for granted all those around you, like *myself*, who make it that way."

"Oh, come off it, Adrien. It's not like I don't work my ass off for everything we have."

Adrien turns to look at him, stone-faced.

"Okay, *you* do help. A lot," Sergio concedes. "And I couldn't be where I am without you."

"Do you really mean that?"

"Of course I do!" His words echo over the treetops, creating a more dramatic effect for his attempt to get out of hot water. "Look, Adrien," he says gently as the chairlift deposits them at the top of the black diamond run. "Ever since Mom and Dad died, I've taken it upon myself to keep you and me together. I can't bear losing you as well."

To Sergio's credit, this is true. Adrien took the death of their parents hard, but Sergio took it way harder as he was the reason they were out on that country road late at night on a quest to hunt him down after he'd run off with a local politician's daughter to their East Hampton home for a weekend of juvenile amusement. "So, I'm sorry if I sometimes come across as overbearing. I like having you around."

"Look, Sergio, I like being around you, too, and I don't want anything to come between us …" He pauses and looks at Sergio. Adrien's eyes are dark under his lowered brows, and the corners of his mouth are turned down. He takes a deep breath, and his exhalation sends a slow stream of condensation around him like smoke. "Which is why I think I have to quit working for you. I'm sorry."

Sergio, stunned, says nothing. He's left in silence to watch his brother head down the mountain, zooming away from him at an impressive clip. This isn't the first time Adrien has quit. It is, however, the first time Sergio realizes he truly means it.

"Did you guys have fun?" Holden asks them once they find each other on the bunny hills.

Sergio doesn't get a chance to answer as Henry is already calling his name. "Uncle Sergio! Look!" He zooms past him down the hill in a perfect miniature replica of his father's crouched skiing stance. Perfect, that is, until he has to come to a stop that he hasn't mastered yet. His solution is to flip forward, doing a complete somersault that lands him on his rump. "Did you see?"

"Yeah, Henry! I saw," Sergio says as he skis over to him and pulls him back up onto his feet. "That was very impressive. You're gonna be an Olympian like your dad."

"Do you think I can be?" Henry asks, looking up at Sergio, who's still holding his hands.

"Definitely. It's in your blood. It's what you are destined to be. If that's what you want, of course."

"It is!"

"Then you will," Sergio assures, crouching down to click Henry's skis off. He lifts him up with one arm, then grabs the skis with his free hand and starts skiing them to where Holden and Adrien are waiting, already unburdened of their skis by the lodge. Their demeanor is casual yet serious, and Holden claps Adrien on the shoulder, as if assuring him he made the right decision. Sergio doesn't need to be there to know what they're discussing. He wonders how long Holden has known of Adrien's intention. By logic, he figures Adrien probably told Holden last night. But it's possible Adrien's been wanting to do it for longer.

Feeling unsettled, Sergio squeezes Henry a little tighter. "Can I ask you something, buddy?"

"Yes," Henry says and rests his head on Sergio's shoulder.

"You like me, right?"

"Yes." He lets out a little giggle as if the answer is obvious.

"Am I still your favorite?"

"Mommy says it's not nice to have favorites."

"Okay, she's not wrong. But you have a favorite toy, right?"

"No," Henry says solemnly, lifting his head away from Sergio's shoulder to look him in the eyes. "I don't want to hurt my toys' feelings."

"That's fair." Sergio nods his understanding. "But you have a favorite food, right? Pizza has to rank higher than, let's say, something like broccoli."

"Nobody's favorite is broccoli." Henry's face twists in disgust.

"Right!" Sergio agrees. "Broccoli is awful! So you can be honest with me, I'm your favorite, right?"

But Sergio doesn't get the answer he was expecting. Instead, he gets inner ear damage as Henry excitedly screams out another name, "Jeremy!"

and begins squirming in Sergio's arms in an apparent bid to get down. So much for being the kid's favorite.

With Henry squirming in his arms, Sergio sees the apparent primary subject of Henry's affection. Jeremy is holding onto the guardrail as he ascends the steps towards the lodge, with Allison walking beside him and Rose leading the way. He stops in his tracks and looks around, obviously trying to find Henry. Eventually, his eyes locate him in Sergio's arms. He lifts his free hand and gives a wave. His cheeks are flushed from the cold, and his hair comes out in wisps from underneath his grey toque.

Sergio lets Henry down and watches him as he runs over to meet Jeremy. With the aid of Rose's outstretched hand, he's brought to a stop before he can barrel into his target. Apparently, preventing Henry's inevitable collision course with Jeremy is a full-time job around here.

"Hungry?" Holden asks Sergio, clapping him on the shoulder.

Keeping his eyes on Jeremy instead of turning to look at Holden, Sergio says, "I didn't know Jeremy was coming to lunch."

"Oh yeah, he's gonna take Henry back to the house after we eat for a nap so Rose can join us for more skiing."

"Is he like your babysitter or something?" Sergio isn't sure if he wants the answer to be yes or no, and he's half tempted to offer to take Henry home himself and ensure his placement back on the top of Henry's list of favorites, well above broccoli.

"No," Holden says. "He helps out when he can. He's really nice. You should make an effort to get to know him while you're here. You two would really get along."

"I have made an effort to get to know him. Years ago. And he rejected me."

"Is that what this is all about? Your bruised ego?" Holden laughs.

"No," Sergio mutters, trying to defend himself. Though the truth is, the memory of Jeremy's rejection has occasionally crossed his mind ever since he'd given Sergio the brush off at the games four years ago. And each time he's been confronted with the memory without Jeremy around, it has fueled his resentment. It wasn't until he saw him yesterday on the ice in person at the barn that he'd began to remember how well they'd originally hit it off instead of only remembering the rejection. That the banter between them had been fun and stimulating. That they'd laughed and enjoyed themselves and shared an impassioned kiss tucked away in an alcove beneath the stands of the ski slopes while waiting for Holden to make another aerial run. The same alcove where Jeremy pulled away—his face flushed, his lips chapped, his hair askew—and told Sergio that he couldn't risk losing his focus. Because he was under so much pressure, and as fun as their flirtation was, he needed to put a pause on it until after the games.

Had Sergio been thinking with more than his dick, he would have seen it: the slight rigidity in the way Jeremy walked that was beginning to encroach on his natural grace, the way Jeremy would intermittently tug at the corner of his eye as if trying to clear something from it, the exhaustion that constantly painted his face. To Sergio, like any other outsider looking in, it appeared to be the symptoms of someone succumbing to the pressure of the world watching their every move. The pressure of being not only America's darling, but America's gay darling. A good one, a poster boy, someone who could make little boys on figure skates—as opposed to hockey skates—an admirable thing to see. So much was pinned on Jeremy at the time that of course, Sergio knew who he was. Of course, Sergio wanted to be the bad boy attached to the good boy's image. Of course, Sergio wanted to add Jeremy's name to the notches on his bedpost. And of course, when Jeremy turned him down, Sergio switched gears and chased after the entire Norwegian women's snowboarding team instead.

"I think it's curious that Jeremy is so firmly planted in your life, is all."

Holden shrugs. "It's the least we could do for him."

Holden's words eerily echoed the ones Holden's parents had spoken in regard to Sergio and Adrien over a decade earlier. When asked why they wanted to take the boys in, the answer was simple: "It's the least we can do for them." But Jeremy Owens is no orphan; he's a full-grown man. The circumstances are entirely different.

"Come on. This place has a great turkey burger," Holden says, breaking Sergio from his thoughts and leading them all inside, where the hostess awaits their arrival and leads them right to a large round table in the middle of the sunlit restaurant that overlooks the mountains. Sergio, wanting to be as far away from Jeremy as possible, sits opposite him with Holden on one side and Allison on the other. He tries not to seethe when he sees Henry climb onto Jeremy's lap, apparently using him as his chair for lunch.

"How long are you in town?" Allison asks once they've placed their orders.

"A week," Sergio says, curling his lips into his most charming smile, grateful for the distraction. A very pretty distraction. He thought he'd gotten a good look at her the day before while she was on the ice, but now, up close, he sees he missed a few very alluring details. Like her deep, soulful brown eyes with long lashes set above high, sharp cheekbones that would make every emaciated model he photographs green with envy. To go with that, she has a pleasant voice and a shy laugh that she hides behind her hands when Sergio says, "Plenty of time for us to get to know one another."

"I thought I warned you about that, Sergio Durand," Rose says from where she's seated between Holden and Jeremy. It's been a long time since anyone used his full name to scold him. Not even Mr. and Mrs. Haring ever used it whenever he caused them trouble.

Sergio brushes her off with his hand without looking her way. "Don't mind her," he says to Allison, his lips pulling into a wicked grin. "We're just two people talking."

The talking is what keeps Sergio from reaching across the table and yanking Henry out of Jeremy's lap and placing him onto his own. Even while talking to Allison, he can't keep himself from listening in on Jeremy and Adrien's conversation two chairs away.

"Oh! She's in Paris. How nice," Jeremy says. "I've only been there once. Years ago, for a competition, but I didn't really get to enjoy it. I got a picture of myself in front of the Eiffel Tower, though. So I guess that's something."

"You need to go again," Adrien says. "In fact, we should plan something. Daphne's family is always open to having guests. You would only need a plane ticket."

Jeremy sighs wistfully. "That'd be lovely. I'll think about it."

"Have you ever been to Paris?" Allison asks Sergio, apparently picking up on what Sergio has actually been listening to instead of her.

Sergio gives her his attention again. "I have," he says. "Many times. Would you like to go?"

"She can't go to Paris with you until after the Olympics, Sergio," Rose teases, then adds under her breath, "Or ever."

Holden laughs.

"Can I go to Paris?" Henry asks.

"Yes!" Sergio says, figuring this will help him win his nephew back. "I'll take you whenever you like."

Rose raises an eyebrow at him. "I won't let you abscond with my protégé, you think I'll let you leave the country with my kid?" Everyone at the table laughs, but something in her voice and raised eyebrow indicates this isn't a joke at all.

"I'll take him," Adrien chimes in.

Rose points her finger at him. "Now *that* I approve of!"

Sergio's jaw drops, and his eyebrows knit together. He sits back in his chair and brings a hand to his chest. "Rose, you wound me."

"She has a point, mate," Holden says, then jostles Sergio's shoulder with his hand. "You know I love you like a brother, but you and Henry would both need a babysitter in Paris."

Sergio shrugs. "As long as it's someone hot to look at."

Rose turns her attention to Allison. "You see. Didn't I tell you? Total player this one is."

Allison averts her eyes and giggles behind her hand. Rose has obviously been preparing the young twenty-year-old skater for Sergio's arrival.

"Oh, I don't know about that, Rose," Jeremy says, surprising Sergio, and apparently Adrien as well, who turns to look at him while bringing his hot tea to his lips. "Is it still a play when it's a one-man show?"

Adrien nearly chokes on his tea, and the rest of the table bursts out laughing. Even Henry lets out a guffaw when he sees everyone else's reactions. Everyone except for Sergio, who replies, "You're all jealous."

Holden claps him on the shoulder, again, and harder this time. "Not me!" he exclaims with pride lighting up his face so that it practically sets the table aglow. He grabs Rose's hand with his other hand and holds it up. "Nabbed my win on my first try."

Rose lets go of his hand and pats him on the head, playfully messing up his hair. "Keep telling yourself that, babe."

"Oh, please," Jeremy says with a pretty smile tugging at his lips. "You two are equally smitten."

"Yeah, they are," Allison agrees.

"The model couple," Adrien chimes in and raises his tea. "A relationship we all aspire to have."

Holden lifts his beer, prompting the rest of the table to do the same. "Here, here!"

"Yes, yes," Sergio says, holding back the urge to fake gag. He can feel Allison staring at him, but instead, he can't help but look at Jeremy over the brim of his pint and wonder what would have happened if he'd played his cards right during the Olympics.

Whatever. It was in the past. He shakes it all off, then turns his attention back to Allison, where he spends the rest of lunch flirting in an attempt to ignore the way that Jeremy so easily fits in with his family. He tries not to get mad at Adrien for choosing to chat with Jeremy instead of reassuring Sergio that he was merely joking less than an hour ago when he said he was quitting. He tries to stay positive when he sees Henry falling asleep in Jeremy's lap. And he tries to avoid Rose's glare and Jeremy's snicker when he hops onto the chairlift with Allison, slinging an arm around her as they are carried up the slopes to take a black diamond run together.

However, for once, having a beautiful girl under his arm isn't enough to distract him from memories of the two days from his past he desperately wishes he could do over.

The first is the day his parents died. At the time, having just turned seventeen, he was young and dumb. These last ten years, he's thought of that day often and how monumentally he screwed up. How with one poor decision, he ruined four people's lives. How he turned not only his, but Adrien's world upside down. And for what? To get off? To get the girl who'd been stringing him along and playing hard to get with him in his first experience of fumbling adolescent love alone in a lavish beach house? And then, when it was all over, she hadn't even been there for him during his grief?

Not only was that the day he lost his parents, but it was also the day he said *fuck it* to love. Forever vowing from that moment on not to waste his time with anyone who could have a hold on him and cloud his decision-making.

The second day, which isn't a surprise either, was the day he kissed Jeremy Owens. He doesn't regret kissing Jeremy. He regrets letting him go, even though he'll likely never admit that out loud.

He genuinely liked Jeremy, right from the get-go. Jeremy was charming and smart and held himself with such composure, even under all the pressure that was placed on him, the perfect definition of stoic. He was incredibly talented on the ice and photographed beautifully. He was the first person since the death of his parents that had Sergio thinking, *You know, maybe I can give dating someone a try*. And then, WHAM! He kissed him, and it was perfect, and he felt it from his lips all the way down to his toes, and the first thing Jeremy did when they pulled apart was reject him.

Of course, the truth was that Jeremy didn't reject him, he only wanted them to put a temporary pin in what was forming between them. But Sergio, unfortunately, hadn't seen it that way and went right back to swearing off a connection with anyone from that moment forward. Hook-ups, one-night stands, and no-strings-attached arrangements cause far less grief and heartache.

That is what he keeps in mind as he texts Allison a photo he'd taken of them from the ski slopes with a declaration that he's looking forward to seeing her later tonight at the New Year's Eve party. It's a huge soiree thrown at the Grand Olympian Hotel every year. Holden and Rose are co-hosting for the fourth year in a row since returning home as champions from the last Olympics.

"Can you grab Henry from Jeremy?" Rose asks Holden when they pull into the garage after their afternoon of skiing. "I need to get cleaned up and start getting ready for tonight."

"Sure thing," Holden says, then turns to look at Sergio and Adrien in the back seat. "Do either of you want to come with? Maybe Jeremy has Henry up and on skates. You should see him. He's terrible."

"Jeremy seemed careful on his skates last night, but I wouldn't call him terrible," Sergio says. He briefly does a mental side-by-side comparison of the Jeremy of old with the Jeremy of now. Yes, he looked less sure of himself, but nothing close to terrible.

"I meant Henry, but good to know you were paying close attention to Jeremy," Holden teases, then asks again, "So are you coming down or not?"

Sergio nods. "Yeah, I'll come."

"Adrien?"

"Nah. It's almost midnight in Paris. I'm gonna call Daphne and wish her a Happy New Year."

"Alright, send her our love," Holden says and exits the car. Sergio follows him out of the garage and around the house to head down to the barn.

"Awfully presumptuous of you to assume I send any love to Daphne," Sergio says once they are out of earshot of Adrien.

"Oh, come on. She's nice."

"So nice she turned my brother against me."

Holden lets out a sigh. "Sergio, she didn't do that, and you know it."

Sergio shrugs and slips his hands into his coat pockets. "I don't know what I know anymore, except that Adrien has quit on me."

"He didn't quit on you," Holden assures and blows on his hands to warm them up. "He's doing what's right for him. And, honestly, for you too, even though you don't see it."

Sergio shrugs again. "Maybe. I guess I could hire someone else."

"Or you can start doing more of this on your own. Stop hiring people to make your life easier."

"Isn't that the purpose of hiring people?"

"Isn't that the real reason Adrien quit? You may have been paying him, but you never treated him like he had a choice in being there." Holden opens the barn door, effectively ending the conversation as he ushers Sergio through.

Upon entering the rink, Sergio is met with something unexpected. He thought he was going to see Henry clumsily scooting around on skates, not sitting on the low, raised ledge on the entrance side of the ice, watching Jeremy skate in graceful loops and turns. His legs, his body, his arms are making impossibly lovely shapes that move in time with the sound of Chris Issack's voice crooning, *Wicked Game,* which is softly playing over the speakers.

"Well, this song is a little on the nose, don't you think?" Sergio says to no one in particular as he watches Jeremy move, carrying himself on the ice with more confidence and comfort than he seems when he's in shoes on regular ground. It's not an advanced routine, he's not doing any jaw-dropping jumps, fast spins, or overly complicated footwork, but it is soothing to watch regardless. Perhaps even more so without the heightened stakes of show-stopping tricks. It's pure unbridled movement, flowing to the melody and punctuating the lyrics. It's also surprisingly sexy.

"Hey, guys!" Holden yells out, announcing their arrival. Jeremy puts a pause on his moves, and Henry waves so enthusiastically from his seat on the low ledge that he falls onto the ice, laughing. Holden moves quickly to help him off the ice and back onto the low ledge to sit. He looks at Jeremy. "Routine is looking good. Legs feeling alright today?"

"Yeah," Jeremy says, smiling. His cheeks are flushed, but not from exertion or the cold needed to maintain an ice rink. This is a happy blush. One Sergio hadn't realized he missed seeing until now.

"I thought you weren't competing anymore," Sergio says, standing against the waist-high wooden wall that lines the rest of the rink.

"I'm not," Jeremy says and grabs a bottle of water that's resting not far from where Sergio is standing.

"So, what's with the routine?"

"Just an excuse to skate, I guess," Jeremy says, the attractive blush disappearing from his cheeks as he takes a sip of water and averts his eyes from Sergio's. He turns his attention back to Holden and Henry. "What time are we leaving tonight?"

"A little before eight," Holden says. "We gotta drop Henry off at the Weirs' on the way."

"Alright. I'll meet you up at the house in a bit, then," he says, sliding a blade guard onto his right skate before he steps off the ice, holding onto the wall by Sergio for balance and continuing to avoid Sergio's attempt to make eye contact. He then slides a guard onto his left skate and walks away from them.

"See you later, Jeremy," Holden calls after him as he lifts Henry off the ground and places him on his shoulders.

"Did I say something wrong?" Sergio asks.

"Well, you didn't say anything right," Holden answers, laughing lightly.

Sergio is sulking, licking his wounds by way of a whiskey neat at the far corner of the bar at the goldenly lit Grand Olympian Hotel. The New Year's Eve party is effervescent and alive with the who's who of Lake Placid elites preparing to count down to the start of a promising new year. Millionaire sports stars and businesspeople are mingling together, glad-handing and verbally promising endorsements or appearances, or soliciting sponsorships.

With the Winter Olympics fast approaching once again in only six short weeks, the rush to associate oneself with the next big star in sports is running at full tilt. This should be where Sergio shines. Showing off his connections and who he knows, and most importantly, taking pictures of everyone and making sure the right ones land on the right pages of the right sports magazines, gossip columns, or business press releases is his specialty.

But instead, he's moping and nursing his drink.

"What's wrong?" Adrien asks as he squeezes in beside him. "You're not still upset about earlier, are you?"

"No," Sergio lies and takes another sip of his whiskey, draining his glass. The acute burn of the drink as it slides down his throat is soothing.

Adrien orders him another one and a gin and tonic for himself. "As your assistant—"

"*Ex*-assistant."

"Soon to be *ex*-assistant. I'm not leaving you in the lurch," he assures him with a tinge of sympathy in his voice. "Regardless, the assistant in me wants to lecture you for not taking pictures. But the larger part of me that is your brother is glad to see you taking an actual break from work."

Sergio shrugs and grabs his fresh drink from the bartender. His eyes wander to where Jeremy and Rose are speaking with a group of sports reporters. Rose is doing most of the talking. Jeremy seems to be holding his own, but he hides behind his glass of sparkling water with a twist of lime more often than he speaks. That glass is near empty, and Sergio is tempted to bring him a new one. But given his track record over the last twenty-four hours of mess-ups every time he talks to Jeremy, he decides to focus his attention on Allison instead.

Allison, standing not far from Jeremy and Rose, is being chatted up by Chadwick Levinson, the French-Canadian who won the men's gold medal in figure skating four years ago after Jeremy had to exit the competition. She's only half paying attention to him, her eyes flitting between Chadwick and the rest of the room. Her eyes catch Sergio's, and she quickly averts them. A faint blush rises in her dark cheeks before she draws her attention back to Chadwick, who's likely either trying to talk her into switching training camps or leaving the party in favor of his room. The way he's crowding her space suggests to Sergio it's the latter.

Grabbing his drink and one of the many complimentary glasses of champagne off the bar, Sergio bids his brother goodbye with a dismissive nod of his chin, then ambles over towards Allison. He slides into the space beside her and offers her the drink.

"Thanks," she says, her cheeks still aglow as she takes it. She turns her attention back to Chadwick. "If you'll excuse me, I need to speak with Sergio."

"Sergio? Sergio Durand?" Chadwick asks. He beams at Sergio and turns his head in a way that only people who are used to having their good side photographed do automatically. His chin is lifted slightly, his left cheekbone is angled higher than his right, and a full set of pearly whites is gleaming under the soft glow of the chandeliers.

Sergio feigns ignorance, looking at him quizzically. "I'm sorry, who are you?"

"It's me! Chadwick Levinson!"

"Doesn't ring a bell," Sergio says, enjoying the way Chadwick's face falls.

"You know me!" he exclaims and playfully swats Sergio's shoulder. "Chadwick Levinson! You took my gold medal photos at the Olympic Games four years ago in Nagano."

"Did I? You know, I take so many pictures at events like that. I can hardly be expected to keep track."

"But it's me, Chadwick Levinson! I was the underdog. No one thought Jeremy Owens could be beaten."

"I couldn't," Jeremy says, startling Sergio as he steps into their conversation.

Chadwick stands up a little straighter and eyes Jeremy up and down. "Sorry, I didn't see you there," he says with a haughty lilt to his voice.

Sergio has the sudden urge to punch him in Jeremy's defense. A slight ding of an alarm goes off in his head. This is what everyone must have felt about him yesterday.

"I should really thank you," Chadwick says. "Nike was so focused on making you the future face of figure skating that they completely overlooked me for ages. Once you walked away from that endorsement, I took off. Now, look where I am!"

"I didn't walk away," Jeremy says bitterly, and now Sergio *really* wants to punch the smug look of satisfaction off Chadwick's face. Perhaps it will be the thing that lightens the tension Sergio has caused between himself and Jeremy all day. He does, despite evidence to the contrary, want Jeremy to like him.

"It's fine. You can admit you couldn't handle the pressure—"

The sound of Sergio's fist hitting the flesh of Chadwick's nose was louder than he expected.

Allison gasps, and the party comes to a screeching halt. The room goes silent except for the Sonny and Cher cover band mercifully continuing to play on the stage that Holden is now jumping onto to divert the crowd's attention.

"Alright, everyone," Holden says into the microphone. "Grab a glass of champagne. The countdown starts in less than a minute."

"What the fuck did you do that for?" Chadwick bellows, clutching his nose—and, to Sergio's surprise, Jeremy.

"He was being a prick!" Sergio exclaims to Jeremy, pointing at a moaning Chadwick as he's offered napkins by a caterer to soak up the blood pouring from his nose.

"From where I stand, you are both guilty of being pricks," Jeremy says.

Sergio throws up his hands in his defense. "I didn't like the way he was talking to you."

"I didn't either, but I can take care of myself. I don't need you, of all people, to go all Jeff Gillooly on him for me," Jeremy says right as Holden yells, "Ten!" from the stage, and a team of security guards comes rushing into the ballroom, heading straight through the packed crowd towards where Sergio, Jeremy, and Allison are standing.

Sergio hangs his head and mumbles, "Why can't I get anything right today?"

"Nine!"

"What was that?" Jeremy asks over the din, his tone still accusatory.

"Eight!"

"I said, why can't I get anything right today?"

"Seven!"

"Well, there's always tomorrow." Jeremy shrugs and offers him a bit of a smirk with an annoyed stare.

"Six!"

"See you later, Sergio," Jeremy says and walks away with Allison, who wrinkles her nose at Sergio from his side.

"Five!"

"Yeah, maybe tomorrow," Sergio says to himself.

"Four!"

He eyes the security team as they begin to close in on him and blindly grabs a glass of champagne off a server's tray as they walk by.

"Three!"

He drinks it all in one gulp, not bothering to wait until midnight, then puts the glass down and braces for the incoming impact of the hotel's security team.

"Two!"

"One! Happy ..."

Chapter Three

"Uncle Sergio! Wake up!" Henry shouts, kneeing Sergio in the balls and jolting him awake.

Sergio shoots up, confused and wincing as he grabs his aforementioned balls. Gus hisses and runs out from underneath the bed and bolts out the door. This is not the knock-down tackle he was bracing himself for. Though given the pointiness of Henry's knee, it does perhaps hurt more than getting laid out by four hulking security guards. That said, they must have hit him pretty hard for him to wake up in his own bed and not remember anything that happened after midnight.

"Henry, my boy," he manages to say through gritted teeth. "Good rule of thumb. Let adults sleep in on New Year's Day."

"That's tomorrow, silly!" Henry laughs.

"No. That's definitely today," Sergio says, still wincing. *I should know, I had a rough night last night*. Which, now that he thinks about it, if he was drunk enough to black out and forget the rest of the evening, shouldn't he be feeling worse than he does right now? Well, worse than he does outside of getting kicked in the balls for the second day in a row by a five-year-old's knobby knee. He really is going to need to talk to Henry about that if this is going to be his standard wake-up call for the week. Or maybe the solution is to lock his door. Too bad he hadn't done that the night before.

"Come on, Uncle Sergio," Henry pleads, pulling at Sergio's arm. "Dad said to come get you. Breakfast is almost ready."

"Is it another big spread like yesterday?"

Henry stops pulling and looks at Sergio, his face scrunched up in bewilderment. "You weren't here for breakfast yesterday."

"Yes, Henry, I was," Sergio says impatiently. He's in no mood for whatever little game Henry is playing. It would have been nice to be able to sleep in today before he goes on his apology tour for last night's foibles. His focus is on Jeremy, but second, he needs to talk to Holden, who likely had to bail him out of jail if Chadwick decided to be an asshole and press charges. *Oh, shit*. Maybe it's not Henry that's confused. He pulls the kid in close to his chest. "How mad is your dad at me this morning?"

"Daddy's not mad at you."

"No? What about Mommy?"

"Mommy's always mad at you." Henry giggles.

"Okay, that's true," Sergio says, lightly laughing along with him. "Did you wake up your Uncle Adrien yet?"

"No." Henry continues to giggle as Sergio tickles his side.

"Good. Go wake him up like you did me again, please," he says, then remembering his brother quit on him the day before, adds, "Maybe put a little extra kick into him for me, would ya?"

"Okay!" Henry yells as he jumps out of Sergio's arms and off the bed, throwing his thumbs into the air as he then goes thundering down the hall.

Sergio waits until he hears the telltale *oof* of Adrien being woken up in Henry's special manner before he rises and exits the room. He smiles and snickers to himself, trying to figure out how he even got to bed last night clad in his sweatpants and T-shirt. It's not the first time he's woken up somewhere, unsure of how he got there. But he is sure Holden and Adrien will be more than happy to tease him about it as they retell the drama of the evening over coffee and breakfast before hitting the slopes again for another day of skiing.

Once downstairs, the reception Sergio gets from Rose is as chilly as it was the day before. Clearly, Henry hadn't picked up on his parents being upset with Sergio's antics last night. That's fair, he reasons. They were likely hiding it from Henry. No use telling a five-year-old his favorite uncle is a complete degenerate who punches Olympic gold medalists—no matter how much they deserved it—in the face.

"Good morning, shithead!" Holden says, loud and bright, as Sergio trips once again over Gus underfoot.

"Goddamn it, Gus!" he yells.

"Hey! Don't yell at my cat," Rose scolds, picking Gus up and kissing the space between his ears before she places him on the nearby couch and then moves back into the kitchen.

"Sorry," he says to her, but doesn't mean it. He turns back to Holden, "And, sorry about last night as well. I hope I didn't cause too much damage. I'll pay you back whatever I owe you if you had to bail me out or something?"

"Bail you out?" Holden questions.

"Money isn't going to fix this," Rose says, taking plates from the cabinet.

Sergio, attempting to move the Gus incident behind them, turns on the charm. He grabs the plates from her and hopes it doesn't fail him today like it did yesterday. Maybe this time she'll let him drink his coffee. "Lemme get that."

"Thanks," she says, avoiding his eye contact before she spins around and whips him across the chin with her full, red ponytail.

"Listen," Sergio continues as he goes about setting the table. "I am really sorry about last night. I was drunk."

"You weren't that drunk," Rose says.

"I obviously was if I punched someone," Sergio says with a laugh, trying to lighten the mood.

"Punched someone?" Holden flips a pancake, then looks over his shoulder at Sergio. His eyebrows rise, and his lips quirk up at the corners. "Maybe you were drunk."

"Yeah, I punched Chadwick Levinson last night. Did you all not see that?"

"Sergio, what are you talking about?" Rose asks him.

Confused, he takes a seat, dropping his task of setting the table. "Last night," he says, holding his hands out in front of him, palms up. "I punched Chadwick Levinson for insulting Jeremy."

"Umm ... that was *you*, mate," Holden says slowly, placing a pot of coffee on the table that Sergio begins to pour a cup from.

"What?"

"Yeah," Rose says, taking the full mug of coffee he poured out of his hand. He frowns and starts pouring another. "You were the asshole who insulted Jeremy last night."

"Okay, I may have been thoughtless—"

"You're always thoughtless," Adrien says as he enters the kitchen with Henry dangling upside down from his shoulders, laughing in delight.

"That's for sure," Rose says and steals the second cup of coffee as well, then holds it out to Adrien as he places Henry back down on the ground.

Sergio, frustrated, pours yet another cup. All of this is feeling way too familiar for him, and he's starting to think everyone is fucking with him, which he supposes he deserves. "But I punched the guy!"

"Sergio, dude, you didn't punch anybody last night. And definitely not Chadwick Levinson. That man isn't even allowed on our property," Holden says, delivering plates of pancakes, bacon, and sliced fresh fruit. Rose points at Holden, as if punctuating his statement about Chadwick's ban from their haven in the Adirondacks. She then takes Sergio's latest mug of coffee and places it in front of where Holden takes a seat.

"I did!" Sergio practically shouts. "At the New Year's Eve party!"

"Sergio, the party's not until tonight," Holden says solemnly.

"What? How? It was last night." He pulls his phone from his sweatpants pocket, ready to show them that they're all wrong. When he looks at it, he gets the shock of his life. There, right beneath the time, eight-thirty am, is the date, December thirty-first.

"Alright, quit fucking around, Sergio." Holden laughs and mercifully hands Sergio back his cup of coffee. "Here, it looks like you need this more than I do." He then claps him on the back. "Eat up! We're gonna need all the calories we can get for the slopes today."

Once on the slopes, Sergio starts to wonder if yesterday was all a dream. No one has any recollection of the events of yesterday as he seems to. But he does remember taking pictures, documenting the whole day. Most notably, he had snapped a few shots of himself and Adrien from the chairlift he finds himself perched on beside his brother again right now. He pulls his GoPro out of his pocket, sure that he'll find photographic evidence of the existence of yesterday in the camera's memory bank.

"What the fuck," he mutters as he flips through the photos, finding no trace of the previous day's activities. *Did someone erase them?*

"What the fuck, what?" Adrien asks, sounding exhausted. "You've been weird all day."

Sergio starts shaking his camera as if, like a magic eight ball, the photos will appear to tell him his fate. "The photos I took yesterday! Where the fuck are they?"

"They're on your work camera, the EOS. Not your GoPro. Why would you even think you could find them there?"

"Not the fashion shoot from two days ago!" Sergio says, frustrated. "The ones I took of you yesterday from this lift while we were skiing."

"Sergio, what are you talking about? We didn't go skiing yesterday."

"Yes, we did!"

"No, we didn't!"

"We did!" Sergio shouts, his voice escalating louder and louder the longer this conversation goes on. The two teenagers in the chairlift in front of them turn and look at Sergio like he has two heads. He flips them off, but they continue to stare and watch the show, whispering to each other.

"Sergio," Adrien says gently, and grabs the camera from Sergio's shaking hands, then places it in his coat pocket for safekeeping. Which is a smart call, considering Sergio is two seconds away from throwing it into the trees. "We didn't go skiing yesterday. We woke up, we did the Dior photoshoot, we hopped on a plane, and we came here. Holden and Henry picked us up, we had dinner, you insulted Jeremy, and we all went to bed. Are you having some kind of mental mind snap I need to know about?"

"Pfft. As if you'd care even if I did. You quit on me yesterday."

Adrien shifts in his seat uncomfortably. "I didn't quit on you yesterday."

"That's funny because I distinctly remember you quitting right here, sitting beside me on this fucking chairlift like you are right now."

Adrien shifts again. "Sergio, I didn't quit ... not yet, at least."

Sergio whips his head around and looks directly at his brother beside him. "You're still quitting?"

Adrien holds his hands up in defense in front of his shoulders. "Still? Sergio, I haven't had a chance to talk to you about that yet and given your"—he gestures his hands in opposite circles at Sergio— "*state* right now, this isn't the time to have this conversation."

"So, you *are* quitting?" Sergio asks again as the chairlift drops them off at the top of the slope.

"Look, Sergio," Adrien says, skiing to a stop and taking a deep breath. "I don't want anything to ever come between us. Which is why I have to quit working for you."

"Fine. Whatever, asshole," Sergio says and propels himself forward to ski down the mountain and away from Adrien. Shouting over his shoulder as he goes, "But just so you know, you quitting is something that *will* come between us."

"Did you guys have fun?" Holden asks once they find each other on the bunny hills.

Sergio, the same as from *his* yesterday, doesn't get a chance to answer as Henry is already calling his name. "Uncle Sergio! Look!" he shouts, then zooms down the hill past him, flipping forward to a stop like he'd done the previous day before to land on his rump. "Did you see?"

"Yeah, I saw," Sergio says, planting a fake and rigid smile on his face in an attempt to remain positive in Henry's presence. Whatever is going on is not Henry's fault, which gives him an idea. Elaborate joke or not that might be being played at his expense, it is unlikely that Henry is in on it. There's no way he could ever remember to keep the terms of some complicated prank clear in his head for longer than five minutes.

Sergio skis over to the fallen and giggling child and lifts him back onto his feet, then crouches down and helps him out of his skis. "Henry, what day is it?"

"Thursday?"

"No." Sergio laughs, the first genuine one of his day. "Well, actually yes, it is Thursday. But what's the date? It's a holiday, right?"

"It's New Year's Eve!" Henry answers excitedly. "I'm going to the Weirs' for a party. Do you want to come?"

Sergio twists up his lips and considers. Given how he remembers the events of New Year's Eve going yesterday, a child's celebration is likely to be far more fun, though not necessarily plausible. Frowning, he says, "I think I have my own party I have to go to."

Henry nods in understanding. "The one my mom and dad and Jeremy are going to."

"That's the one."

"You should tell Jeremy you're sorry there."

Sergio's frown deepens, his lips pulling down farther, and he wonders how his faux pas is still so fresh on Henry's mind. After all, to Sergio, it was two days ago. But, he supposes, if nobody seems to remember yesterday, his incident with Jeremy only happened last night. And if apologizing to Jeremy is all it will take for everyone to be on the same page, or God help him, the same day, he can suck up his pride—what's left of it at this point—and utter the magic words before the clock strikes twelve.

At the party—filled with the same revelers as before, the same who's who of winter sports mingling with the who's who of hangers-on and sponsorships, all glad-handing each other like this is the first time they've ever met—Sergio watches from where he's perched once again at the bar. He'd be bored if he weren't so frustrated.

The rest of his day carried on the same as the morning, with everyone acting like Sergio was losing his shit. The effect of which has Sergio really wanting to lose his shit. Instead, he's opted for drowning himself in whiskey, hoping that at some point he'll get the chance to do what Henry suggested earlier and apologize to Jeremy for his insensitivity. But what insensitivity is he meant to apologize for? His blunder in assuming Jeremy had too much to drink instead of a neurological disorder, or his punch to Chadwick Levinson's nose in Jeremy's honor, that nobody seems to remember. Reasonably, he figures it's the former as he watches Jeremy work the room with Rose while Chadwick, completely lacking any evidence of having been punched, works Allison into his good graces in a nearby corner.

"What's wrong?" Adrien asks him. "You're not still upset about earlier, are you?"

"No," Sergio says, and this time he means it. It seems his brother's quitting is an inevitable fact he's going to have to accept. He finishes what's left of his drink in one large gulp.

"Then what are you moping about?" Adrien asks and orders another whiskey from the bartender for Sergio, as well as a gin and tonic for himself.

"I'm not moping," Sergio grumbles.

"You kind of are," Adrien says, and pauses. He looks at Sergio with his head tilted slightly to the side in thought. "I get it, though. It's been a rough twenty-four hours."

With his gaze back on Jeremy, Sergio blindly grabs his drink from the bartender and takes a sip. "You don't even know the half of it."

"This isn't easy for me either, you know?" Adrien says, sipping his drink as well. Sergio can feel his brother's eyes boring a hole into his temple. "It's not a decision I came to lightly."

"I'm sure it's not." Sergio brushes him off. He may have accepted Adrien's resignation, but that doesn't mean he's in the mood to hear his reasoning. Especially when that reasoning is likely Daphne.

"Daphne and I—"

"Adrien, please. Not tonight."

"Alright," Adrien says with a light pat on Sergio's shoulder. "We can talk about it tomorrow."

"If there even is a tomorrow." Sergio goes back to his grumbling.

"What was that?"

"Nothing, Adrien. Go have fun." He grabs his drink and walks away from his brother. He pauses his steps once he reaches the center of the room and debates which way to go. Allison is trying to catch his eye with a slight lift of her hand and a pleading raise of her right eyebrow, as if to say, 'Please get me away from this blowhard.' He could go that route and help her, but he'd wind up ending tonight in much the same manner as he did the night before. His other option is to cut straight to Jeremy, who's being slowly pushed out of the conversation going on with Rose and the gathered sports reporters. The reporters have all but muscled him out of their circle. Looking to heed Henry's advice, Sergio begins to make a beeline, albeit a slightly stumbling one reminiscent of a bumblebee and less a productive and determined worker bee gathering pollen, to where Jeremy is standing with his feet shuffling awkwardly as he tries to re-ingratiate himself into the conversation. A pang of something that resembles pity hits Sergio in the chest, stiffening the area around his heart. It's uncomfortable to watch Jeremy get shunned by the same people who followed him around like he was a god four years ago.

"Listen, Jeremy," he says as he approaches him. "Can I talk to you?"

"This isn't really a great time," Jeremy says, gesturing at the nearby reporters.

"It's alright, Jeremy," one reporter says. "We're done with you."

"Oh, alright then," Jeremy says and turns to Sergio, looking dejected. "I guess now is a fine time."

Sergio winces internally, feeling that after that, this is absolutely not the right time to bring up his own callous misstep regarding Jeremy. But forge on, he will in his desperation to lighten this awful feeling of sinking he has in his chest. "Look," he starts with as they begin to walk away from the reporters and Rose. "About the other night."

"You mean last night?" Jeremy's lips press together. He eyes Sergio up and down, and Sergio can't help but notice how tired Jeremy looks. There's something in his eyes, a harshness that says he wishes he were anywhere but here right now. Not only talking to Sergio, but at this party.

"Yeah, last night." Sergio agrees. He offers him a soft smile, hoping to warm Jeremy in his favor before he continues. "I'm sorry about that."

"It's fine." Jeremy sighs. "I'm pretty used to it by now."

"Well, I didn't mean to offend."

"You didn't."

"I kind of think I did," Sergio presses on. "And I didn't mean to."

"Nobody ever *means* to," Jeremy says, carefully making his way through the crowd with Sergio keeping step beside him. Each of his steps is deliberate, and Sergio suppresses the urge to grab onto Jeremy's elbow to keep him steady and lead him somewhere quieter and less crowded. But Jeremy seems to have his own determined destination in mind.

It's not until he hears Chadwick Levinson's voice that Sergio realizes where Jeremy has led them.

"Nobody thought Jeremy Owens could be beat," Chadwick blusters to an annoyed-looking Allison. Sergio groans at his words. Apparently, he's doomed to hear this conversion between the two rivals no matter how it's provoked.

"I couldn't," Jeremy says, stepping in beside Allison.

Chadwick stands up a little straighter and looks Jeremy up and down. "Sorry, I didn't see you there," he says with a haughty lilt to his voice. Sergio immediately remembers why it felt so good to punch this asshole the night before.

"I should really thank you," Chadwick says. "Nike was so focused on making you the future face of figure skating that they completely overlooked me for ages. Once you walked away from that endorsement, I took off. Now, look where I am!"

"I didn't walk away," Jeremy says.

Sergio can taste the bitterness radiating off of Jeremy. Despite how thick it is, he keeps his cool. Sergio's punch did not go over well last night. If he wants to make any inroads with Jeremy, he needs to keep his fists to himself.

Chadwick lifts his hand as if lazily swatting a fly on a hot summer day. "It's fine. You can admit you couldn't handle the pressure."

"I handled the pressure just fine," Jeremy says. "And you damn well know it."

Sergio looks at Allison standing on the other side of Chadwick. She seems to be having the same reaction that he is: careful silence and a clenched fist at her side. He's half tempted to wait this out and see if Allison throws the punch this time.

"Maybe," Chadwick says, his tone bored. He shifts his attention back to Allison. "Remember what I offered. My coaching staff would love to take you on."

Allison positions herself beside Jeremy. "I'm fine where I am."

"Well, if you change your mind, you know how to reach me," Chadwick says and turns to walk away from them. When he does, he finally notices Sergio. "Sergio? Sergio Durand!"

"Yeah, yeah. It's me," Sergio says in defeat right as Holden hops on stage to announce the beginning of the countdown.

"Ten!"

"It's good to see you," Chadwick says.

"Nine!"

"Don't tell me you know Allison, too?" Chadwick asks.

"Eight!"

"Yeah, I know her ..."

"Seven!"

"... well, I know Rose and Jeremy."

"Six!"

Chadwick leans in a little closer. "It's a shame she's training with them ..."

"Five!"

"... I mean, Rose is great and all ..."

"Four!"

"... but Jeremy." Chadwick winces.

"Three!"

"He's lost whatever magic people thought he had."

"Two!"

Sergio can't help himself. It feels even better to hit him this time.

"One! Happy ..."

Chapter Four

"Uncle Sergio! Wake up!"

"Fuck," Sergio coughs out as he jumps out of bed, then doubles over in pain for the third day in a row from Henry's insanely accurate knee to the balls. He narrowly misses stepping on Gus as the cat hisses and shoots out from under the bed. "Fuck!" he cries again, clutching himself. Which, despite the near vomit-inducing pain, is not why he's cursing. His fucks come more out of the frustration he's feeling that he's found himself waking up on New Year's Eve again. He doesn't even need to check the date on his phone. He's been awake for thirty seconds, and it's already painfully obvious he's back to yesterday, as he has no memory of anything happening after the clock struck midnight.

"What's wrong?" Henry asks, looking up at him with wide, innocent eyes.

"Nothing," Sergio grumbles, knowing full well Henry will never understand. "Can you go wake up your Uncle Adrien and send him downstairs? I need to talk to him."

"Okay!" Henry yells and runs out the door, his thumbs raised high above his head. Sergio waits for the telltale *oof* of Adrien being awakened and then slinks out of his own room, tired, defeated, and in desperate need of a cup of coffee.

"Good morning, shithead!" Holden says brightly as Sergio shuffles into the kitchen, tripping over Gus while going straight past Holden and Rose, heading right to the coffeepot.

He pulls it off the warmer before it's finished brewing and pours himself a cup, chugging it black and piping hot, acknowledging no one in the room. When his cup is empty, he pours himself another one.

"Thanks for pouring me a cup," Rose says, reaching for it.

Sergio jerks it away. "Oh no, you don't. Not today."

"It's like no one ever taught you to share."

"We've tried," Adrien says as he enters with Henry hanging upside down from his shoulders. "Some dogs can't be housebroken."

Sergio rolls his eyes. "I'm not a dog."

"Jury is still out on that one." Adrien laughs.

"Jury is still out on you," Sergio bites back.

"Now, now, boys," Holden says, walking between them, his arms laden with food to place on the table. "There's too much to do today for you two to be fighting."

"Yes, we have a full day," Sergio says, annoyed. He puts his cup of coffee down, then holds up his hand and ticks through his fingers as he lists. "We eat breakfast, then we go skiing," he says, pausing to look directly at Adrien, "which is when Adrien quits on me." All the color fades from Adrien's face. "Then after that, we have lunch. Then more skiing. Then I go with Holden to grab Henry from Jeremy and make an ass out of myself. And after that is the New Year's party where I punch Chadwick Levinson, and this day starts all the fuck over again."

The room goes silent, and everyone looks at Sergio with varying levels of confusion on their faces. Holden is the first to speak. "Any particular reason you have 'punch Chadwick Levinson' on your agenda, mate?"

And that's when it hits him. Maybe if he can get through today without throwing a punch, he can wake up tomorrow.

"Five!"

Don't hit him.

"Four!"

Don't hit him.

"Three!"

You can do this.

"Two!"

Oh, thank God it's almost over.

"One! Happy ..."

"Uncle Sergio! Wake up!"

"Fuuuuuuck," Sergio bemoans into his pillow as he rolls onto his side, cradling his freshly smashed balls in his hands while Gus hisses underneath the bed before bolting out the bedroom door.

"It's time for breakfast."

"I know, buddy," Sergio says, his face still obscured by his pillow as he tries to catch his breath. "I'm sitting this one out."

"Uncle Sergio! Wake up!"

"Goddamn it."

"*Hiss...*"

"Uncle Sergio! Wake up!"

"*Fuck!*" Sergio yells out in pain and jumps out of bed, missing Gus by an inch as the cat runs out from under the bed and through the bedroom door.

Henry looks up at him, frightened.

"I'm sorry, buddy," he says hastily, leaning back over the bed to muss up Henry's hair. "Go wake up Adrien. I need to go talk to your dad."

Henry, still stunned, blinks at him and makes no attempt to move.

"Go on," Sergio encourages, and watches Henry get off the bed and make his way slowly out of Sergio's room, looking over his shoulder once as he goes. Sergio gestures for him to continue with a few flicks of his hand. Once Henry's gone, he turns on his heel and runs out of the room and down the stairs, not even listening for the telltale *oof* of Adrien being awakened.

"Good morning, shithead!" Holden beams.

"We need to talk," Sergio grunts out, tripping over Gus, then grabbing Holden by the shoulder and pulling him towards the back door.

"Hey!" Holden tries to pull it from his grasp. "What the fuck, man? I've got breakfast going."

"I know." Sergio huffs. After all, it's not like he hasn't been through this before. With more force, he tugs Holden halfway out the door. "But I need to talk to you."

Holden tosses the spatula in his hand onto the counter. It bounces off the granite and lands on the floor as the back door clicks shut. The cold air outside gives Sergio a sobering shock, but it's not enough to jolt him back to a timeline that makes sense.

"Alright, what the fuck is up with you?" Holden asks as he rubs his exposed arms. Like Sergio, he's outside in only sweatpants and a T-shirt. Unlike Sergio, he's at least wearing slippers.

Sergio peers over Holden's shoulder and can see Rose peering out the glass at them. He starts walking them further away from the house, moving them more towards the barn. "I know this is going to sound crazy," he says, yanking at his hair. "But I'm living the same day, over and over again."

"As in, your day-to-day life is monotonous? Sergio, that's called being an adult. Why are you so bent out of shape?"

Sergio stops in his tracks and rubs harshly at his face. "No, not like that. I'm literally living the same day over. This is the sixth time I've lived today."

"Well, yeah," Holden says, giving Sergio a fleeting moment of hope. "This is our sixth New Year's all together up here."

"No!" Sergio shouts. "I mean, I keep waking up on the same day! Today. New Year's Eve. And no one else seems to notice."

"I'm still not following. Do you want to go back to bed or something? We can talk about this tomorrow."

"Aren't you listening? There is no tomorrow. Tonight the clock will strike midnight, and I'll wake back up right here."

"Well, yeah," Holden says again. "That's kind of how going to sleep works. One tends to wake up where they fell asleep. Unless they were drugged." He pauses and looks at Sergio, furrowing his brows. "Are you on drugs?"

"No! I don't know what I am! All I know is that I've woken up right here at your house for the past six days."

"That's impossible, though. You only got here yesterday."

"Yesterday to you, maybe. But to me, it's been six days."

"So, you're telling me that you've been here for six days and none of us has noticed?"

"Yes!" Sergio yells out.

"Wow. Sorry, mate. That sounds like a real kick in the dick."

"Funny you should say that because your son wakes me up with a literal kick in the dick every morning."

"That sucks." Holden winces. "He's got one hell of a kick on him. Have you tried locking the door before you go to bed?"

Sergio looks at him with a blank expression, eyes narrowed, and his lips set in a line.

"I'm only saying, it might help." Holden shrugs, then rubs his arms some more before he blows into his hands.

"What part of 'I wake up on the same day' are you not getting? Even if I lock the door tonight, it won't change the fact that I didn't lock it last night. So no matter what, Henry is going to burst into my bedroom tomorrow morning and knee me in the nuts."

"I thought you said he kicked you in the dick."

"Are we really going to split hairs here?"

"You're right. It's the same thing." Holden holds up his hands in defense, then stands a little taller. His eyes shine bright as if a light bulb was flicked on somewhere inside him with an idea. "Wait a minute." He grabs Sergio's shoulder and looks him directly in the eyes. "Are you fucking with me? Is this some kind of prank? Because if it is, it's hilarious! You really got me on this one. I was actually concerned for a minute."

Sergio's blood boils. "This. Isn't. A. Prank."

"It kind of feels like a prank."

"If anyone is being pranked, it's me!"

Holden lets out a whistle. "I wish I'd have come up with this."

Sergio jolts out from under Holden's hold on his shoulders and rubs harshly at his face. "Trust me, I wish you had, too."

"Okay, so let me try to get a handle on this. What you're telling me is that today feels exactly like yesterday, even though you weren't here yesterday?"

"No. I'm telling you that I have woken up here for six days in a row on a perpetual Mobius strip of New Year's Eves, and I'm the only one who notices."

"So, like a time loop?"

"I don't know. I guess. How does something like that even work?"

Holden shrugs again. "Not sure, man. We don't even have a hot tub."

"A hot tub!" Sergio exclaims, not sure what Holden could possibly be talking about.

"Yeah, you know. Like that movie! *Hot Tub Time Machine*."

"I don't think this equates," Sergio says and hangs his head in defeat as he realizes he's talking to a moron.

"Oh!" Holden's eyes widen and his mouth drops open into an oh shape to match his word. "Maybe this is more like *Groundhog Day*?"

"Like with the rodent?"

"Yeah! I mean, sort of. Like how Bill Murray had to repeat the same day over and over again to learn how to be a better person or something."

"Is that what that story was about?" Sergio asks, trying to remember the details.

"It definitely wasn't about him continuing to be an asshole," Holden points out, right as something catches Sergio's eye over Holden's shoulder. It's Jeremy looking like he's fresh from waking up, coming out of the barn with a steaming mug held in his sweatshirt sleeve-covered hands. He blows on it and then takes a sip. "I mean, I'm no expert here. But if what you're saying is true, I'm thinking you've been given the opportunity to change yourself."

Sergio keeps his eyes on Jeremy, unable to look away. His cheeks are flushed from the cold, and Sergio has an urge to warm them with his hands. Not that it would help. He is woefully underdressed for the morning chill, and he's pretty sure his toes are frozen. At least Jeremy was wise enough to wear a thick hoodie over his practice gear.

"Yeah, I think you might be right."

"Great." Holden claps Sergio on the shoulder. "Now, can we please go back inside? I'm freezing and my bacon's probably burning."

"Yeah," Sergio says, slowly taking his eyes off Jeremy. As he looks away, something deep inside him tingles in the pit of his stomach. He looks over his shoulder and catches Jeremy stepping through the barn door, heading back inside. The sunken feeling in the pit of his stomach is practically screaming, telling Sergio that having a second chance with Jeremy is key.

Chapter Five

"Uncle Sergio! Wake up!"

"Oof ..." Sergio coughs and wheezes, then rolls onto his side, curling into a ball, and tries to catch his breath. The sound of Gus's familiar hiss rings out below him before the cat goes running out the door like an angry, furry specter. "Morning, Henry ..."

Henry tilts his head, looking at him quizzically. "Are you alright?"

"I've been better," Sergio says around a labored breath.

Henry's head tilts the other way. "Are you sick?"

Sick of this shit. "No. It's been a rough morning."

"But you just woke up!" Henry throws his hands up, exasperated with his uncle.

Sergio repositions himself to sit up against the headboard and pulls Henry into his lap. "It was a long night."

Henry's eyes go wide. "Did you have a bad dream? I had one of those once. Mommy says to not be scared."

"You know what, kid? You're right. It was only a bad dream." It's more like a living nightmare, but Henry doesn't need to know that.

Henry leaps off Sergio's lap, narrowly missing kneeing him in the balls again. "Stay here. I have something to help," he says as he runs out the door. His footsteps thunder across the hall to his bedroom. There's a brief pause in the noise before his footsteps start up again in quick succession.

Sergio, now a little wiser, braces himself for Henry's approach and holds his arms out when he sees Henry come careening into his room, holding a stuffed dog the size of his torso. The sight almost catches him off guard, but Sergio still manages to grab Henry and control his landing as he leaps back onto the bed.

"Here!" Henry yells, holding the toy out for Sergio. Sergio takes it and looks at it. It's reminiscent of a Saint Bernard except it has comically long, droopy ears.

"What's this?" Sergio asks.

"It's a dog."

"Yes, I can see that." Sergio chuckles and flaps the stuffed dog's ears. "But what does it do?"

Henry shrugs and floats his hands up to shoulder height. "Keeps the bad dreams away?"

"Hmm ..." Sergio hums, nodding with his lips pulled into a tight line to make himself look serious about what Henry handed him as a solution. He knows full well there is nothing this stuffed dog can do about his current predicament, but he's certainly not going to crush Henry's spirit with a reaction that conveys that. "Thank you, Henry," he says, and places the toy beside him on the bed, tucking it in so only its head is peeking out from underneath the covers. "I believe this dog will be most helpful in fighting off bad dreams."

Henry's lips pull into a wide and confident grin.

Sergio ruffles his hair. "Should we go get some breakfast?"

"Yeah!"

"Good," he says and gets out of the bed, helping Henry down in the process. "I'm starving. Now, go wake up your Uncle Adrien."

"Okay!" Henry bounds out the door, holding two very enthusiastic thumbs up over his head.

In a rare moment of awareness, Sergio cranes his head out the door and yells, "Gently!"

Henry raises his thumbs over his head once again, then bursts through the door to Adrien's bedroom. He is greeted by Adrien with a sleepy, "Hey, buddy." Thankfully, it is not accompanied by the 'oof' of Henry kicking Adrien in the balls.

Sergio, wearing the self-satisfied grin of a man who feels like he accomplished a good deed, leaves his bedroom and heads down the stairs. Having done something altruistic—no matter how minor—he's ready to take on this repeated day with a new attitude.

"Good morning, shithead!" he says in chorus with Holden as he enters the kitchen, trips over Gus, recovers, and makes a swift move to grab the flatware from Rose to lie across the table. Unlike his failure to avoid tripping over Gus, he does manage to deftly dodge the whip of Rose's ponytail by leaning back. After finishing setting the table, he grabs the coffee and begins filling up the mugs, starting with a cup for Rose.

She raises a suspicious eyebrow at him as he hands her the steaming cup.

"What? Did you expect me to only pour coffee for myself?" he asks as he fills a second mug and holds it out to Adrien as he enters the kitchen with Henry hanging from his shoulders.

"I suspect that's exactly what she thought," Adrien says as he takes the mug after placing Henry back onto his feet.

"You all have such little faith in me." Sergio shakes his head. He has a smile on his lips and thinks, *See? This isn't so hard.*

"I have faith in you," Holden says, and places the plates full of pancakes, bacon, and sliced fruit onto the table. He even refuses the mug of coffee Sergio is holding out for him. "You take that. I'll drink the sludge at the bottom of the pot."

"Seriously?" Sergio, Rose, and Adrien all ask together.

"Yeah. I like it when I can chew it," Holden says, pouring himself the last remnants of the coffee. He takes an exaggerated sip from his mug and smacks his lips after he swallows. "Ahh. Delicious."

"You're disgusting," Rose and Adrien say together as everyone begins to grab food.

"So," Sergio says, dishing up his plate and looking toward Rose. "Jeremy. What's his day look like?"

She barely looks at him while she pours syrup over Henry's pancakes. "Why? Are you looking to insult him again?"

Sergio feels his cheeks get slightly hot. "No. I was ..." He pauses, and his shoulders creep up towards his ears. "Hoping to apologize, actually."

"Really?" she says. "I've never known you to ever say you're sorry."

"You and me both," Adrien says, with a tight laugh.

Sergio snaps his head to look at his brother. He takes a quick breath before retorting. Saying something snarky at his moment isn't going to keep his brother from quitting on him later. "Don't worry," he says. "I'll be saying I'm sorry to you later."

"Doubt it," Adrien says and takes a long sip of his coffee.

One person at a time. Sergio lets out a small, quick sigh. He turns his attention back to Rose. "Really, though. Should I go talk to him before or after skiing?"

Rose shrugs. "After, I guess. Allison is gonna be at the barn any minute now, and we need to get right to work with no distractions." She takes a bite of her food and then washes it down with coffee. "Which, speaking of, I better get going."

"You didn't finish your breakfast," Holden says, looking rejected as if there's something wrong with his spread.

She rises from her seat and grabs her plate, then kisses him on the cheek. "I'll take the rest of it to go. You boys have fun. And maybe while you're on the mountain, you can feed this idiot"—she ruffles Sergio's hair with her free hand as she walks by— "a proper script on how to apologize to someone."

In the chair lift high above the snow-covered mountain, with their legs and skis dangling in the air, Adrien teases Sergio. "Do we need to talk about what you're gonna say to Jeremy today to apologize to him? Or are you going to act like a grown-up on your own? We could pull a Cyrano De Bergerac if you need?"

"Nah." Sergio laughs, enjoying the lightness between himself and his brother. "I think I can manage."

"I don't know," Adrien says with a slight sing-song nature to his voice. "Have you ever actually apologized to anyone?"

Sergio scoffs. "Yes." He has. Sort of. It's arguable if he's ever really done it without the ulterior motive of aiming to get his way, though.

"Well, a word of advice. Don't make it about you."

"I would never."

"You would always." Adrien playfully jostles him with his shoulder, making their airborne chariot sway back and forth.

Sergio turns to look at his brother and gives him a quick wink. *Keep it light and playful,* he reminds himself. Every other time the two brothers have been on this lift, Adrien has quit on him when he hasn't managed to keep the mood fun. With his brother in a seemingly good and lighthearted mood, Sergio is feeling amiable.

"So, I've been thinking," he begins, jostling Adrien back with his shoulder and creating more sway back and forth on the chairlift.

"About?"

"I'm giving you a raise," Sergio says.

"Sergio." Adrien laughs with a tinge of bitterness that makes Sergio nervous. "I don't need a raise."

"Sure you do. You're the reason I stay afloat. Anyone can see that."

"I'm the reason you make your deadlines. The money from our bottomless trust keeps us afloat."

"Maybe so," he says, dropping all pretenses and bluster. "But without your help behind the scenes, I'd be nowhere." Sergio looks over his shoulder at his brother. His profile is striking against the backdrop of the high trees and ice blue sky. Sergio can't help but want to take a picture. He pulls out his camera and captures it. Holding the screen to his brother, he shows it to him. "You always did photograph well."

"You've always known how to take an excellent shot." Adrien shrugs.

"Anyway, as I was saying, we make a good team. And it's high time I started making you feel like you were an equal partner."

Adrien lets out a sigh, and his cheeks lose some of their rosy color. "That's the thing, though, Sergio. I don't want to *be* an equal partner. I need to branch out on my own." He pauses and takes a deep breath, then turns to look at Sergio with a bit of sadness. "I've been putting this off. But it's time for me to stop working for you."

Defeated, Sergio moves his gaze to their dangling skis. "How long have you felt this way?"

"I can't pinpoint when, but it's been a while."

"Like since Daphne?"

"No," Adrien snaps. "This has nothing to do with Daphne. This is about me wanting to realize my own dream. I can't keep leeching off of you."

Sergio turns and half smiles at his brother. "Technically, as you pointed out, we're leeching off our trust fund."

"Yeah, well, I can't keep leeching only off that either and maintain any sense of dignity."

Sergio nods. He can't necessarily say he gets it, but at least he's got a better answer as to why Adrien is quitting before he goes zooming down the mountain.

———♥———

"Did you guys have fun?" Holden asks when Sergio and Adrien come to a stop at the bottom of the bunny hills.

"Could have gone better," Sergio says, looking out for Henry's impending crash arrival at the same time Adrien says, "It could have gone worse."

"Uncle Sergio! Look!" Henry shouts as he zooms down the hill in a perfect miniature replica of his father's crouched skiing stance before he somersaults to a stop. "Did you see?"

"Yeah, Henry. I saw. That was *very* impressive," he says as he lifts Henry back onto his feet. He crouches down in the compacted snow to come to eye level with him and starts to unlatch his skis from his boots. "Did you and your dad have fun?"

"Yup!" Henry says. "Maybe tomorrow I can ride the big lift with you and go down the mountain from the top."

Sergio raises an eyebrow at him, then lifts him up with one arm so his other hand is free to carry Henry's skis as they make their way to the lodge. "That's pretty high, and it's a long way down."

"I know," Henry says, dropping his head back and looking at the mountain in question upside down.

Sergio redirects his head to look at him. "We'll have to check with your mom and dad first."

"Just Dad."

"Just Dad?"

"Yeah." Henry laughs. "Mommy will say, 'No way!'"

"Then I might have to agree with Mommy on this one. She's mad enough at me already."

"No duh," Henry says seriously.

Sergio squeezes Henry firmly around the middle. "Thank goodness you're not mad at me."

Henry stares directly at him. His features scrunch together, mustering up an intensity Sergio is surprised by. It's a very serious look for a five-year-old. Especially one as happy-go-lucky as Henry. "You still need to say you're sorry to Jeremy."

"I know, buddy." Sergio gives him another squeeze, and Henry drops his head back again, looking at his surroundings.

"Jeremy!" he yells from upside down.

At least he didn't do that in my ear this time.

"Hiya, Henry!" Jeremy yells back, and Sergio takes Henry to him.

When they get close enough, Sergio places Henry back down on the ground and then takes off his skis as he watches Henry run towards Jeremy before he's cut off at the pass by Rose's outstretched arm. "Careful," she says.

"I know!" Henry says and wraps his arms around Jeremy's legs right as Sergio arrives to the metaphorical applause of no one.

Well, maybe not no one. Allison looks at him with curiosity from where she's standing beside Jeremy. She's dressed for skiing in baby blue gear that looks exquisite next to her rich, dark skin. Sergio, unable to break old habits, smiles at her even though he'd much rather be giving his smile to the coach beside her. However, ignoring her would be rude, and he's pretty sure that Rose would find a way to be upset with him for being rude to her skater almost as much as if he were trying to sleep with her. Which he isn't. Tempting as it may have been when he first arrived, the combination of Rose's wrath and his own reawakening feelings for Jeremy is more effective at getting him to cool his jets than the snow all around them.

From the side of his eye, he watches Jeremy as he listens to Henry tell him all about skiing. Jeremy is giving Henry his rapt attention, something Sergio would give anything to have focused on him again. He wishes they were back in that coffee shop nestled in the valley under the mountains of Nagano, Japan.

Four years ago

With his favorite vintage camera loaded with black and white film around his neck, Sergio entered a small coffee shop located a few blocks outside the Nagano, Japan Olympic Village. He'd been shooting athletes and elite fans with expensive tickets to the festivities all morning, and he wanted to take some time to photograph the locals who still needed to go about their day while the Olympic caliber chaos ensued around them. These photos weren't going to be used for a feature or a spread. They were for Sergio and Sergio alone. Because again, despite all appearances, Sergio has a big heart, and he does find great comfort in witnessing the average person engage with the world through the lens of his camera. He likes the way it feels to create stillness in those moments of bluster and business with the click of his finger. Even more, he likes revealing that stillness days later while developing the film within the enclosed space of his darkroom.

Perhaps that's a better metaphor for Sergio Durand's heart. It's held within the confines of a dark room, kept very safe and away from anyone who could ruin the contents inside by simply opening the door and shining in too much light.

Once at the café's counter, with a series of points and awkward grunts in foreign words, he ordered a cappuccino and a chocolate donut covered in a layer of chocolate frosting and another layer of chocolate sprinkles. Not because that's what he wanted, but because it was the easiest thing to order through the language barrier he found himself having to navigate with the young woman behind the counter. He tipped generously and held up his camera to show his interest in taking her picture. Through smiles, nods, and hand gestures, she communicated her permission, and he held the camera to his eye. She smiled the enormous smile of someone truly flattered to be asked, instead of the practiced smile Sergio was more accustomed to photographing when the subject was someone so used to having their photo taken they always appeared bored.

With his coffee and donut in his hands, he scanned the café, looking for a place to sit. It was packed, but one seat caught his eye. Tucked in the corner, as hidden away as someone could be in a place like this, was none other than the men's figure skating gold medal favorite, Jeremy Owens, reading a book.

Odd, Sergio had thought. It seemed strange for one of America's Olympic darlings to be hiding out. He should have been reveling in the fame like Holden and Rose.

His curiosity piqued, Sergio went to the corner table and very politely, as he does understand social graces, softly cleared his throat to grab Jeremy's attention. When Jeremy looked up, Sergio was almost unable to speak, having been taken aback by Jeremy's soulful brown eyes peeking out from under the front wisps of his hair pushed forward by his toque.

As distracted as he was by how handsome he found Jeremy's face, Sergio did muster up some words. "Sorry to interrupt your reading," he said. "But there's no other place to sit. Would you mind if I joined you? I don't bite, and I can entertain myself if you'd prefer to continue reading."

Jeremy closed his book while slyly looking Sergio up and down, appearing to quickly do an assessment. He put his book down, tugged at the corner of his left eye, then gestured with his other hand for Sergio to take a seat. Once he did, Jeremy brought his coffee-filled mug to his lips and continued to eye Sergio over the brim.

"Thanks," Sergio said, putting his coffee and donut down. He then slid into his seat, letting his knees brush Jeremy's underneath the table. Holding out his hand, he said, "Sergio Durand."

"Jeremy Owens," Jeremy said, sliding his hand into Sergio's grasp. He locked eyes with Sergio, and to Sergio, like the shutter of his camera flitting open to capture a moment, everything seemed to freeze for one split second.

Breaking that pause in time, he asked, "I'm not keeping you from anything interesting, am I?"

Jeremy cracked his cookie in half and, while taking a bite, he continued to study Sergio. His gaze skated over Sergio's jawline, then traveled down his neck, and finally lingered at the juncture where Sergio's neck dipped into the collar of his shirt. He looked back up at Sergio with a glint in his eyes and a redness on his cheeks. "That remains to be determined. It's not every day a handsome man asks to join me for coffee."

Interesting, Sergio thought. Jeremy Owens is bolder than Sergio had presumed he would be for someone hiding in the darkened corner of a coffee shop.

"Really?" Sergio asked. "That surprises me a bit."

"How come?"

"Well, I've been documenting these Olympics. I find it hard to believe that an athlete with as high a profile as you have is in short supply of people wanting to join him for coffee."

Jeremy raised an eyebrow at him. "So you knew who I was when you asked to join me?"

"I did," Sergio confessed. "But I'd have asked to join you for coffee even if you weren't on the cusp of becoming the next face of Wheaties."

Jeremy's eyes flicked to the camera around Sergio's neck before he tugged at the corner of his left eye with the heel of his hand as though trying to clear an irritant. "Is this your angle to take the promotional photo?"

"No." Sergio laughed, though if given the opportunity, he'd happily photograph Jeremy for any sponsorship or endorsement deals given to him after his predicted gold medal win. "I'm not even on assignment right now. This roll of film is for me."

"Good," Jeremy said with a light sigh in his voice. "I'm so tired of having my picture taken."

Sergio broke off a piece of his donut and popped it into his mouth. "Why's that? Most everyone I've run into is begging me to take their photograph."

After letting his gaze flick to Sergio's lips, the glint returned to Jeremy's eyes. "I'm sure that's not all they want from you."

Sergio, having not missed the clear signals of Jeremy's interest, sat forward in his chair and shifted his legs so he could knock his knees against Jeremy's once again underneath the table. "What do you mean?"

Jeremy pulled slightly back in his seat, though he didn't remove the firm presence of his legs against Sergio's. With his hand, he gestured at Sergio in an upward sweeping motion. "I mean, come on, look at you."

"Look at me, what?" Sergio teased and sat back in his own chair, not to pull away, but to get another eyeful of Jeremy. *He* was something to look at. Those deep brown eyes under that light, caramel colored hair. His full lips and his long neck led down to a slender, yet muscular frame. A frame that Sergio could partially feel against his knees. Jeremy's legs were solid, strong, and sturdy. And Sergio wanted nothing more than to run his hand roughly over the firmness of Jeremy's thighs.

Jeremy smiled and shook his head. "Don't make me say it."

Sergio grinned like the devil. "Oh, I'm definitely going to make you say it."

Jeremy's cheeks blushed, and Sergio, in a rare display of restraint, didn't reach to brush his fingertips over Jeremy's creamy skin.

"Good-looking guy like you," Jeremy finally said, with a tip of his chin. "I'd expect you to be beating them off." He paused as a small smile crept across his lips, then looked at Sergio more directly and winked. "Pun intended."

"Cheeky, aren't you?"

"Oh, you have no idea." Jeremy took another bite of his cookie.

"What about you?"

"What about me?"

"Oh, come on. You can't be in any short supply of men asking you for a date."

Jeremy shrugged. "My life doesn't really leave a lot of room for dating."

"Is that something you would like?"

"Doesn't everybody?"

Sergio brought his cappuccino to his lips and took a long, contemplative sip. Like Jeremy assumed, he'd never struggled with finding a date. And maybe because of that fact they'd never been important to him. It's hard to long for something one never misses. "I guess I've never thought about it."

"Never?"

"Not really."

"Hmm ..." Jeremy hummed and took a sip of his coffee. "I guess I'm a bit of a romantic then."

"What, like you're waiting for someone to come and sweep you off your feet?" For some reason, as he waited for Jeremy's answer, Sergio's heart beat a little faster.

Jeremy laughed and tugged at his left eye again. "Yeah, I don't think that would be so bad."

For whatever reason. Call it fate. Call it an alignment of the stars. Call it Sergio Durand meeting someone who, for once in his adult life, didn't appear to want anything from him they couldn't provide for themselves, Sergio felt his heart try to peek out from its place of hiding.

"Any chance I can interest you in dinner tonight?"

Tugging at his eye once more, Jeremy said, "Yeah, on one condition, though."

"What's that?"

"You leave the camera in your room. They make me nervous."

"I can do that," Sergio promised and broke another chunk off of his donut before he popped it into his mouth.

"Okay." Jeremy smiled and nodded his head. "Pick me up at the practice rink tonight around eight, and we can grab a bite once I'm off the ice."

"It's a date."

Later that night, with no camera in his hands as requested, Sergio arrived at the practice rink at seven-thirty instead of eight. Not only was it the first time in his life he'd ever arrived early for a date, but it was also the first time he wasn't beyond fashionably late.

It was well worth it. Outside of occasionally accompanying Holden to Rose's events, where Sergio usually scrolled through his phone instead of paying rapt attention, it was the first time in his life he ever really watched the sport of figure skating. The first time he ever really watched another person in an element Sergio didn't understand.

Jeremy glided across the ice at impossible speeds. He made fast turns and giant jumps where he spun in the air and landed on one blade with ease before turning around and doing it again and again and again, never ceasing. His skin was flushed, more than it had been at the café while flirting heavily with Sergio. It was mesmerizing. Sergio didn't miss having his camera at his disposal, not even for a second. He was so enthralled with what he watched that he almost missed the way Jeremy winced every time he landed. The way he would hold his breath to adjust his posture. The way he would tug at his eye intermittently between more attempts of his tricks or in lulls of his choreography. He barely saw the look of concern that washed over Jeremy's coach's face as he observed his skater. He didn't know that Jeremy was silently praying to the skating gods every time he stepped on the ice to make it so no one would notice something was wrong.

Holden claps him on the shoulder, breaking Sergio from his thoughts. "Hungry?"

Sergio looks away from Jeremy and Henry and nods. "I can eat."

"This place has a great turkey burger," Holden says and leads them all inside, where the hostess awaiting their arrival leads them right to a large table in the middle of the restaurant.

This time, looking for an opportunity to make things less awkward and maybe apologize, Sergio tries to jostle for the seat beside Jeremy at the table. He's quickly thwarted.

"Here," Allison says, touching his arm with light fingers and grabbing his attention. "Next to me."

As he goes to rebuff her request, Jeremy takes the seat next to Rose, then Adrien—likely figuring that Sergio is about to do the predictable thing for him and indulge in the very pretty face of Allison—slips into the chair on Jeremy's other side.

Damn it. Sergio lets out a sigh as he takes the only seat left, placing him between Holden and Allison and sitting with a perfect view across the table of Jeremy holding Henry in his lap.

"How long are you in town?" Allison asks him once they've placed their orders.

He turns in his chair to look at her. Maybe she simply wants to engage in polite conversation? Maybe she's tired of seeing and talking to the same people day in and day out while training in Lake Placid? It's a small town. The monotony has to get to everyone at some point.

"A week."

"That's nice," she says, smiling at him. She leans in like she's waiting for him to say something else.

He doesn't. He takes his attention to the rest of the table. His eyes briefly meet Rose, who's looking at him with tight, pursed lips and a raised eyebrow. Silently, he mouths at her, "I can behave."

"Prove it," she silently says back, making it clear she doesn't believe he's capable of not indulging in the charms of Allison. She is, after all, quite pretty, but for the first time in Sergio's life, a pretty face isn't enough to distract him from his task at hand. Mainly, apologizing to

Jeremy and maybe, with some luck, getting a second chance to rekindle an old flame.

Taking his attention away from Rose, he hears Jeremy say, "Oh! She's in Paris. How nice. I've only been there once. Years ago, for a competition, and I didn't even really get to enjoy it. I got a picture of myself in front of the Eiffel Tower, though. So I guess that's something."

"You need to go again," Adrien says. "In fact, we should plan something. Daphne's family is always open to having guests. You would only need to purchase a plane ticket."

Jeremy sighs wistfully. "That'd be lovely. I'll think about it."

"Have you ever been to Paris?" Allison asks Sergio, grabbing back his attention.

"I have. Many times. It's not that great." He slumps in his seat and crosses his arms over his chest.

"Not that great?" Holden laughs. "Sergio, you love Paris. Remember that time you got so drunk you slept through your room being robbed?"

Sergio groans.

Various forms of, "He what!" are exclaimed by Rose, Jeremy, and Allison.

"Oh, god." Adrien hangs his head, laughing. "Don't remind me. What a nightmare."

Agreed. Sergio wants to sink even lower into his chair. This is very quickly turning into yet another roast at his expense.

Rose grabs her wine and sits back in her chair. "Oh, I'm going to need to hear this *entire* story."

"It's not that great of a story," Sergio says.

"If it involves your humiliation, I'm betting it is." She nudges her chin at him.

Holden, still laughing, points at Adrien, stretching his arm across the table. "Remember, they even took his underpants." Tears of mirth leak from his eyes.

"He ran down the hall to get me in a hand towel, not even a full-sized one," Adrien wheezes out.

"Hahaha. Laugh it up," Sergio says with a crisp shake of his head and his nostrils flaring. "They stole my best camera."

"Well, that is a shame," Jeremy says, his face soft and voice sincere. It catches Sergio off guard.

"Don't let him fool you," Adrien says, catching his breath. "After I bought him enough clothing to get through the rest of the trip, I bought him a replacement camera as well."

Jeremy shrugs. "It's still a loss." He looks across the table at Sergio and offers him a small smile. "I mean, if someone stole my skates, sure, I could buy a new pair, but they wouldn't be the same. Even if they were seemingly identical. The tools of your craft always hold a piece of your soul when you use them as an extension of yourself."

"Very true," Rose says and grabs his hand on the table. She turns to look at Sergio again. "But dammit if it isn't funny when it happens to Sergio."

The whole table bursts out laughing some more. Well, almost everyone. Sergio and Jeremy stay quiet, eyes locked in their shared knowledge of what it's like to hide your true self beneath your craft. Together, they share a pair of genuine, albeit shy, smiles for the first time since before Jeremy put the brakes on their fledgling courtship underneath the stands of the aerial ski event four years ago.

"Can you grab Henry from Jeremy?" Rose asks Holden when they pull into the garage. "I need to get cleaned up and start getting ready for tonight."

"Sure thing," Holden says, then turns to look at Sergio and Adrien in the back seat. "Do either of you want to come with? Maybe Jeremy has Henry up and on skates. You should see him. He's terrible."

"Yeah, I'll come." Sergio nods. Jeremy's smile at him from lunch is still in the forefront of his mind, helping him to feel hopeful that there is a path for an apology to be accepted.

"Adrien?"

"Nah," he says and begins the spiel Sergio is so familiar with. He says it silently along with him. "It's almost midnight in Paris. I'm gonna call Daphne and wish her a Happy New Year."

"Alright, send her our love," Holden says and exits the car with Sergio following after him out of the garage and around the house to head down to the barn.

"What's the deal with Jeremy?" Sergio asks when the barn comes into view. "Is he seeing anyone?"

Holden stops in his tracks and turns to look at Sergio. "You're not looking to rekindle an old flame, are you?"

"No. Not at all," Sergio lies, a ghost of a memory of what Jeremy's lips felt like pressed against his tickles his skin.

"Good. Because if you think Rose is protective of Allison, you have no idea how fierce she is when it comes to Jeremy." Holden's whole body quakes, and he continues walking. "I shudder at the thought of your castration."

"Why is everyone in your family out for blood with my balls?" Sergio asks.

"Huh?" Holden looks at him, confused.

Sergio, recalling his daily wake-ups, shakes his head. "Let's just say your son has one hell of a kick."

"He's got his mother's legs," Holden says by way of explanation while opening the door, wafting the sound of *Wicked Game* by Chris Isaak through the air.

After they enter, Sergio pauses at the rink's wall and watches Jeremy move. The way he carries himself on the ice is confident, even though the moves he makes are relatively simple and not showy. But nonetheless, they are beautiful. There are no jumps or complicated tricks. It's pure unbridled skating done perhaps the way it's meant to be, with smooth gliding footwork carving large loops into the ice and body movements flowing to the melody and finding pauses in the downbeats. Like the first time he saw Jeremy working this routine, it's soothing. The moves and the music, though haunting, are perfectly aligned.

"Hey, guys!" Holden yells out, announcing their arrival. Jeremy puts a pause on his moves, and Henry waves so enthusiastically from his seat on the low ledge that he falls onto the ice, laughing. Holden moves quickly to help him back onto the low ledge. "Routine is looking good. Legs feeling alright today?"

"Yeah," Jeremy says, smiling. His cheeks are flushed with that happy blush that Sergio has never noticed on anyone outside of Jeremy ... ever.

"You really look good out there," Sergio says. "Best I've ever seen you skate."

"Don't tease," Jeremy says. The smile drops from his lips.

"I wasn't teasing. I meant it." He pauses and tries to find his words. "It's like, when you watch the competitions, you can always read the nerves, and fear, and stress on the skater's faces. But not you. Not here. You skate like you're doing what you love because you love it."

Holden dramatically turns, doing a big sweeping motion with his head, and looks at Sergio. His eyebrows are raised high, and he has a hint of a smirk pulling at his lips. "Excuse me, but who are you and what have you done with my friend Sergio?"

"Oh, fuck off." Sergio jabs him in the shoulder. He looks back at Jeremy. "I mean it. You look good."

Jeremy dips his head and turns away. "Thanks," he says. "I'm really only out here playing around. I shouldn't even be on the ice."

"No," Sergio protests. "You're exactly where you belong." He reaches across the half wall in an attempt to turn Jeremy to look at him again, craving a glimpse of those flushed cheeks once more.

Jeremy starts at Sergio's hand touching his shoulder. He shifts, twists, and loses his balance, landing on the hard ice floor with a thud. Sergio winces, but before he can stammer out an apology, Henry yells at him, "Not cool!"

Holden hoists himself waist-high onto the half wall so he can lean over it and offer Jeremy his hand.

Jeremy waves him off, clearly embarrassed. "I got it." Once standing again, he places one hand on the wall and keeps his eyes averted, chewing on his lip while he carefully makes his way to the low ledge. "What time are we leaving tonight?"

"A little before eight," Holden says. "We gotta drop Henry off at the Weirs' on the way."

"Alright. I'll meet you up at the house in a bit, then," he says, sliding a blade guard onto his right skate before he takes a hesitant step off the ice, holding onto the wall by Sergio for balance. He completely avoids Sergio's attempt to make eye contact as he slides a guard onto his left skate and slowly, with rigidity in his steps, walks to a place where he can sit and unlace his boots to take them off. His expression makes it obvious that he's done with having an audience.

"We'll see you later, Jeremy," Holden calls after him as he lifts Henry off the ground and places him on his shoulders.

"Fuck," Sergio mutters, knowing full well exactly how he's going to be woken up again tomorrow. Perhaps during his next shot at this day, he can at the very least not knock Jeremy over.

Chapter Six

"I mean it," Sergio says, looking directly at Jeremy on the ice and ignoring Holden's smirk beside him. "You look good."

Jeremy dips his head and turns away, but the faint blush of his cheeks doesn't sneak past Sergio. "Thanks," he says. "I'm really only out here playing around. I shouldn't even be on the ice."

"No," Sergio protests, wanting to see his face again. "I think the ice is exactly where you belong." Then, remembering the disaster from yesterday, he resists the urge to reach over the half wall and touch Jeremy, even though he wants nothing more than to feel Jeremy underneath his fingertips. To run his hands down Jeremy's soft sweatshirt and enjoy the resistance of his toned muscle structure beneath his palms. "Come here."

Jeremy looks over his shoulder at Sergio as he begins to skate away. "I'm not your dog. You can't just beckon me to you and expect me to come because you said something nice."

Sergio's mouth drops open. "That's ... that's not what I was trying to do at all." He shakes his head and looks at Holden for help. Useless. He's barely stifling a laugh. "I was going to try to apologize."

Jeremy stops near Henry and grabs his blade guards off the half wall. "Sergio, I don't have time for this right now." He slips a guard onto one skate and takes his attention to Holden as he steps off the ice. "What time are we leaving tonight?"

"A little before eight," Holden says. "We gotta drop Henry off at the Weirs' on the way."

"Alright. I'll meet you up at the house in a bit, then." He slides a blade guard onto his right skate before he steps completely off the ice, avoiding Sergio's attempt to make eye contact. Once seated, he keeps his head down and focuses on unlacing his skates, making it clear he's done having Sergio as part of his audience.

"We'll see you later, Jeremy," Holden calls after him as he lifts Henry off the ground and places him on his shoulders.

"Yeah, we'll see you later," Sergio says, thankful this time that he at least didn't knock Jeremy over.

∞

"I think the ice is exactly where you belong," Sergio says with twice as much sincerity. There's no denying it. After catching yet another glimpse of Jeremy's skating and seeing that blush redden his cheeks at the slightest compliment, nothing has ever been clearer. To Sergio, getting Jeremy to see that is the most important thing to him, second only to apologizing.

Jeremy moves away from him, heading to where he can collect his things and get off the ice. Sergio pushes past Holden, practically knocking him over in his haste to catch Jeremy before he can put his first blade guard on.

"What the hell?" Holden laughs.

Sergio flashes him an annoyed look, then turns his attention back to Jeremy. "Listen, Jeremy. Can you give me a second? I want to apologize."

Jeremy pauses and gives a pointed nod in Henry's direction, then another one at Holden before staring at Sergio. "Now really isn't the best time."

"There is no better time. I should know. I've been trying to do this for days now."

"Days?" Jeremy's face scrunches up in confusion. "You just got here."

Fuck. Sergio swallows. "I meant all day."

"It's fine, Sergio."

It feels anything but fine.

Jeremy turns his attention to Holden. "What time are we leaving tonight?"

∞

Sitting beside his brother in the back of Holden's Range Rover, Sergio replays yesterday's disaster apology attempt to Jeremy in his head. He has to try something new.

"Can you grab Henry from Jeremy?" Rose asks Holden when they pull into the garage after yet another day on the slopes. "I need to get cleaned up and start getting ready for tonight."

"Sure thing," Holden says, then turns to look at Sergio and Adrien in the back seat. "Do either of you want to come with? Maybe Jeremy has Henry up and on skates. You should see him. He's terrible."

"Yeah, I'll come." Sergio nods.

"Adrien?"

"Nah. It's almost midnight in Paris. I'm gonna call Daphne and wish her a Happy New Year."

"Alright, send her our love," Holden says and exits the car.

"Actually, do you mind if I go do it? Alone?" Sergio asks Holden, following him towards the garage exit.

"Sure." Holden shrugs and turns around. "It's your funeral."

Rose stops in her tracks on the garage steps leading into the house. She looks at Sergio skeptically. Her eyes narrowed in. "Why do you need to go alone?"

"I'd like to apologize to Jeremy," Sergio says with urgency. He figured out yesterday that having Holden there doesn't help. He doesn't need Rose standing in his way, either. He raises an eyebrow at her in challenge. "And I don't need a chaperone."

"Fine," she relents, opening the door and stepping through. Over her shoulder, she calls out, "But I swear to God, Sergio, if you hurt him again, I will kick you in the nuts."

Under his breath, Sergio says, "Don't worry, your son's already done that multiple times for you."

"What was that?" Holden asks.

"Nothing," Sergio says as he exits the garage in the opposite direction and heads towards the barn. The entire way there, he reminds himself to stay calm and not to make any movements that might lead to Jeremy falling or comments that might cause Jeremy to shut down.

Pulling the door open, he hears the familiar crooning of Chris Isaak. Despite his nerves, the song pulls a sense of calm and comfort over him like a blanket. Even through its haunting and cut-throat lyrics, which are accurate to his predicament, he's beginning to crave the song. Then, same as he's done the other times he's walked in on this sight, Sergio pauses at the rink's wall and watches the way Jeremy moves. It's beautiful in its simplicity.

Taking a deep breath, he slowly makes his way over to where Henry is sitting, watching Jeremy glide around the ice. Not wanting to startle him or pull Jeremy's attention away from his skating, which he is obviously enjoying, Sergio stays quiet. Once he reaches Henry, he carefully sits beside him and pulls him into his lap. He rests his chin on Henry's head. "He's great out there, isn't he?"

"The best," Henry says, then looks up at Sergio to amend, "After mommy."

Sergio lets out a soft laugh and whispers, "Yeah, after Mommy. Of course."

Jeremy's skating has taken him closer to where Sergio and Henry are sitting and when he loops around in his choreography, he slows in his tracks, gracefully dropping his arms to his sides and coming to a stop a few feet away, blushing. "I thought Henry was my only audience."

"Sorry," Sergio says, realizing now he could be seen as an interloper. "I snuck in. I didn't want to disturb you. You look good out there."

"Don't tease," Jeremy scolds.

"I wasn't teasing."

Jeremy bites at his lip, looking like he doesn't believe him and like he wants to change the subject to anything besides talking about himself. "Where's Holden? I figured he'd grab Henry."

"I told him I wanted to do it instead."

"Well, I won't hold you up," Jeremy says as he steadies himself against the low rink wall and slips a blade guard on one skate, then steps off and does the same with his other before he begins to walk away.

With Henry still in his arms, Sergio awkwardly rises and steps to catch up with Jeremy. "Actually, I wanted to talk to you."

Jeremy pauses and looks over his shoulder. "Really?"

"Yeah. About last night."

Jeremy turns away again. "Don't worry about it. It's fine."

Sergio grips Henry a little tighter with one arm, then reaches for Jeremy with the other. "It's not fine. It was insensitive, and I shouldn't have said it."

Jeremy's shoulders creep up towards his ears as he turns to face Sergio again. "It's not like you knew."

"No, but I should have," he says, and he means it. Any decent human being would have continued to follow their love interest's story even after they had asked them to put their mutual interest on hold, no matter how briefly.

"Why?" Jeremy asks sincerely, tugging at his left eye in his familiar way. "Would it have made a difference anyway? Would you have come to my hospital bedside and held my hand after I collapsed from that migraine? Would you have helped me stand up when I woke up from it, and my right foot no longer worked as it was supposed to, and my back ached and refused to straighten with ease, making me hunch like a rigid old man? When I was released from the hospital and shipped back to the States, would you have taken me to endless physical therapy appointments and rehab only so I could function as a shadow of myself?"

He tugs at his eye again, and Sergio grabs his hand and cradles it in his own. "Why do you do that?" he asks gently.

"Because I can't always see out of it," Jeremy snaps and pulls his hand back.

Henry, always intuitive, reaches for Jeremy in Sergio's arms. Jeremy smiles at him and ruffles his hair. "Listen, I gotta rest up," he says. "It's gonna be a long night. Do you know what time we're leaving?"

"A little before eight," Sergio says, feeling worse than he had before he tried to apologize. "We gotta drop Henry off at the Weirs' on the way."

"Alright." Jeremy nods. "I'll meet everyone up at the house in a bit." He turns on his heel and walks away, presumably to take his skates off and head up to his little apartment in the barn.

"Well, that went horribly," Sergio mutters as he watches Jeremy go.

Henry shrugs and looks at him. "You tried."

"Yeah, kid. I did try." But not nearly hard enough. Thankfully, there's always tomorrow.

∞

Spotting Sergio sitting on the rink's ledge with Henry on his lap, Jeremy slows in his tracks, gracefully dropping his arms to his sides, and comes to a stop a few feet away, blushing. "I thought Henry was my only audience."

"Sorry, I didn't mean to intrude," Sergio says and places his best smile on his face, reminding himself to get it right this time.

"It's alright, I guess," Jeremy says. "Honestly, I haven't had an audience in four years. I was hoping I'd never have to get used to that again."

"I hardly count as an audience," he says, hoping that not mentioning how much he was enjoying watching Jeremy skate yields better results.

"Anyone other than Rose counts as an audience."

"What about Allison? Does she get to watch you skate?"

Jeremy shrugs and braces himself against the half wall as he slips a blade guard on. "Not like this, no."

"Then I guess I should consider myself privileged." With one arm wrapped around Henry, Sergio rises to his feet and offers his free hand to Jeremy to help him step off the ice.

Jeremy takes it. "Where's Holden? I figured he'd grab Henry."

"I told him I wanted to do it instead." Sergio pauses as Jeremy places a guard on his other blade.

"What for?"

"I wanted to take a moment and apologize to you for yesterday."

Jeremy tries to brush him off. "Don't worry about it."

"Well, I have been worrying about it. All day, in fact. And I want you to know that I'm sorry."

Jeremy looks at him with his head cocked slightly to the side and his brows pinched together. "Are you?"

Even after days of experience, he's still not prepared for Jeremy's skepticism. He tries not to show his frustration on his face. After all, it's not Jeremy's fault that he keeps living the same day over and over and over again. And even though he's been trying and failing to do this for several days now, it's not as if Jeremy knows that. Nor does he even want to try to explain it to him. Nothing ruins an apology more than an unhinged proclamation of living in a torturous time loop as an excuse for unacceptable behavior.

"I really am," he says sincerely and feels his stomach make a small leap when Jeremy flashes a shy and nervous smile at him. His cheeks are still flushed from the cold and his exertion on the ice. It's a smile so similar to the one Sergio saw flit across Jeremy's face the moment they broke their kiss, right before Jeremy asked Sergio if they could put a pin in what they were doing until after the Olympics. It makes him want to go back in time—not to yesterday, but to that very moment. The day he screwed up. This stupid time loop is keeping him trapped in correcting the wrong mistake. But perhaps he can fix it now. "And I'm sorry for ditching you four years ago. I shouldn't have done that."

The smile leaves Jeremy's face, and he tugs at his left eye. "It was for the best," he says, sighing.

"I don't think that it was."

"Why?" Jeremy asks, his expression blank, his tone flat. *At least this time he's not yelling at me.* "Would it have made a difference anyway? Would you have come to my hospital bedside and held my hand after I collapsed from that migraine? Would you have helped me stand up when I woke up from it and my right foot no longer worked as it was supposed to and my back ached and refused to straighten with ease, making me hunch like a rigid old man? When I was released from the hospital and shipped back to the states, would you have taken me to endless physical therapy appointments and rehab only so I could function as a shadow of myself?"

Sergio stands with his mouth agape, almost forgetting Henry latched onto his hip. How did Sergio end up here again? Why is Jeremy so hellbent on having this conversation during his apology? And why does he doubt him so much? Is it that hard to take Sergio's words today at face value?

Truth is, Jeremy is right. Sergio wouldn't have handled what happened to Jeremy well at all. In fact, he would have made it worse with his chronic selfishness and inability to see any situation outside of how it affects him. However, fate and time have a funny way of forcing someone to learn the lessons they need to, no matter how painful the experience. Learning how to consider others beyond his own needs is a long and arduous process. He's simply going to have to take it day by repeated day.

"I thought Henry was my only audience."

"Sorry, I didn't mean to intrude."

"It's alright, I guess. Honestly, I haven't had an audience in four years. I was hoping I'd never have to get used to that again."

"I hardly count as an audience."

∞

"Where's Holden? I figured he'd grab Henry."

∞

"I told him I wanted to do it instead."

∞

"What for?"

∞

"I wanted to apologize to you for yesterday."

∞

"I owe you an apology."

∞

"I shouldn't have said what I said last night."

∞

"I wanted to tell you that I was sorry."

∞

Sergio takes a breath. Maybe the fourteenth time be the charm. "I need to apologize to you for yesterday."

Jeremy looks him up and down. "Go on," he encourages.

"I'm sorry."

"Are you?" Jeremy asks for what feels like the one hundredth time. But who's counting?

Feeling defeated and frustrated yet again, Sergio pushes on. "I am," he says, this time leaving out any mention of the past and trying to focus only on his current mistakes in Jeremy's present.

"No offense, but I'm not exactly keen to believe you."

Goddamn it. How hard is it to get someone to accept an apology?

The honest answer when it comes to Sergio is very hard. But, as he's slowly figuring out, when it comes to forgiveness, saying sorry is hardly ever enough. A person needs to show they mean the words. They need to back it up. Cash the metaphorical check their mouth wrote with their actions.

No one wants an empty apology. Or one made under duress. Even if that duress is an endless loop of tries.

∞

"I thought Henry was my only audience," Jeremy says as he spots Sergio sitting on the rink's ledge with Henry on his lap once again. He slows in his tracks, gracefully dropping his arms to his sides, and coming to a stop a few feet away, blushing.

"Sorry," Sergio says. "I should have announced myself."

"It's alright, I guess. Honestly, I haven't had an audience in four years. I was kind of hoping I'd never have to get used to it again."

"I hardly count as an audience," Sergio says, then having an epiphany and finally remembering what he promised Jeremy years ago before he watched him on the ice the first time at the Olympic practice rink, he adds, "Besides, I followed your request and didn't bring my camera."

Jeremy flashes him a genuine smile that causes Sergio's stomach to flip. *Come on, Sergio, you can do this.*

"I can't believe you remember that."

"Of course, I remember. And you were right to request it. It was a real treat to watch you skate without the barrier of the lens." Feeling bold that this little twist to the conversation hasn't led to him being shut out yet, Sergio takes a risk. "And I'm glad I don't have it with me this time, either."

"Even if you did," Jeremy says, giving a soft shake to his head, "no one would be asking you for the prints."

"That's not true. You were made for the ice."

Jeremy averts his gaze and braces himself against the half wall as he slides a blade guard on. "Maybe before," he says, his chin tucked towards his chest. "But not so much anymore."

With one arm wrapped around Henry, Sergio rises to his feet and offers his free hand to Jeremy to help him step off the ice. "You'll probably tell me you're out there playing around—"

"I am," Jeremy interrupts before Sergio can finish voicing his praise. He doesn't let that stop him.

"I know. And that's what makes you so beautiful to watch." Sergio pauses as Jeremy places a guard on his other blade, giving him time to steady himself again and face Sergio directly. "You look ... free."

Jeremy tilts his head, giving Sergio a contemplative look. "I guess I am," he says and holds Sergio's gaze, even while tugging at his left eye.

Together, they share a moment of silence, standing and staring at each other while Henry looks back and forth between them like he's watching a tennis match and waiting for one of them to make a match set point.

Sergio lets go of Jeremy's hand, then reaches to cup Jeremy's cheek. He runs his thumb across his cheekbone and waits for Jeremy to pull away. He doesn't.

Sergio leans in, placing the gentlest of kisses on Jeremy's lips. Gentler than any kiss he's ever placed on Jeremy's or anyone else's lips for that matter, worried that anything too fierce will burst this first moment of perfection Sergio has experienced in he no longer even knows how many days.

He holds his breath, waiting for Jeremy to respond. When Jeremy opens his mouth slightly and kisses him back, it takes all of his strength not to drop Henry and scream out in joy.

Chapter Seven

"So," Rose says, surprising Sergio later that night as she appears beside him by the bar at the New Year's Eve party. He's still riding the high from the success of his kiss while waiting for the whiskey neat he ordered for himself and a sparkling water with a twist of lime for Jeremy. "Henry told me you kissed Jeremy."

This is new. She's usually too busy talking to sports reporters and chatting up potential sponsorships for Allison to pay any attention to what Sergio is doing at the New Year's Eve party. And honestly, going by the look of judgment on her face and the way she's crossed her arms, he's one hundred percent sure he preferred it when she paid him no mind at all in the last hours counting down to the New Year. It's none of her business that he and Jeremy shared an innocent kiss.

"So what if I did?" He shrugs and lays a tip down on the bar for the bartender who's sliding Sergio his drinks. "You're the one who was so adamant that I make nice with him."

"Make nice, not make out," she quips and uncrosses her arms to grab a glass of champagne for herself. She takes a sip, keeping her eyes on

Sergio the entire time, making him apprehensive about whatever it is she's about to say next. She is his best friend's wife and therefore family. But in the context of family dynamics, to Sergio, she feels more like a younger sister who can do no wrong in everyone else's eyes, but goads her older brother when no one is looking, always making him look as if he's the problem. "I don't know what you're playing at, Sergio. But whatever it is, I don't like it."

"Why do you assume I'm playing at anything?" Sergio rolls his eyes, averting them from Rose and over to where Jeremy is standing, awkwardly dealing with Chadwick Levinson. He catches Sergio looking at him, and a smile plays across his lips, lifting his cheeks and causing his eyes to slightly crinkle.

"Because I know you too well, Sergio."

"You obviously don't know me well enough if you can't see that I genuinely like Jeremy."

It's Rose's turn to roll her eyes. "You only like someone for as long as it takes for you to get your dick in their mouth."

"Come on, Rose, you know that's not true. I like *you* and I've never once considered doing what you just suggested."

That's a lie. He very much did once think about it at the moment he, Holden, and Adrien all first saw her two Olympics ago in Calgary. That lasted only a fleeting second as Holden immediately proclaimed his love for her while she rushed by, carrying all her skating gear on her back to the practice rink. Holden's heart eyes were so large that Sergio's interest in Rose went right out the window. Instead, he relentlessly teased Holden about his crush for the entirety of that Olympic Games. So naturally, Sergio doesn't think that counts. And thankfully, he's never mentioned it to anyone. Sometimes he can manage not to dig his own grave.

"I seriously doubt that," she says. "But regardless. Can we please get through this week without you breaking my best friend's heart?"

"Why do you assume I'll break his heart?" Sergio asks, genuinely wondering why everyone except Holden seems to think so little of him. Even Henry has expressed his disapproval in matters that concern how Sergio interacts with Jeremy. In Henry's defense, however, up until this afternoon's kiss, all interactions have been less than stellar.

Though, to Sergio, at least by his reasoning, none of this casual judgment of him is fair. He knows himself and his motivations better than any of them could ever pretend to. Sergio *is* capable of falling in love with someone other than himself. At one point, he thought that was going to be Jeremy. And now here fate is giving him a second, well, thirtieth, fiftieth, eightieth chance at rekindling their connection and potentially fanning their flame.

Rose sighs. "Because history repeats itself."

"I didn't come here intending to break anyone's heart. Hell, I didn't even know Jeremy was going to be here, let alone living with *you*," he says, pointing at her. He grabs the two drinks he ordered from the bar. "Now, if you'll excuse me. I would like to take Jeremy his drink and save him from having to continue talking to that insufferable Chadwick Levinson asshole. And *maybe* even seal myself a second kiss from Jeremy when the clock strikes twelve."

With a huff, Sergio walks away. After a breath and a few strides, he stands tall, shoulders back, proud of himself for standing up to her. He makes his way across the party to Jeremy, arriving as Holden hops on stage to announce the countdown.

"Alright, everyone," Holden says into the microphone. "Grab a glass of champagne, the countdown starts in less than a minute."

"Here you go," Sergio says, handing Jeremy his drink and inserting himself in the space between Jeremy and Chadwick, effectively blocking Chadwick from being able to talk to Jeremy anymore.

"Thank you," Jeremy says, clearly relieved.

"Sorry, that took so long. Rose had some words for me."

Jeremy smiles and brings his drink to his lips. He sips through the thin black straw, then says, "I'm sure she did."

"She thinks I'm bad for you," Sergio says right as Holden starts the countdown from the stage with a "Ten!"

Jeremy leans in close. "She might be right."

"Nine!"

"What if I want to prove her wrong?"

"Eight!"

"Then I guess you better get to work."

"Seven!"

"And how would I do that?"

"Six!"

"You can start by taking me out on a date."

"Five!"

"How about tomorrow? I'll take you anywhere you want."

"Four!"

"Anywhere?"

"Three!"

"Anywhere."

"Two!"

"Kiss me again before I say yes."

"One! Happy ..."

Chapter Eight

"Uncle Sergio! Wake up!" Henry shouts, kneeing Sergio in the nuts and jolting him awake.

"Why!" he cries out as he curls into a ball while Gus hisses and runs away from the scene of this repeated crime against Sergio's favorite part of his anatomy.

"Because breakfast is ready," Henry says slowly.

Sergio buries his head into his pillow. "Henry, I need you to go away right now."

The sound of Sergio's own crying isn't enough to mask the sound of Henry wailing as he jumps off his bed and goes running down the hall.

"What's with you today?" Adrien asks from the chairlift carrying them further and further upward.

Sergio doesn't answer him. Instead, he lifts the safety bar, then leans forward and pitches himself off the lift, headfirst into the snowy mountain below, hoping this grants him yet another do-over.

***

"Uncle Sergio! Wake up!" Henry shouts, kneeing Sergio in the balls and jolting him awake.

Sergio, relieved his dramatic exit worked, but also still in pain from having his junk smashed in, whimpers as he curls into his now customary ball. Gus hisses as always and bolts out the door.

"Uncle Sergio, are you okay?" Henry asks, crawling on top of him.

"Yeah, buddy, I'm okay," he says, pulling Henry in for a cuddle. He takes a deep breath, then sobs a little harder, hating himself for how he treated Henry yesterday. Even knowing Henry has no recollection of it isn't enough to ease his guilt.

"You don't seem like you're okay."

"I don't?"

"No," Henry says, shaking his head. "Are you sick?"

"Maybe." *Sick in the head.*

"You should stay in bed and get some rest. That's what Mommy makes me do when I don't feel good."

"You know what, Henry? That's a good idea." He lifts the covers, letting Henry go free. "Can you go tell your mom and dad that I'm sitting out today?"

"Okay!" Henry yells, then hops off Sergio's bed and goes running out the door.

Sergio rolls back over, pulls the duvet close to his chin, and closes his eyes. A small part of him wonders if he'd find peace if they never opened again.

But they do open. And thankfully for Sergio, it's to a quiet house, because people are not something he can deal with right now. Well, people outside of Jeremy, as he can still feel the way Jeremy's lips felt against his two of his days ago. They were warm, soft, and ever so lovely.

He almost wants to laugh. Almost. He'd been so convinced that after he and Jeremy had shared that kiss, that this hell of a day was going to be over. He'd course-corrected. Where was his reward?

Hungry, he gets out of bed and heads downstairs to raid the kitchen, hoping some food in his belly will help him figure out a solution for his current predicament. Surely there has to be a way to break this loop.

Inside the refrigerator is a plate of pancakes that Holden must have left for him. He places it in the microwave. While the food spins around and around in circles as it warms, he contemplates the events of this day he keeps living.

It always starts the same, that he can't change, no matter how much he and his balls wish he could. But everything after that seems to be malleable. He was able to fix things with Jeremy, but obviously, that wasn't enough. And looking back, he does have the brains to realize that the idea of one kiss breaking his loop was a naive notion. Who does he think he is? A Disney princess? He's far from it in every way possible. So, obviously, he needs to do more, but what does that entail?

The timer goes off on the microwave, and he pulls out his food, then begins eating it standing at the counter. "Okay," he says out loud around a mouthful of food to an empty room. "It's not only Jeremy I need to fix things with. So what else is there?"

He furrows his brow as he chews, and his mind immediately goes back to Rose scolding him about the kiss at the New Year's Eve party. "Ahh, Rose," he says, laughing for the first time today. "I'm kind of starting to think she hates me." He takes another bite. "I wish Adrien were here. He could tell me how to fix that. She likes him ... fuck, Adrien."

He sighs, then rubs at his temple with his free hand. "I gotta figure out a way to keep him from quitting." The prospect of solving his dilemmas with both Rose and Adrien is something he's designating for Sergio of another New Year's Day. This version of today is already a wash in his eyes. He may as well give himself a break.

He takes the last bites of his food, then wipes the remnants of sticky syrup from his mouth with a nearby towel. The feel of the towel on his lips makes him think of Jeremy again. Not because the towel feels at all similar to the way Jeremy's lips felt. But more so because he doesn't want the feeling of the slightly scratchy dish towel to replace the feeling of Jeremy's plump and perfectly moisturized lips pressed against his own. Sure, it's too late for him to try to fix his life on this version of this day, but seeing as how it's still well before noon, it's not too late for him to steal another kiss from Jeremy.

Cleaning up his plate, he concocts a half-baked plan, one that doesn't involve fixing anything, but does ensure he can feel Jeremy's lips pressed against his once again and again and again and again, for however long it takes for him to fix everything wrong in his present life.

With a skip in his step, he heads back to his room, taking the stairs two at a time. He grabs some clean underwear, realizing he hasn't actually changed his since the night before, far too long ago. He quickly undresses, then grimaces as he brings his briefs to his nose, expecting them to be completely rank given the circumstances. To his relief, they are perfectly fine. Fresh even, as if he had only put them on the night before. *That's a perk. No laundry while I'm stuck here.* Not that Sergio has ever concerned himself with laundry before. Having his clothes cleaned by a service falls under the purview of Adrien's job description.

Nevertheless, he takes the clean underwear and a towel with him to the bathroom across the hall and takes a steaming hot shower. While in there, he indulges in a jerk off session that he normally would stretch out for ages, but given his current circumstances, finishes in an embarrassingly short few minutes. Regardless, he does feel better having relieved some of the tension he's been carrying around, repeated day in and repeated day out.

After his shower, he dries off and changes into a simple pair of jeans, a dark green, long-sleeved Henley that matches his eyes, and his black leather boots. He relishes in the comfort of being dressed in something other than his ski gear or his sharp New Year's Eve party suit.

By the time he's finished with all of this, he hears Jeremy return home from lunch with Henry in tow. *Not too much longer,* he thinks and goes back downstairs where he finds Gus eyeing him warily as he walks back and forth in front of the back door, as if, like his mom, he wants to create an obstacle between Sergio and Jeremy.

Sergio crouches down and reaches his hand out to stroke Gus between the ears. The cat seems to enjoy it when everyone else does it. No such luck. Gus hisses loudly and bears his claws, swiping at Sergio's hand. He makes contact, drawing blood.

"Asshole," Sergio says, standing up. He walks to the sink and rinses the wound. It's not too bad, only a scratch, but it still stings. As he dries off his hand, compressing the scratch with a paper towel, he watches Gus walk away with his tail swishing high behind him. He yells out to the cat before he disappears out of the room, "I'm not apologizing to you!"

He checks his scratch again to make sure the bleeding has stopped. It has, but panic washes over him. What if he's stuck in this loop because of that damn cat?

He shakes his head. "No. There's no way." But just in case, he vows to maybe not call the cat an asshole again. It's worth a shot. But right now, he's not going to let Gus impede his mission. He has lips to kiss and no amount of 'cattiness' is going to stop him. So instead of having a battle of wills with a feline, he patiently waits for the time to be right for him to head down to the barn and collect young Henry.

When the time finally does come, Sergio practically sprints through the trees to get to the barn. He's out of breath when he opens the door, but the sound of *Wicked Game* resounding through the speakers causes his world to slow back down. It slows even more as he watches Jeremy glide across the pristine ice. It occurs to Sergio that this ice appears like glass, preserved and untouched by the outside world. Sure, there are the deep edge marks from Jeremy's skating, and from Allison's earlier today, but it's still so smooth comparatively to other rinks he's seen. There's something beautifully intimate about it. No one else in the world knows this little piece of heaven exists outside of their little rag-tag group of family and friends. No one else has ever set foot on this ice and marred its surface. Suddenly, the vision of Jeremy skating seems to be that much more of a marvel. Sergio is lucky. For all the millions who watched Jeremy skate when he was competing, Sergio gets to watch him now when it's for nobody else but whoever Jeremy invites in.

Which reminds Sergio that he is, in fact, an uninvited interloper. So he better always remember that witnessing Jeremy in his element is a gift.

"I thought Henry was my only audience," Jeremy says when he spots Sergio walking towards the half wall. He slows in his tracks, gracefully drops his arms to his sides, and comes to a stop a few feet away with flushed cheeks.

"Sorry," Sergio says, hurrying over to grab Henry and pick him up off the ledge. "I should have announced myself."

"It's alright, I guess." He shrugs. "I haven't had an audience in four years. I was kind of hoping I'd never have to get used to it again."

"I hardly count as an audience," Sergio says. "Besides, I followed your request and didn't bring my camera."

Jeremy flashes him that genuine smile that causes Sergio's stomach to flip. "I can't believe you remember that."

"Of course, I remember. And you were right to request it. It was a real treat to watch you skate without the barrier of the lens. I'm glad I don't have it with me this time, either."

"Even if you did," Jeremy says, giving a soft shake to his head, "no one would be asking you for the prints."

"That's not true. You were made for the ice."

Jeremy averts his gaze and braces himself against the half wall as he slides a blade guard on. "Maybe before," he says with his chin tucked towards his chest. "But not so much anymore."

With one arm wrapped around Henry, Sergio offers his free hand to Jeremy to help him step off the ice. "You'll probably tell me you're out there playing around—"

"I am."

"I know. And that's what makes you so beautiful to watch." Sergio pauses as Jeremy places a guard on his other blade, giving him time to steady himself again and face Sergio directly so he can tell Jeremy the truth of what he sees. "You look free."

Jeremy tilts his head, appearing to contemplate Sergio's words. "I guess I am," he says, holding Sergio's gaze, while tugging at his left eye.

Together they share a familiar moment of silence, standing and staring at each other while Henry watches on. Sergio's heart rate kicks up, along with his hope and anticipation.

He lets go of Jeremy's hand, then carefully reaches to cup Jeremy's cheek. He runs his thumb across his cheekbone, then leans in, placing the gentlest of kisses on Jeremy's lips. As gentle as the kiss he placed there a few days ago.

He holds his breath, waiting for Jeremy's response, hoping it's the same as the time before. When Jeremy opens his mouth slightly and kisses him back, it takes all of his strength to once again not drop Henry and scream out in joy.

∞

"You look free," Sergio says, smiling as Jeremy tilts his head, looking at him in contemplation.

"I guess I am."

∞

"I guess I am."

∞

"I guess I am."

∞

"I guess I am."

Chapter Nine

"Uncle Sergio! Wake up!"

"Oof ... morning, buddy."

"*Hiss ...*"

"Dad said to come get you. Breakfast is almost ready."

"You know," Sergio begins, thinking about how he'd rather be kissing Jeremy Owens than eating pancakes, bacon, and fruit yet again, "I don't think I'm that hungry today."

Henry pouts. "But breakfast is the most important meal of the day."

"Did your mom tell you that?"

"No." Henry laughs. "My dad did."

"Probably because that's the only meal he can cook."

Henry holds his hands at shoulder height and shrugs.

Sergio pats him on the head. "Breakfast might be the most important meal of the day for you now, but when you're older, you'll learn there are far more important things than breakfast."

For one, getting more intimate with Jeremy, who he's been kissing every day for the last however many days, with no release. At least, that's what's on Sergio's brain this morning over pancakes. After all, how long has it been since Sergio last hooked up with anyone? He's lost count at this point. That's like taking heroin away from a junkie. Lou Reed should be playing softly in the background to soundtrack his detox.

"Like brunch!" Henry yells.

"What?"

"Something more important than breakfast," Henry says, nodding his head with his lips pressed tight as if he's understanding Sergio on a soul level. "Mommy gets very excited to have brunch with Jeremy."

"Who wouldn't?" Sergio smiles.

Henry's eyes go large, and his mouth drops open. "Are you and Jeremy having brunch?"

"Do you think he would want to go with me?"

"No." Henry shakes his head.

"Yeah." Sergio laughs. "I don't think so either."

"You should go tell him you're sorry."

"Why do you think I'm skipping breakfast?"

"I thought you weren't hungry."

"I'm hungry for something besides pancakes."

Henry shakes his head again and hops off the bed. "I don't understand grownups."

"You and me both, kid," Sergio says as he flings the covers off himself and gets out of bed as well. "Go wake up Adrien, then tell your mom and dad I'm skipping breakfast, will ya?"

"Okay," Henry agrees, then goes running out of the room with both of his thumbs held enthusiastically over his head, thundering towards Adrien's room.

Sergio pokes his head out the door. "Gently!"

Running, Henry raises his thumbs up even higher, then bursts into Adrien's room.

Shaking his head and feeling magnanimous, Sergio changes out of his sweatpants and into his jeans and long-sleeved Henley. After returning from the bathroom to brush his teeth, he steps into his boots and loosely laces them. He sneaks out of his room and creeps down the stairs to head outside through the front door. This way, he can avoid Rose and her judgmental eyebrow and whip-like ponytail that she'd definitely aim in his direction if he had to tell her face-to-face that he was skipping breakfast in favor of sweeping Jeremy off his feet. She'd see right through him and block any and all Sergio's attempts to spend more time with Jeremy, leading to perhaps even more satisfying results beyond kissing.

At the door, before he goes through it, he looks towards the kitchen. Holden and Rose are readying breakfast and are completely oblivious to his presence. Gus, however, spots him and hisses. Sergio flips him the bird, then ducks out the door. He's careful to close it with the quietest of clicks.

Once outside, the cold crisp morning air hits his lungs, so he blows into his hands then slides them into his pockets. Even though he's barely been outside, his hands are freezing, and he wishes he would have thought to have Henry sneak him a cup of coffee to hold between his palms to keep them warm. Not that Henry would have been capable of being discreet or delivering the coffee to him without spilling it everywhere. Nevertheless, as he approaches the barn through the trees, he's jealous of the steaming, warm mug he sees Jeremy grasping. With any luck, Jeremy will offer him a cup and a multitude of warm-up activities inside his lofted abode.

"Hey! Jeremy!" Sergio calls out as he approaches.

Jeremy looks at him with his brow furrowed and his lips pressed in a hard line. A puff of air escapes through his lips as he lets out an audible sigh. "What are you doing down here?"

Stopping a few feet from him, Sergio brings his hands to his mouth and cups them before he blows into them again. "I came to talk to you."

Jeremy rolls his eyes and turns his focus back to looking between the trees. "About what?"

"About last night," Sergio says as gently as he can. This is rapidly not going as well as he had envisioned. Where's the gracious Jeremy of the days he spent kissing him? The Jeremy who smiles at his charms. The Jeremy who lets his guard down. The Jeremy who would have been possibly more amenable to the idea of Sergio tearing his clothes off and ravishing them both to orgasm.

Jeremy takes a sip of his drink. Apple and cinnamon tea by the smell of it. "Don't worry about it," he says, and takes another sip, still not looking at Sergio.

Damn it, this is not going well. Where's Henry when I need him? He begins to panic and changes the subject. "I hear you're skating again," he tries, hoping that acknowledging something Jeremy loves will bear better fruit.

"And you care about that? Why?"

"I ... I guess I would ... I imagine it's freeing for you to skate again."

Jeremy turns his head to look at Sergio again and takes another sip of his tea. "Freeing from what? Failure? Disappointment? My life as everybody's pet pity project?"

"No." Sergio hangs his head and rubs his temples. "Why is this going so badly?" He looks back up at Jeremy. "You're not understanding me."

"Oh, I'm understanding you perfectly well." Jeremy takes another sip. "You thought you could come down here and butter me up by showing some faux sympathy. But I don't need your sympathy, Sergio. Nor do I want it."

Sergio looks around, stunned. "That's ... that's not what I was doing at all. I really only came down here to apologize and see if you wanted to spend the day with me or something."

"And why would I want to do that? You think I want to get tangled up with *you* again? So you can ditch me the moment things are out of your control?"

Sergio, looking back at the successful days he's had with Jeremy, nods.

Jeremy takes one last gulp of his tea, emptying the contents of his mug into his mouth, then swallows thickly. Staring right at Sergio, an eyebrow raised in a manner frighteningly similar to Rose, he says, "Look, you're hot and, in the past, you have shown rare signs of being a human being capable of caring about somebody else. However, until I see that more sincerely from you, we're not spending any more time together than we have to." He pauses, tugs the corner of his left eye, and stares at Sergio. And now it's Sergio's turn to swallow. His pride slides down his throat like a frozen, jagged rock. "Now, if you'll excuse me, I need to get ready for Allison's practice. Enjoy your day, Sergio."

Mouth agape, Sergio watches Jeremy turn around, open the barn door, and disappear behind it before it shuts with a slam.

"What the fuck was that?" Sergio asks no one, then turns and walks back up to the house with his tail between his legs. How did everything go so wrong so quickly? He can get it right in the afternoon. Maybe Jeremy isn't a morning person. Maybe Sergio chose the wrong outfit, even though this one works fine in the afternoon. Who the fuck knows?

Or maybe, what works in the afternoon is that Sergio comes to Jeremy at a moment when both of their guards are down. Henry is always there, which brings out Sergio's softer side. Jeremy is on the ice, and though that is his element, having an audience at this point in his relationship with figure skating is not something to which he is accustomed. And both of them, always in that moment with one of their metaphorical walls broken down, are able to see each other more clearly.

This morning, it was right back to Sergio feeling cocky after a few solid days of success and Jeremy feeling exhausted by the arrival of the man who has managed at every turn—as far as his memory and knowledge of their history goes—to disappoint him. *Fuck,* Sergio curses his damn ego.

"Well, look who decided he wanted breakfast after all!" Holden exclaims around a mouth full of pancakes as Sergio enters the kitchen through the back door.

"Jeremy didn't want brunch, did he?" Henry says from his chair.

"No. No, he didn't," Sergio says and takes a seat, and then pours himself the last of the coffee.

"That's because Jeremy Owens is smart," Rose says over the brim of her own mug, with her eyebrow raised.

"Yeah," Sergio says, defeated, and avoiding everyone's eyes on him at the table.

Holden claps him on the shoulder with one hand and shovels more food into his mouth with his other. "Don't worry, Sergio. You're smart, too."

"Smarter than a bag of hair," Adrien adds, then takes a sip of his coffee.

Sergio sighs and loads a plate up with a small amount of food, wondering how and why this day always seems to devolve into pick-on-Sergio day. He supposes that maybe he deserves it. And also supposes that tomorrow he'd be better off going back to what he knows works instead of trying to reinvent the hamster wheel he's on.

But since he's here, and he's feeling pretty shitty, a thought crosses his mind. There's another way he can release some of this tension in his body. Another way he can get a jolt of adrenaline and serotonin. Something he can do with Holden and Adrien that will bring them all together, even if it is only for one day, the other two will forget. But he'll have it, and maybe if he can get past the guilt of that, it will be enough to get him through these repeated failures.

"Hey, Holden," he says. Holden turns to look at him and gives him a goofy grin while he chews his food. "You got any helicopter hookups around here?"

Holden's grin seamlessly morphs from goofy to serious. He wipes his mouth with his napkin, then places it onto the table. "Heli trip?"

Sergio nods his head up and down and stares right at Holden, grinning like the devil. "Heli trip."

Standing at the top of the world while snow and wind whip around them from the helicopter blades whirling back into the air, Sergio no longer feels defeated. He swings his arms over Adrien and Holden's shoulders. "Isn't this great?"

"It's amazing," Holden says.

"It's a terrible idea," Adrien says.

Holden reaches around Sergio with his long arms and jostles Adrien by the back of his neck. "Don't worry so much, Adrien."

"I'm not worrying," Adrien says.

"Yes, you are," Sergio and Holden say and laugh together.

"You've got this," Holden says. "You're a better skier than almost everyone else on the Adirondacks today."

"My track record on these types of trips says different."

Sergio looks around. "Are we still even in the Adirondacks?"

Holden shrugs. "This might be Canada."

"Great," Adrien says. "I'm sure the mounted police will be super stoked to see me get tomahawked down this ridge."

"You're not gonna tomahawk," Holden says, then looks at Sergio. "But just in case, should we set up the drone to make sure we catch it on film this time."

"Way ahead of you, my friend." Sergio laughs, swinging his backpack forward off his back and pulling out his gear. He holds the camera out in front of them and clicks a picture, then turns it around to look at the captured moment. Despite his nerves, Adrien did manage to smile for the shot. "See? It's not so bad. Now who's going first?"

"Holden," Adrien says. "Let the professional carve the first line."

"You better be right after me," Holden says. "The helicopter is waiting for us at the bottom."

"I'll push him if I have to," Sergio says.

"Please don't push me," Adrien says. "That's how I went ass over teakettle last time."

"I didn't push!"

"You didn't *not* push him," Holden says. "Now quit arguing. There's a few more untouched runs I want to hit."

"How about this?" Sergio puts his camera back into his backpack, then swings it over his shoulders. "No filming. No pushing. Let's hit this first run together." He pauses and holds his hand out to Adrien. "Deal?"

Adrien eyes him up and down, then grabs his hand and shakes it. "Deal."

"Good," Sergio says, then turns to face the edge of the slope and points down. "I'll take center line."

"Perfect," Holden says. "There's a cliff to the right I want to flip off of."

"And I'll be staying as far away from that as I can on the left." Adrien uses his poles and pushes himself forward and away from the other two men. With a quick look over his shoulder, he says to Sergio, "And by the way, I quit!" Then, like he's pulling off a Band-Aid, he takes off.

Sergio shrugs. He should have seen that coming. He chooses to ignore it and looks at Holden. "Race you to the bottom?"

"Last one down buys the first round of drinks," Holden says with a clap to Sergio's shoulder before he propels himself forward, leaving Sergio alone at the top.

He waits a moment before he follows and reserves this day as a memory, a snapshot in his mind only for him. Because after all, he is the only one out of the three who will remember it. He admires Adrien's perfect switchbacks and catches the moment Holden does a double backflip off the dodgiest cliff.

"If I ever make it out of this loop," he says to the glimmering snow. "I promise to pay for the three of us to do this together tomorrow."

Chapter Ten

"Uncle Sergio! Wake up!"

"Oof... morning, buddy."

"*Hiss...*"

"Dad said to come get you. Breakfast is almost ready."

"Mmm... I love breakfast."

"Me too!" Henry exclaims.

"Do you know who else loves breakfast?"

Henry's eyes go wide. "Who?"

"Uncle Adrien!" Sergio says as he tickles Henry's sides. "Go wake him up."

"Okay!" Henry yells again and jumps off the bed, running out of the room with his thumbs raised high.

Sergio is quick to his feet and shouts out through the open door, "Gently!"

Henry lifts his enthusiastic thumbs even higher, then Sergio hears him burst into Adrien's room to be greeted by a very sleepily uttered, "Hey, buddy."

He smiles to himself and sets his eyes back on the proverbial prize: Jeremy. Yesterday's adventure did the trick. He is feeling refreshed and ready to tackle his dilemma. With a whistle and a skip to his step, Sergio makes his way downstairs.

With each step he takes, he goes through a mental checklist of everything he needs to do, and how he needs to do it, *and* in what order. All of which, if done correctly, he knows will lead to Jeremy kissing him back later when he picks up Henry from him this afternoon. He needs that kiss. He needs to know that somewhere, somehow, in some way, Jeremy is capable of seeing him as someone worth kissing. The kisses they shared in the many days before yesterday were not a fluke. They were not in his head. They were not hallucinations brought on by whatever mechanism is going on that keeps him in this hell of a tortuous loop on what should be an insignificant day.

Step one of that plan is to be nice and help Rose set the table. He grabs the plates out of her hands. "Let me help you with that."

"Alright," Rose says, handing him the plates before she whips him in the face with her ponytail.

Step two. Let Adrien quit without protest and ignore the fact that this somehow still feels wrong. "If that's what you think is best, I won't stop you."

"I really do think it's for the best," Adrien says, then gestures with his chin for them to ski down the mountain.

Step three. Do not engage in flirtation with Allison. Show humility by letting the table make fun of him. "I still can't believe they stole my underwear."

"It is a shame about your camera, though," Jeremy says with a sympathetic smile.

Step four. Volunteer to retrieve Henry from Jeremy. "I'll go get him."

Holden claps him on the shoulder. "It's your funeral."

Step five. Enter the barn unnoticed. Breath in the crisp air and let the music wash over him.

Step six. Sit beside Henry quietly and marvel at the beauty of Jeremy Owens on the ice, skating with grace and strength and joy in his heart.

"He's the best after your mommy, isn't he?"

Step seven. Compliment him, but don't bring up *anything* that has to do with his past or present physical abilities.

"You look free and full of joy out there."

Step eight. Offer him a hand to help him off the ice.

"Here, let me."

Step nine. Let him know that he sees him. That he truly sees him. That it's not a game. That he's not teasing. That the only place he wants to be right now in this entire world is in this semi-frigid barn with his thumb gently caressing Jeremy's cheek.

"This is where you're supposed to be, with or without an audience."

Step ten. Hold his breath while he presses his lips against Jeremy's and waits for Jeremy to kiss him back. *Please, whoever is listening, give me a sign I didn't fuck this up.*

Step eleven. Don't drop Henry in relief the moment Jeremy's lips yield to him.

Failure.

"Ouch!" Henry yells. "Uncle Sergio. You dropped me."

Fuck! Sergio winces. "Sorry, buddy," he says, then quickly kisses a laughing Jeremy one more time before he picks Henry back up.

Chapter Eleven

"Uncle Sergio! Wake up!"

"Oof ... morning, buddy," Sergio says and despite his discomfort, a small smile pulls at his lips while Gus hisses and runs out the door. He is back to kissing Jeremy Owens once every day. He's done that by carefully following his eleven-step plan for the last three days. And also, luckily for Henry, he only dropped Henry that one time. Though, it's not like Henry remembers it anyway.

"Dad said to come get you. Breakfast is almost ready."

"Pancakes, bacon, and fruit?"

Henry nods with the carefree exuberance of a five-year-old, shaking the bed.

"I guess we better not keep him waiting then," Sergio says and gets up. He ruffles Henry's hair. "Go wake up Uncle Adrien."

"Okay!" Henry yells and throws two very enthusiastic thumbs up into the air, then runs out of the room.

"Gently!" Sergio yells, poking his head out the door.

Running, Henry holds up his thumbs higher, then bursts into Adrien's room.

"Hey, buddy." Sergio hears Adrien's groggy voice as he walks past his room and heads down the stairs.

Once in the kitchen, he's greeted by Holden's usual and jovial, "Good morning, shithead!"

"Good morning to you, too!" Sergio greets, slapping Holden a high five. He's feeling so high off those three kisses, he doesn't even get frustrated when he trips over Gus yet again. After he regains his footing, he grabs the plates out of Rose's hands without a word of explanation and starts to set the table, properly now, no longer forgetting his task not even a quarter of the way through. Once the coffee is ready, he grabs four mugs and begins to pour, making sure to lead with Rose's.

"Thanks ..." she says, raising one eyebrow and tilting her head slightly.

"You're welcome." Sergio winks at her and then holds out a mug of coffee for Adrien at his arrival, with Henry hanging off his shoulders.

"You didn't poison this, did you?" Adrien asks him as he takes it.

Sergio laughs. "Adrien, you are the last person on this earth I would want to poison."

Adrien takes a slow sip, squinting at Sergio over the brim of the mug. "Doubtful."

"Seriously. I would be lost without you," Sergio says with emphasis on his seriousness. He pours another cup of coffee and places it down in Holden's spot.

"You take that," Holden says. "I'll drink the sludge at the bottom of the pot."

"You sure?" Sergio asks, already knowing what Holden's disgusting answer will be.

"Yeah," Holden says, grabbing the coffeepot and pouring himself the last remnants of the coffee. He takes an exaggerated sip from his mug and smacks his lips after he swallows. "Ahh. Delicious."

"You're disgusting," Rose, Adrien, and now Sergio say together as everyone begins to grab food.

Alright. So far, so good, Sergio thinks, figuring he's finally got this whole breakfast thing down. Everyone around the table is happy. No one is glaring at him yet. And as long as he stays on this track, he's well on his way to kissing Jeremy at precisely 6:14 this evening.

There's only one problem. Sergio isn't exactly content with only kissing Jeremy at 6:14. And he's tired of being denied that second kiss as the clock strikes midnight. And he's even more tired of being promised a date for a next day that never seems to ever be happening.

Rose rises from her seat, breaking Sergio from his thoughts. "I'll take the rest of this to go." She kisses Holden on the cheek and then heads for the back door. "You boys have fun."

"Will do!" Holden calls out after her. "We'll see you for lunch."

Sergio swallows his food, then takes a long sip of his coffee and decides to take advantage of Rose's departure. "Holden," he says. "Why does your wife hate me?"

Holden coughs and chokes on his coffee. "She doesn't hate you." He waves Sergio off and shakes his head no.

"She thinks you're a bit of a self-centered prick," Adrien says and takes a sip of his own coffee.

"What's a prick?" Henry asks.

Adrien gulps, and Holden pats Henry on the head. "Nothing you need to worry about." He turns his attention back to Sergio. "Honestly, she doesn't hate you. You know you're like family to us."

Sergio shrugs. "Not all families get along."

"She's just stressed right now with Nationals coming up in two weeks and then the Olympics after that, assuming Allison makes the team."

"She's been stressed before," Sergio reasons.

Holden shovels the last of his pancakes into his mouth. He talks as he chews. "She has a lot riding on this Olympic season."

"More than she did the two years she competed and won?"

"It's different, I guess." Holden pauses and drinks what's left of his coffee before he wipes his mouth with his napkin. "It's not only her she's worried about this time. She has to think about Allison and Jeremy."

An image of Jeremy being enraged at Sergio's pity floats through Sergio's mind. Someone else being responsible for him is the last thing Jeremy would ever want. "Jeremy is more than capable of taking care of himself."

"He is," Holden agrees.

"Everyone in this family knows that," Adrien adds, then shovels more food onto Henry's plate, keeping him distracted while the grownups talk.

"But the rest of the skating world doesn't know that," Holden says, filling in the part no one wants to say.

Sergio sighs. "I wish there was a way they could see him skate. He still looks beautiful on the ice."

Holden tilts his head and looks at Sergio with his brow furrowed. "How would you know that?"

Sergio gulps, realizing what he accidentally did. "Oh ... I ... I guess I figured he was still skating."

Holden rises from his seat and grabs his plate, taking it to the sink. "Well, he is. But don't ask him about it."

"Why?" Sergio asks.

"Because nobody knowing is the only way he can still enjoy it."

"Okay, I can understand that," Sergio says. After all, Jeremy has made it clear to him that he hates having an audience, and now he has a better understanding as to why. "But that still doesn't explain why your wife hates me."

"She doesn't, Sergio. It's less to do with you and more that she doesn't want to see Jeremy get hurt."

"Why does everyone assume I'm going to hurt him?"

Adrien lets out a whoop of laughter. "Why would anyone assume you wouldn't?"

Sergio glares at his brother, and for the first time in all of these repeated days, he actually wants to fire him.

Holden claps Sergio on the shoulder, then grabs his empty plate, before taking Adrien's. "Listen, guys, we better get going if we want to get some slope time in before the hills fill up with day tourists."

"Alright," Sergio says, then grins at Holden. "Not today, but some day this week if we want to avoid the tourists, we should take a heli trip."

"Absolutely not," Adrien says at the exact moment Holden grins maniacally and says, "Absolutely!"

With the knowledge that Adrien will, in fact, have fun on said trip, Sergio smiles and finishes his coffee. His smile doesn't last long, though. He may be able to take some comfort knowing that, according to Holden, Rose doesn't hate him. She's merely protective of Jeremy. However, proving to her that he's not out to hurt Jeremy in the sixteen waking hours he gets each version of this day will be no easy feat.

Hanging high above the mountain top, his legs and skis dangling from the chairlift, Sergio still can't stop replaying this morning's conversation in his head. He turns to look at Adrien.

"I'm not convinced that Rose doesn't hate me."

Adrien shrugs. "She might."

"Wow, way to reassure me."

Adrien twists his head and shoulders to face Sergio, looking at him in exasperation. "What do you want me to do? Lie to you like everyone else does?"

"Well … no. But—"

"No, but what, Sergio?" He rolls his eyes and takes a breath. "Listen, you know I love you. But come on, man, you have a reputation for a reason."

"I've changed!"

Adrien stares at him with his lips set in a hard line. "Have you?" He doesn't let Sergio answer. "And while I don't actually think that Rose hates you, I also don't think she wants you flirting with her assistant coach *or* her skater for that matter."

"I'm not flirting with anyone!" Sergio lies. Well, it's technically not a lie, as he hasn't flirted with either of them yet during this version of today.

"Day's still young," Adrien says dryly and turns in his seat to take his gaze back to the space above the treetops.

Sergio frowns and keeps his eyes on his brother. "Do you hate me?"

"Jesus Christ, Sergio. I told you that I love you not even two minutes ago."

"I know, but ... you could hate me, too."

Adrien takes a deep breath, then slowly turns to face Sergio again. "Sergio, I could never hate you. You're my brother, my family, and the most important person in this world to me." He pauses as the chair lift deposits them at the top of the mountain, then, after taking another deep breath, says, "Which is why I think I have to quit working for you."

Sergio, stunned that Adrien still managed to quit on him, even in this conversational context, says nothing as he watches his brother take off down the mountain, speeding away from him as fast as the snow will whisk him away.

"Did you guys have fun?" Holden asks them once they all meet again on the bunny hills.

As always, Sergio doesn't get a chance to answer as Henry is already calling his name. "Uncle Sergio! Look!" He zooms down the hill and flips forward to a stop. "Did you see?"

"Yeah, Henry. I saw," Sergio says, downtrodden as he approaches and picks him up.

"You alright?" Henry asks him.

Sergio plasters a fake smile on his face. "Of course I'm alright. I'm with you!"

"You don't look alright."

Sergio laughs. "Between you and me, Henry, sometimes I think you're the only person who likes me around here."

"Uh-uh." Henry shakes his head. "Everybody likes Uncle Sergio."

"You think so?"

"I know so!" Henry says with complete confidence. "They talked about you all day yesterday."

Well, this is new and exciting information. Sergio perks up. "Did they now?"

"Yep! Even Jeremy was excited to see you."

Sergio's heart soars, and then abruptly sinks. Fuck. He blew it from the start.

With wide, slightly watery eyes, he looks directly at Henry. "He was?"

"Yeah!" Henry says excitedly before his face falls, and he looks at Sergio seriously. "You should tell him you're sorry."

"Ugh ..." Sergio groans. "I know, buddy. I'm working on it," he says, trying to hold Henry tighter as he squirms in his arms.

"Jeremy!" Henry yells, prompting Sergio to put him down. He takes off running.

"Hungry?" Holden asks, clapping Sergio on the shoulder as he watches Henry close in on Jeremy.

Sergio nods his head. "Starving. I could go for a turkey burger."

Holden's face lights up. "This place has a great turkey burger!"

"Yeah, I know, you've told me," Sergio says, hanging his head and walking towards the lodge with Holden oblivious and keeping stride next to him. He leads them all inside, where the hostess is waiting for their arrival.

From here, Sergio hits autopilot. It gets easier and easier every time he repeats this portion of the day. He knows precisely when to laugh, when to brush someone off, and most importantly, the exact moment when Jeremy will look at him with softness in his eyes right before he says, "It's still a loss. I mean, if someone stole my skates, sure, I could buy a new pair, but they wouldn't be the same. Even if they were seemingly identical. The tools of your craft always hold a piece of your soul when you use them as an extension of yourself."

And, same as the first time he said it, Sergio feels a deep crack burrow its way through his heart. A crack that gets deeper and deeper every time they sit across from each other at this table for lunch.

A crack that he has to sit with and smile through every time Rose breaks the shared moment between him and Jeremy when she says, "Very true. But, damn it if it isn't funny when it happens to Sergio."

"Hahaha." Sergio laughs as he's supposed to and rolls his eyes. Once his eyes settle back into place, he lets his gaze linger on Jeremy, who is back to talking to Adrien as their food arrives. Thankful for the distraction, Sergio digs in and eats, and goes right back into autopilot mode.

But today he has an extra layer of distraction. Henry said Jeremy was looking forward to seeing him. He can recognize now that he fucked that up. From moment one. Looking back at his actions on the day that he and Adrien arrived, he can now understand why Jeremy seems to run hot and cold with him on this day. That the times that he approaches him and most importantly, the *ways* that he approaches him make a difference. That he is naturally on guard with Sergio from the moment Sergio opens his mouth to speak, never sure which Sergio he's going to get.

"You need help with him, Jeremy?" Rose asks.

"No." Jeremy shakes his head, smiling softly and directing Henry's head to rest on his shoulder. "I got him."

"Okay, well, we'll see you later," Rose says and waves goodbye. Prompting everyone else to do the same. They all take their turns, one by one bidding Jeremy adieu.

"See you in a bit," Sergio says, then, losing himself in the moment, he kisses Jeremy on the cheek. He's as frozen as the steps they are standing on as Jeremy flinches away. "Sorry." Sergio winces. "Force of habit."

"It's not a habit I'm familiar with," Jeremy says, a hint of accusation in his tone. "You must have me mistaken for one of your other guys."

"Or girls," Adrien adds, tugging Sergio away. "Come on, Casanova. You've humiliated yourself enough for one day."

"Ten!" Holden shouts into the microphone on stage.

Sergio hangs his head and mumbles, "Thank fucking Christ this day is ending."

"Nine!"

He swallows an entire glass of champagne in one gulp.

"Eight!"

"How could I be so fucking stupid?"

"Seven!"

"Will this hell ever be fucking over?"

"Six!"

"How hard is it to get one thing fucking right?"

"Five!"

He looks up and finds Jeremy across the room.

"Four!"

He lets out a little sob.
"Three!"
"I just want to be with you."
"Two!"
"Please ..."
"One! Happy ..."

Chapter Twelve

"Uncle Sergio! Wake up!"

"Oof ... morning, buddy."

"*Hiss ...*"

"Dad said to come get you. Breakfast is almost ready."

"Mmm ... breakfast. Can't wait," Sergio says with sarcasm that Henry is thankfully too young to catch dripping off his tongue. If Sergio never has to eat another pancake or slice of bacon, it'll be too soon. The same goes for turkey burgers at the lodge or whiskey and bulk champagne at the New Year's Eve party.

He's suddenly struck with an idea. "Hey, Henry. Do you think you can ask your dad to make me an omelet?"

Henry looks at him with his eyebrows pinched together. His lips move as if he's silently trying the word omelet out in his mouth for the first time. He tips his head to his shoulder. "What's an omelet?"

"It's like scrambled eggs with vegetables and stuff inside."

Henry pulls a disgusted face that causes his nose to scrunch up. "Why would you want *that* instead of pancakes?"

"In the mood for something different, I suppose." Sergio laughs. "Could you ask him?"

Henry shrugs, flipping his hands up at shoulder height. "I guess so," he says, then runs out the door with his thumbs raised enthusiastically in the air above his head.

"Thank you!" Sergio calls out after him, listening to Henry's thundering footsteps as he goes careening down the hall past Adrien's room and then down the stairs.

Stretching, Sergio sits up in bed and swings his legs out from underneath the covers. From where he's sitting, he can see out the window; the sun is already shining brightly between the high aspen treetops and reflecting off the higher mountains glimmering behind them. He lets out a light breath, and a soft smile lingers on his lips. It's quite peaceful here. He could even consider staying permanently. As long as he's not trapped in this godforsaken loop.

He rises from his seat and steps closer to the window, taking in the full scene. As he's scanning the horizon, the barn comes into view, and with it, Jeremy Owens standing right outside the main door with his mug of hot tea in his hands. He looks serene as he takes a sip. Sergio touches the glass with his fingertips, trailing Jeremy's outline like he's a picture on a screen. A photograph frozen in time.

"Are you coming?" Adrien asks from the doorway.

Sergio hastily removes his fingers from the glass, but he keeps his eyes on Jeremy for a second longer. "Yeah," he says. "I'll be right down."

"You think you can order off-menu while you're here?" Rose chides, her voice clipped and snippy when Sergio and Adrien step into the kitchen. She's finishing setting the table and is on her way to grabbing the coffee pot.

"It's no big deal," Holden says as he flips Sergio's requested omelet in one pan, then a pancake in another. "I'm a man of many skills."

"That may be true," Rose says and kisses him on the cheek as she walks past with the coffee in hand. "But it still doesn't mean Sergio gets to make demands."

"Pfft ... you should try working for him," Adrien says. "Some days I wish an omelet were all I had to procure."

Sergio, used to the two of them picking on him, ignores them and grabs the coffee from Rose to begin pouring everyone a cup. She steals the first one for herself, so he offers the second to Adrien. He saves the third for himself and gives the last to Holden as he places the made-to-order omelet down in front of Sergio at the table.

"Thanks, bud," Sergio says. "This looks perfect."

Holden stands a little prouder. "I do make a mean omelet."

"Is that omelet going to be mean to Uncle Sergio?" Henry asks, looking concerned.

"Of course not," Holden assures him right as Adrien says, "God, I hope so," and takes a sip of his coffee.

"Why would I need my food to be mean to me when you and Rose already do such a good job of it?" Sergio asks as he begins to dig in. He may be trapped in this day and doomed to repeat it tomorrow, but dammit if he's not going to enjoy this omelet. Chewing, he turns to look at Holden. "Delicious!"

"Don't mention it," Holden says, clapping him on the shoulder with a crisp crack. He gestures to the table. "Eat up! We're gonna need all the calories we can get for the slopes today."

On the slopes, after enjoying new food in his belly, Sergio is feeling rather optimistic about his plight. Well, not necessarily optimistic about anything along the lines of him being released from this loop, but he is capable of appreciating some of the finer things about his predicament. Most notably that by the time he and Adrien make it down to the basin after this last run for the morning, he will be well on his way to seeing Jeremy and hopefully kissing him again.

He smiles to himself in anticipation and starts kicking his feet, causing the chair lift to gently sway forward and back.

"You're oddly chipper right now," Adrien says, eyeing him out of the corner of his eye.

"Am I?"

"Yes." Adrien laughs. "You're kicking your feet like a school kid with a crush. But I know that can't be right."

"You think so little of me, huh?"

"When it comes to things like feeling a connection with someone? Yes." Adrien laughs again.

With Jeremy still on his brain, Sergio shrugs. "I'll prove you wrong one of these days."

"Doubtful," Adrien says and looks off into the trees.

Despite it being a futile effort, as all traces of today will be gone tomorrow, Sergio pulls out his camera and takes a picture of his brother looking contemplative. Sergio can practically see the gears grinding in Adrien's head. He turns the camera so Adrien can see the picture on the screen. "For Daphne."

Adrien smiles, but it doesn't meet his eyes. "Thanks, that's a good one."

Sergio recognizes something in his brother's sad smile that he's starting to feel in himself. A longing for someone else. In some ways, Sergio has it easier. Jeremy is not only in the same town, but he's also staying on the same property. Adrien's longing has to travel a far greater distance. It requires translation into another language. It needs to be quenched in a bolder way. Sergio must only walk to the barn. Adrien requires a slow slog through TSA lines and border customs after an eight-hour flight.

"You miss her, don't you?"

Adrien shrugs. "I don't know. We spend so much time apart that I think I'm always missing her. It's kind of our standard."

Something clicks inside of Sergio, like a puzzle piece finding its home. Having always been single and never wanting to share himself or his life with anyone, it was easy to overlook. But now that he pines for Jeremy like this forest of needle trees, he has a newfound understanding of his brother's needs outside of their familial relationship.

"It doesn't have to be."

Adrien rolls his eyes and looks at him straight on for the first time on this particular lift ride. His expression is blank and tired. "Don't tell me *you* have a solution."

"I think I might," Sergio says, knowing exactly what he needs to do. He braces himself for the end of the lift coming and dismounts effortlessly, then waits at the top of the mountain for Adrien to join him. Once standing at his side, he continues, "Adrien. You know I love you, but I think it's time for you to stop working for me."

"Are you firing me?" Adrien asks, his face lighting up in a genuine smile that bursts the bubble of tension that's been festering between them for all these days.

"Afraid so," Sergio says, then takes off down the mountain, feeling almost as light as he did the first time he kissed Jeremy. Maybe things are going to be alright between him and Adrien after all.

"Did you guys have fun?" Holden asks them once they all find each other on the bunny hills.

"Tons. I fired Adrien," Sergio says as he skis past Holden to get to the bottom of the little hill to catch Henry who is already calling out for him.

"Uncle Sergio! Look!" Henry shouts, then zooms down the hill before flipping forward to a stop onto his rump. "Did you see?"

"Hell yeah, Henry! I saw!" Sergio picks him up and slaps him a high five. He then places him back onto his feet before bending down to release Henry from his skis.

"You fired your brother?" Holden asks, appearing behind Henry.

Sergio looks up at him and hands him Henry's skis. "Yeah. Are you surprised?"

"Sort of," Holden says, looking confused with his lips twisted to the side. "To be honest, I figured he'd quit first."

"Well, it's a good thing you didn't wager on it." Sergio rises to his feet with Henry in his arms.

Holden looks at his feet.

"Wait," Sergio says. "Did you make a bet with someone?"

"Well, the thing is, Adrien kind of mentioned it to me that he was unhappy and that he was thinking about quitting, and then I told Rose and really, *she* was the one who wagered a bet with me."

"Huh," Sergio muses. "So Rose thought I'd fire Adrien?"

Holden cringes. "Not exactly. She guessed Adrien would quit on you today, while I wagered he'd wait until the week was over."

"Good. So, neither of you wins, then," Sergio says, feeling smug as he walks away, carrying Henry to the lodge for lunch.

After lunch, where Sergio ate a Cobb salad instead of a turkey burger, everyone is standing outside, saying their goodbyes.

"You need help with him, Jeremy?" Rose asks, eyeing her sleeping son in Jeremy's arms.

"No." Jeremy shakes his head, smiling softly and directing Henry's head to rest on his shoulder. "I got him."

"Okay, well, we'll see you later," Rose says and waves goodbye, prompting everyone else to do the same.

Everyone but Sergio. "Mind if I come back with you?" he asks Jeremy, and everyone stops in their tracks. He can practically hear a record scratch as they all turn to look at him.

Jeremy shrugs as much as he can with a forty-three-pound sleeping child in his arms. "I guess not."

"Great!" Sergio says, clapping his hands together. He turns to look at the rest of the group, all of whom look stunned. "We'll see you all later."

"Yeah ... see you later," Rose says, though her lips purse and a deep furrow wrinkles the space between her eyebrows. She turns to look at Jeremy. "Don't hesitate to call me if you need help with anything."

Jeremy laughs and winks at her. "I think I can handle these two boys for a few hours."

"You could always put Sergio in his kennel up in the house," Holden says, clapping Sergio on the shoulder. From there, he grabs Rose's hand and leads her towards where their skis are so they can get on the slopes for the afternoon. She's looking over her shoulder as they go, glaring at Sergio the entire time.

Sergio gives her one last little wave as they begin to walk away, resisting the urge to grab Jeremy's hand like Holden grabbed Rose's. It's an odd thought for him. He's never been one to hold someone else's hand, but something about the way Jeremy's hand feels in his whenever he helps steady him getting off the ice has Sergio seeing the simple act of affection as desirable. He could hold his hand. He could walk him to the car, to the barn, through the throngs of people at the New Year's Eve party. But right now, Jeremy is far more likely to rip his hand away from Sergio as if he's been stung than reciprocate the gesture.

"Are you sure you don't want to stay?" Jeremy asks with skepticism in his voice.

"Nah. I'm done skiing for the day."

Jeremy shifts Henry to rest against his other shoulder, then glances at Sergio as they walk. He looks as if he's trying to decipher what angle

Sergio might be playing. "I hope you're not expecting me to entertain you."

"Nope," Sergio says, even though that's exactly what he's hoping for as he opens up the back door of the car. He stands by, watching over Jeremy's shoulder as he straps Henry into his car seat. A task presumably made easier by the fact that Henry is currently out cold.

Once in the car and heading toward home, Sergio continues to make what he hopes is a light conversation, knowing full well that Jeremy could turn on him with one wrong word. It's happened on other versions of this day, and if the history of his never-ending New Year's Eves has told Sergio anything, it's that he never gets a new tactic right on the first try. So, it is best to tread lightly. However, Sergio, always the over-confident man that he is, doesn't let that stop him from forging ahead with something new. After all, there is freedom in knowing that no matter how badly he screws up, there's always another today.

"It's really nice of you to help Rose and Holden out like this," Sergio says from where he sits in the front passenger seat of Rose's Audi.

"It's the least I can do," Jeremy says, his eyes on the road, his hands set at ten and two. "Besides, I love Henry. So, it's not like it's hard."

"Yeah. Henry does make things easier, doesn't he?"

"Yes. Very much so." Jeremy smiles, and it makes Sergio's heart flip. For as long as Henry has been alive, Sergio has imagined himself at all of Henry's milestones. And now, thanks to this second, third, ninety-ninth, two hundredth chance, he sees Jeremy there in some capacity, witnessing them as well.

"And I can tell he really likes you," Sergio says. "He gets so excited when you're around."

Jeremy takes his eyes off the road for a brief second and looks at Sergio. "Same can be said about you."

"What? That I'm also excited to be around you?"

"No." Jeremy laughs and shakes his head as he returns his gaze to the road. "I meant *he* gets excited to see you. You were practically all he could talk about yesterday."

Sergio's cheeks warm and flush slightly, and he thinks about what Henry had told him before about Jeremy being excited to see Sergio as well. "And what about you?" he asks.

"What about me?"

"Were you excited to see me?"

Jeremy pauses and appears to think about this. He removes his left hand from the steering wheel and tugs at the corner of his eye before answering. "In a way, I was."

"But not anymore?"

"Well, we didn't exactly have the kind of reunion I had imagined. So, no."

A frown pulls at Sergio's lips. "I'm sorry about that," he says and takes a breath. "Honestly, I hadn't realized."

"It's fine," Jeremy says with a sigh. "I shouldn't have expected you to keep tabs on me."

"No. I think you're right. Any decent human being would have."

Jeremy chances another glance at him again. "You're not that bad."

"Tell that to Rose," Sergio jokes.

Jeremy sucks in a breath through his teeth. "You are right about that. She may take a little more work to impress than I do."

"A little?" Sergio plays it up. "I'm straight-up terrified of her."

"You should be. She's out for blood."

"I know. But I have it on good authority that she's simply looking out for you."

Jeremy's shoulders slump. He stays quiet as he turns into the Harings' driveway, then hits the button to open the garage door. "It's not her place to do that. I can look out for myself."

"And is yourself telling you to look out regarding me?"

"That is yet to be determined," Jeremy says and brings the car to a stop in the garage.

"I'll do my best not to raise any alarms," Sergio promises and exits the car. From there, he moves to where Henry is in the backseat and opens that door to pull his still-sleeping body out of the car. Jeremy reaches to grab him out of Sergio's arms, but Sergio waves him off. "I'll carry him down the hill."

"Thanks," Jeremy says, closing the car door, then hitting the lock button. Once outside the garage, he shuts the large garage door using the keypad and leads the way down to the barn. He looks over at Sergio again and nods his chin towards Henry. "I'm not sure when he's heavier. When he's dead asleep or wide awake and squirming around."

"Less chance of him kicking me in the balls when he's sleeping," Sergio says, deeply aware of the truth of that statement.

Jeremy lets out a whoop of laughter. "Very true."

"Oh! He's gotten you too, then?"

"Thankfully, no. But I have witnessed Holden be on the receiving end more times than I can count."

"Henry's only doing his part to ensure he never has to be a big brother."

"Yeah. We should probably have Holden checked out. I know Rose has been wanting to have another one soon," Jeremy says as they come to a stop at the barn's entrance. He shuffles his feet and appears to contemplate something. After a moment, he looks directly at Sergio with a nervous expression, brows furrowed together, and his bottom lip trapped between his teeth. "Would you like to come up?"

"Sure," Sergio says, trying not to sound as if being invited up to Jeremy's is the only thing he has ever wanted.

With Henry sleeping on Jeremy's bed, Sergio waits on Jeremy's sofa for him to return from the kitchenette with some tea. The electric tea kettle grows louder as it edges closer to a rolling boil, and Sergio takes the time to admire the little home Jeremy has made for himself here in the barn.

The place itself is warm and cozy with no traces of the climate-controlled chill that is maintained to keep the ice frozen a level below them. To add to the warm atmosphere, Jeremy painted the walls in a deep green, and his furniture is made of rich, brown leather. He's hung artwork on the walls and loaded shelves with plants and his collection of books, most of them obscure titles of the magical realism variety.

But what strikes Sergio as interesting isn't necessarily what Jeremy has displayed. He's more curious about what he doesn't have adorning his walls and shelves. There are no photographs of his days as an Olympian. No medals or trophies, not even a framed commemorative keepsake. It's as if that part of his life never happened. As if Jeremy never skated before he stepped onto the ice in the barn. The rink is the only place left that holds any trace of his blades carving shapes into the ice.

"I hope ginger lemon is okay," Jeremy says, handing a mug of tea to Sergio before he sits beside Sergio on the small sofa. The scent of the lemon wafts around Sergio, and the deep spice of the ginger clears his sinuses which are adjusting to being back inside from the cold.

"Anything is fine," Sergio says, content to still be in Jeremy's presence, especially now that he's gotten a better glimpse of how Jeremy lives, cocooned and private. He settles a little deeper into the sofa, resting his back against the corner so he can maintain a better view of Jeremy beside him. "It's quite cozy in here."

"It's not much, but it works for me," Jeremy says and relaxes more deeply as well. He brings his feet up onto the sofa and tucks them underneath his seat, letting his knees knock together to rest on the cushion. His tea, he holds close to his chest. "Better than any place I could have found on my own, that's for sure."

"Rental market tight around here?"

Jeremy rolls his eyes, but not at Sergio. "Tight and ungodly expensive. Holden and Rose could probably make a killing renting this space out to someone else or using it as an Airbnb."

"I doubt they have any interest in making money off of it."

"Clearly," Jeremy says with a resigned laugh. "Otherwise, they'd have given me the boot ages ago."

"How long have you been living up here?"

"Only since summer," Jeremy says and takes a sip of his tea.

"Where were you living before?"

"With my parents ... in Jersey." Jeremy shudders and tugs at his left eye. "I know. Embarrassing, right?"

"I don't think so." Sergio shrugs, even though he does kind of think so. But he's sure there has to be some sort of explanation as to why a former Olympian was living with his parents.

"It wasn't by choice," Jeremy continues. "Don't get me wrong, I love my folks. They're good people. But it certainly wasn't what I expected for myself in my mid-twenties." He pauses and takes another sip. "But after everything that happened and medical bills piled up and my endorsements all dropped me, I didn't exactly have a lot of other options." He dips his head and looks away from Sergio. "But you don't really want to hear all this."

"Sure, I do," Sergio says with complete sincerity that causes Jeremy to look back at him. There's a glimmer of curiosity in his brown eyes. "Don't forget. I failed to keep tabs on you."

"Well, the tabs on me change day to day, so it's hard to keep up."

"How so?"

"Sometimes I wake up fine. Sometimes I don't. Some days I wake up feeling perfect for me and end up a mess by lunch."

Sergio suppresses a light laugh as this is a wholly inappropriate time to chuckle, but in a strange way, due to his current circumstance, Sergio can relate. Wisely, he says, "And sometimes you go on a nice string of days where everything goes just right. And others are an endless stream of disasters."

"Pretty much." Jeremy laughs and takes another sip of his tea. "That is, until one day, I'll end up being nothing but a stream of disaster days. And that's the part I hate."

"They're only disasters if you think of them that way. And who knows? That might not happen at all."

"I'd like to say that's the case. But most studies show that with males, this only goes one way—and fast."

"Hmmm ..." It's almost a shame that Jeremy has no recollection of all these New Year's Eves. Because, from what Sergio can tell, Jeremy is caught in what would be considered a good day for him. Hopefully, if he ever manages to break this loop, Sergio can help to extend this run into the days and weeks and months and even years out for him.

"But, whatever. It doesn't matter. I can't change anything about my situation. All I can do is go with the flow and take care of myself."

"And if you could change it, would you?"

"In a heartbeat."

"So you could continue to skate professionally?"

"So I could avoid ever having to have this type of conversation with anybody ever again."

"Sorry." Sergio winces. "I shouldn't have pried."

"You didn't. You weren't keeping tabs, remember?"

"Touché."

"Besides, saying it all out loud now, I gotta say, I'm kind of glad you didn't. This shit is depressing." He tugs the corner of his eye again.

"I don't know about that." Sergio admires him as he takes a sip of his tea, enjoying the way the ginger slightly lights up the inside of his ears as he swallows. He lets go of his mug with one of his hands and reaches across the small space between them to grab onto Jeremy's hand, finally satisfying the craving he first felt when they left the restaurant. "I think your story, as it stands right now, is kind of inspiring."

To his relief, Jeremy doesn't pull away. "How so?"

"Look at you," he says, giving Jeremy's hand a squeeze. "Sure, you're not where you thought you would be, and your life took a major, unplanned left turn—"

"To put it lightly."

"But you're still involved in a world you love, coaching someone who is showing promise of being the next great skater. That's rare. Not a lot of people can do what you can."

"Says the world-renowned photographer," Jeremy points out.

"Anyone with a camera can do what I do," Sergio says. "I know for a fact that not everyone on a pair of skates can do what you do."

"Is that so?" Jeremy asks, a conspiratorial smirk spreading across his lips. "You want to put your money where your mouth is?"

Sergio narrows his eyes. "What do you mean?"

Jeremy puts his tea down on the coffee table, then rises to his feet and tugs Sergio up with him. "Come on. Let's get you in a pair of skates."

Sergio gulps. He's never been on the ice even once. "What about Henry?" he asks in a feeble attempt to stop this train.

"He's fine," Jeremy assures. "He'll be out for at least another hour."

"All you need to do is hold my hands," Jeremy instructs once he has Sergio up and standing in a pair of Holden's skates on the ice. His cheeks are lifted, causing the corners of his eyes, sparkling more than the smooth ice, to crinkle.

Sergio, despite his earlier want to hold Jeremy's hands, hesitates and keeps himself braced with his back against the rink's wall. "Oh no," he says. "What if I knock you over? Rose will kill me."

"You're not going to knock me over and, if you do, it'll be our little secret." Jeremy glides forward to be even closer to Sergio. He extends his palms. "Now quit being a wimp and grab my hands."

Sergio eyes him warily, but eventually gives in and grabs hold. After all his longing, he'd be damned stupid to turn down this opportunity for more physical contact with Jeremy.

"Good," Jeremy says, giving Sergio's hands a little squeeze as he begins to skate backward, tugging Sergio along with him. As Jeremy moves, Sergio can feel the way he pulls at him in a rocking motion, steady and comforting. "Now all you have to do is shift your weight with me from side to side. Don't even worry about picking up your feet."

"That's it?"

"That's it," Jeremy says, continuing to sway side to side, setting the rhythm they use for gliding across the ice. Sergio is sure Jeremy's feet are doing more than simply shifting side to side as he instructed Sergio to do, but he's not about to look. He's convinced that any second not spent staring at Jeremy's lovely, smiling face will throw him off-kilter and land both of them on the hard ice below their blades.

"Nice and slow," Jeremy encourages. "Get used to the way your feet feel on the ice. Feel the grip of the blades as they carve and find your balance."

Sergio lets out a tentative laugh. "I'm pretty sure the only reason I'm balanced is because of you."

"Nah, I could let go and you'd be fine."

Sergio grips Jeremy's hands tighter. "Don't. You. Dare."

Jeremy's lips pull up into a playful grin with one eyebrow raised slightly higher than the other. "I can't hold on to you forever, Sergio."

He stares right into Jeremy's eyes and swallows. "Bold of you to assume I ever want you to let go."

Jeremy stops his motions, and slowly they come to a stop in the middle of the rink. His smile fades, and he bites his lip. "Is that so, Mr. Durand?"

Sergio, standing stock still, nods his head yes. Whether it's Jeremy gazing directly at him or his paralyzing fear of losing balance on the ice, right now is the most earnest Sergio has ever felt in his life. His heart beats wildly in his chest as he gazes at Jeremy. Pleading, hoping his little gamble today will be rewarded with a shared moment of exchanged affection in the shape of a kiss with the man he never should have let go of.

"And why is that?" Jeremy pulls at Sergio's hands, drawing him in closer so they are a mere few inches away from standing chest to chest.

Careful not to lose his balance, Sergio releases one of Jeremy's hands. He brings his now free hand to Jeremy's cheek and lets his thumb drag gently at the corner of Jeremy's left eye. "You're so beautiful on the ice," he says, as he slides his hand away from Jeremy's cheek to cup the back of his head with his palm. With his fingertips, he feels the softness of the hair on the nape of Jeremy's neck. "You look ... free."

Jeremy tilts his head and looks at him. He lets out a low hum. "I guess I am."

Daring to lean in, Sergio places the gentlest of kisses onto Jeremy's lips and holds his breath waiting for Jeremy to respond. The moment Jeremy opens his mouth slightly and begins to kiss him back, he feels his head spin. If he gave into it, he would pass out in relief.

"Are you two kissing?" Henry's voice echoes through the rink, causing them to quickly pull apart and for Sergio to lose his footing.

Slam! He lands on his back with a thud, and his legs fling his feet into the air.

"Henry!" Jeremy calls out, visibly trying not to laugh. He holds out a hand for Sergio to grab and helps him up. "You should see your Uncle Sergio on skates. He's terrible."

Chapter Thirteen

Sergio's back hurts from slamming it against the ice, but he's flying so high from his latest kiss with Jeremy that he's able to ignore the pain. He can't, however, ignore Rose as she slides up next to him at the bar at the New Year's Eve party.

"So," she says, staring him up and down with pursed lips. "Henry told me you kissed Jeremy."

"So what if I did?" Sergio challenges, looking at her over his shoulder. One of these days, he's going to have to give Henry a talk about what happens to snitches.

She meets his gaze. "I don't want you messing with him. He has enough going on without having to deal with you." She jabs her finger into his arm, emphasizing her point.

"Maybe he wants to deal with me. Did you ever think of that?" He grabs the sparkling water for Jeremy and the glass of champagne for himself that the bartender places in front of him, then starts to walk away. He's in too good a mood to have this conversation with her.

"Oh, of course." She steps in line with him, not letting him get out of her lecture. "How could I forget. Because you're so irresistible."

With his eyes focused on Jeremy across the room, where he's being cornered by Chadwick Levinson, Sergio picks up his pace and weaves through the crowd. Rose stays right on his heel. She seems as determined to make her point as he is to get another kiss from Jeremy before the clock strikes twelve. So, he makes her point for her. He looks at her over his shoulder as he walks.

"Look, Rose, I get it. He's your friend, and you think I'm a piece of shit."

"I don't think you're a piece of shit," she says unconvincingly. "I just don't want to see Jeremy get hurt."

"And you won't, because I'm not going to hurt him." He dodges a server passing around a tray of canapes. "Now, if you'll excuse me, I need to help him get away from that Chadwick Levinson asshole."

"Ugh." She groans. "He's still here?"

"Yes. And he's been trying to poach your skater all night. So maybe you should worry less about my intentions and more about his."

"Fine," Rose says. "But I swear to god, Sergio Durand, if you hurt him, I'll kick your balls off with my skate blade."

Sergio dodges another server and catches her eye one last time. "Only if your son doesn't beat you to it."

She smiles as if that statement has made her proud. "Like mother, like son!"

"You have no idea!" he yells as he breaks away from her.

He turns and focuses back on Jeremy. When he reaches him, he roughly shoulders Chadwick out of the way. "Excuse us," he says to Chadwick, then hands Jeremy his drink. "Here you go."

"Thank you," Jeremy says, letting Sergio lead him away from Chadwick to a less crowded corner of the room. "How's your back?"

Sergio gives a little twist, wincing at the stiffness. "It's been better."

"Sorry about that."

"Think nothing of it," he says with a light laugh that he feels in the bruised muscles of his back. He puts his arm around Jeremy's shoulders. "It was absolutely Henry's fault."

"I'll agree with that," Jeremy says, leaning into his embrace while Holden starts the countdown from the stage with a "Ten!"

Jeremy brings his lips to Sergio's ear. "And I'll also say it was quite rude of him to interrupt that kiss."

"Nine!"

"Is that so?" Sergio turns to face him, bringing their lips mere inches apart.

"Eight!"

"Definitely."

"Seven!"

"Can I interest you in another one?"

"Six!"

"I think I can be persuaded."

"Five!"

Sergio brings his hand to the nape of Jeremy's neck, pulling him closer. "Promise you won't forget about me tomorrow."

"Four!"

"I couldn't forget about you if I wanted to."

"Three!"

"Let's hope that's the case."

"Two!"

"Now kiss me, damn it."

"One! Happy ..."

∞

"Uncle Sergio! Wake up!"

"Oof ... morning, buddy."

"*Hiss ...*"

"Dad said to come get you. Breakfast is almost ready."

"Mmm ... breakfast. Can't wait," Sergio says, even though what he really can't wait for is seeing Jeremy Owens through the trees when he looks out his bedroom window towards the barn. He sits up and ruffles Henry's hair. "Do you think you can ask your dad to fix me eggs Benedict?"

Henry looks at him with his head tilted to the side. His lips move as he silently tries the words eggs Benedict out in his mouth for the first time. He tips his head to his shoulder. "What's eggs bend-a-dick?"

What you do to me every morning. "Never mind," he says lightly. "How about you ask him to make me an omelet?"

Henry tilts his head back the other way. "What's an omelet?"

"It's like scrambled eggs with vegetables and stuff inside," Sergio says with another ruffle to Henry's hair as he begins to rise out of bed.

Henry pulls a disgusted face. "Why would you want *that* instead of pancakes?"

"Variety, I suppose. They say it's the spice of life," Sergio says. His time spent reliving this day is beginning to teach him that it's not entirely true. Variety is nice when it comes to meal options. After all, it's only natural to tire of the same food day after day after excruciating day. However, variety is very steadily proving not to be the spice of life when it comes to matters of the heart. In fact, having no variety and maintaining a sole focus on the one and only Jeremy Owens is actually proving to be far more exciting for Sergio than hunting tail and notching bedposts.

Speaking of, Sergio moves to the window and peers outside, catching Jeremy right when he steps out of the barn with his tea.

"What are you looking at?" Henry asks him, jumping up and down, trying to get high enough to look out the window.

"The trees." He places a hand on Henry's shoulder to still him. Craving a little bit of peace, he urges Henry along. "Could you go ask your dad about that omelet?"

"Okay!" Henry shouts and gives him two very enthusiastic thumbs ups before he goes thundering out of the room, through the hall, and down the stairs.

Now alone, Sergio smiles to himself and wonders what life will be like without the cacophony of Henry's footsteps if he ever gets released from this loop and returned to the life he was living before. His smile turns into a frown. For as much as he wants to see tomorrow, he no longer thinks his life of yesterday is something to which he wants to return, especially if that life doesn't include being able to gaze upon Jeremy drinking his tea in the morning.

He no longer wants to simply gaze at Jeremy through a window with a thicket of trees and snow-covered ground between them. He wants more. Much more. More than mere chaste kisses in an ice rink barn can ever provide him. But if that's all he can get, for now, he'll gratefully settle. Those few chaste kisses are the best kisses he's ever had.

"Are you coming?" Adrien asks from the doorway.

"Yeah," he says, his eyes lingering on what he desires. "I'll be right down."

"All you need to do is hold my hands," Jeremy instructs, extending his palms forward for Sergio to take.

Feeling more confident than yesterday in his ability to not knock Jeremy down on the ice, Sergio grabs them willingly.

"Good," Jeremy says, giving his hands a little squeeze as he begins to skate backward, pulling Sergio along with him. "Now all you have to do is shift your weight with me from side to side. Don't even worry about picking up your feet."

"Like this?" Sergio asks, getting into the rhythm, trying to remember the little bit he learned during yesterday's lesson.

"Like that," Jeremy says, swaying side to side, his skates carving shallow edges into the ice as he propels them along.

Sergio chances a glance to see what Jeremy is doing with his feet so he may be able to mimic the movements in a few more lessons. With time, hopefully, he'll feel more comfortable and confident on this frozen slab of potential back aches and trips to the hospital for concussion protocol.

"Nice and slow," Jeremy says, moving them a little bit faster. "Get used to the way your feet feel on the ice. Feel the grip of the blades and find your balance."

Sergio lets out a laugh. "I'm pretty sure the only reason I'm balanced is because of you."

"Nah, I could let go and you'd be fine."

Sergio grips Jeremy's hands. "Maybe so, but I'm not willing to risk it yet."

Jeremy's face breaks into a playful grin with one eyebrow raised slightly higher than the other. "I can't hold on to you forever, Sergio."

"Bold of you to assume I ever want you to let go."

Jeremy stops his motions and slowly they come to a standstill in the middle of the rink. "Is that so, Mr. Sergio Durand?"

Sergio, standing stock still, nods his head.

"And why is that?" Jeremy pulls at Sergio's hands, drawing him in closer so they are inches away from standing chest to chest.

Carefully letting go of one of Jeremy's hands, Sergio brings his now free hand to Jeremy's cheek and lets his thumb tug gently at the corner of Jeremy's left eye. "You're so beautiful on the ice," he says, sighing softly. "You look ... free."

Jeremy tilts his head and looks at him in contemplation. "I guess I am."

"I guess you are," Sergio says, leaning in and placing the gentlest of kisses onto Jeremy's lips. This time, he doesn't hold his breath as he knows Jeremy, same as he's done before, when Sergio gets this right, will return the kiss. Instead, he braces himself for their inevitable interruption courtesy of Henry.

"Are you two kissing?" Henry asks, right on cue.

They quickly break apart, but this time, Sergio keeps his footing. He lets his eyes linger on Jeremy, watching him blush as he lets go and pulls away after being caught by young eyes. Sergio winks at him, and that's when it all goes to hell.

Slam! He lands on his back, feet in the air above him, with a thud.

"Henry!" Jeremy calls out, visibly trying not to laugh. He skates back to Sergio and holds out a hand for him to grab, and helps him up. "You should see your Uncle Sergio on skates. He's terrible."

∞

"All you need to do is hold my hands," Jeremy instructs, extending his palms forward for Sergio to take.

Feeling even more confident than yesterday in his ability to at least glide along with Jeremy, Sergio grabs them willingly.

"Good," Jeremy says, giving his hands a little squeeze as he begins to skate backward, pulling Sergio along with him. "Now all you have to do is shift your weight with me from side to side. Don't even worry about picking up your feet."

"Like this?" Sergio asks, getting into the rhythm.

"Yeah! Like that!" Jeremy says, encouraging Sergio along with enthusiasm. He gives Sergio a smile. "Are you sure this is your first time?"

"I've maybe been on the ice twice before," Sergio confesses. "But both attempts ended in a full body slam."

"Well, we all fall down every once in a while."

"Very true," Sergio says, holding Jeremy's gaze as they glide.

"I think you can try pushing off," Jeremy suggests. "Rock your weight onto your right foot, then push off with your left."

Sergio does as he's told.

"Good," Jeremy says, looking very pleased with Sergio. "Now do it again."

Sergio does.

"So good. Keep going," Jeremy lets go of one of Sergio's hands and seamlessly moves himself to skate at Sergio's side. "Just like that."

"What about my other foot?" Sergio asks, not feeling fully steady in his abilities and adjusting to only having one of Jeremy's hands to hold.

"Don't worry about your other foot. Focus on pushing with your left and gliding on your right."

"Alright," Sergio says. "But promise me you won't let go."

"I won't," Jeremy says with a squeeze to Sergio's hand.

With that squeeze of his hand and Jeremy's expressed faith in Sergio's newly acquired abilities, Sergio's confidence in himself under Jeremy's tutelage grows. Though he does miss being able to look upon Jeremy's alluring face as he glides. Chancing a glance, he turns his head. His eyes catch Jeremy looking happy and free as they drift across the ice. Sergio's lips break out into a smile.

"Are you guys skating without me?" Henry's voice echoes throughout the barn.

Slam! This time, it's his toe pick and the forward momentum that gets him, causing Sergio to slide across the ice like he's stealing second base. The irony that this is the closest he's gotten to any form of second base in weeks is not in any way lost on him.

"Henry!" Jeremy calls out. "You should see your Uncle Sergio on skates. He's terrible."

∞

Thunk!

"Henry! You should see your Uncle Sergio on skates. He's terrible."

∞

Slam!

"Henry! You should see your Uncle Sergio on skates. He's terrible."

∞

Crash!

"Henry! You should see your Uncle Sergio on skates. He's terrible."

∞

Bang!

"Henry! You should see your Uncle Sergio on skates. He's terrible."

∞

"All you need to do is hold my hands," Jeremy instructs, extending his palms forward for Sergio to take for what feels like the hundredth day in a row.

"Maybe we should wait until Henry wakes up," Sergio suggests, not wanting a repeat of yesterday and the day before that and the day before that and well, honestly, the last handful of weeks trying to get this right.

He brings his hand to his chin and rubs the skin that had been split open after his last fall, still relieved he hadn't woken up to a gash on his face like the one he went to bed with.

Jeremy rolls his eyes. "He's out cold. Now quit being a wimp and grab my hands."

Sergio, unable to resist having Jeremy's hands in his, does what he's told.

"Good," Jeremy says, giving his hands a little squeeze as he begins to skate backward, pulling Sergio along with him. "Now all you have to do is shift your weight with me from side to side. Don't even worry about picking up your feet."

"Like this?" Sergio asks, settling into the familiar rhythm.

"Yeah! Like that!" Jeremy says with excitement in his voice. "Are you sure this is your first time?"

"I've skated a few times before," Sergio confesses. "But each attempt has ended in a blooper reel-style crash."

"Well, we all fall down every once in a while."

"True. But unfortunately, I happen to do it spectacularly."

"I won't let that happen to you today," Jeremy promises. Sergio would love nothing more than to believe him. "I think you can try pushing off. Rock your weight onto your right foot, then push off with your left."

"Like this?"

"Just like that."

Sergio repeats the motion without being directed.

"So good. Keep going," Jeremy encourages and tries to let go of Sergio's hand to move to his side like he's been doing each day that Sergio's abilities to stay balanced on his skates continue to grow.

Sergio, tired of falling before he gets to the kissing, grips Jeremy's hand harder. "Don't. You. Dare."

Jeremy's face breaks out into a playful grin with one eyebrow raised slightly higher than the other. "I can't hold on to you forever, Sergio."

Holding on tight, never wanting to lose his grip on Jeremy ever again, Sergio says with complete certainty, "Bold of you to assume I ever want you to let go."

Jeremy stops his motions, and slowly they come to a stop in the middle of the rink. "Is that so, Mr. Sergio Durand?"

Sergio, standing stock still, nods his head. He's never been so sure of something in his life.

"And why is that?" Jeremy pulls at Sergio's hands, drawing him in closer so they are standing chest to chest.

Carefully letting go of one of Jeremy's hands, Sergio brings his now free hand to Jeremy's cheek and lets his thumb tug gently at the corner of Jeremy's left eye. "You're so beautiful on the ice," he says, sighing softly, relieved that if things keep going well, he might get to feel Jeremy's lips pressed against his again. "You look ... free."

Jeremy tilts his head and looks at him, a soft smile lifts his lips. "I guess I am."

Feeling quite confident and frankly a bit desperate, Sergio leans in and places a solid kiss on Jeremy's lips, moaning when Jeremy reciprocates it instantly.

"Are you two kissing?" Henry's voice echoes through the rink, causing Jeremy to quickly pull away. Sergio, for the first time, maintains his balance.

"Henry!" Jeremy calls out, his cheeks visibly blushing. "You should see your Uncle Sergio on skates. He's not that bad."

Chapter Fourteen

"Henry told me you kissed Jeremy," Rose says, sliding in beside Sergio at the bar where he's just ordered another whiskey for himself and a sparkling water with a twist of lime for Jeremy from the bartender.

Sergio, not in the mood for Rose ruining his day with a lecture he's already heard enough that he can recite it to her, ignores her accusation. "Shouldn't you be chatting up potential sponsors for Allison?"

She presses her finger against Sergio's cheek and forces him to look at her instead of Jeremy, who's shuffling his feet and standing with his arms crossed while talking with Chadwick Levinson on the other side of the party. "Don't change the subject."

"Fine. So what if I kissed Jeremy? He didn't push me away. In fact, he kissed me back."

Rose groans. "This is exactly what I did not want to happen with your arrival this week."

"What? Two grown men rekindling what they started four years ago?" Sergio asks, annoyed. He lays a tip down on the bar as the bartender delivers his drinks. "Honestly, what goes on between me and Jeremy really isn't any of your business."

"Of course, it's my business," she says and grabs a glass of champagne. She immediately takes a sip, then eyes Sergio up and down when she brings the flute away from her lips. "He's my best friend."

"Some best friend you are." Sergio scoffs. "Your husband Holden is *my* best friend, and I never once stood in the way of the two of you getting together like you're doing to me and Jeremy."

And this, believe it or not, is absolutely true. Short of him teasing his best friend about how smitten he was over a certain red-headed figure skater flitting around the Olympic village eight years ago, Sergio let them be. After seeing Holden's interest, he stopped his own initial thoughts of pursuing her and was thereafter nothing but helpful. They were all nineteen-year-old idiots, and Holden, who'd always been so narrow-eyed focused on his skiing career, had somehow managed to forget girls existed until Rose walked past him. The fact that Holden was suddenly all starry-eyed for someone was a revelation for Sergio. Especially since Holden had spent their entire friendship up to that point making brotherly fun of Sergio, who jumped from girlfriend to boyfriend to girlfriend to girlfriend's brother like he was flipping pages in a magazine.

"Bullshit," Rose says.

Sergio shifts himself to stand in front of her point-blank. "You really don't know me at all, do you?"

Rose laughs bitterly. "I know you too well, Sergio."

"You obviously don't, if you can't see that I genuinely like Jeremy."

"You only like someone for as long as it takes for you to get your dick in their mouth."

Tired of arguing and having this same exact fight with her every night on the rare days that he does get to kiss Jeremy, and subsequently caught by Henry, Sergio sighs, then takes a sip of his drink.

"It's not like that with Jeremy," he says. "I really care about him."

"I seriously doubt that. But regardless. Can we please get through this week without you breaking my best friend's heart?"

"Why do you *always* assume I'll break his heart?"

"Because history repeats itself." Rose raises an eyebrow at him. It's an infuriating move that Sergio now officially takes as a personal challenge to prove her wrong. Not that it matters. Until he finds a way out of this loop, she'll never realize how wrong she is about him.

Taking a sip of his drink, he turns away from her and focuses back on Jeremy. Judging from the history of this evening, Jeremy is currently listening to Chadwick boast about himself and repeat the fallacy that four years ago, he was the better skater, and Jeremy was nothing more than a flash in the pan.

Sergio grabs Jeremy's drink from the bar in his other hand, then takes his attention back to Rose one last time. "I have no intentions of ever hurting Jeremy again," he says. "Now, if you'll excuse me. I would like to take Jeremy his drink and save him from having to continue talking to that insufferable Chadwick Levinson asshole. And *maybe* even seal the deal on a second kiss from Jeremy when the clock strikes twelve."

With both drinks in hand, he sets his shoulders back and stands a little taller than he already is and makes his way across the party to Jeremy, arriving right as Holden hops on stage to announce the countdown.

"Alright, everyone," Holden says into the microphone. "Grab a glass of champagne, the countdown starts in less than a minute."

"Here you go," Sergio says, handing Jeremy his drink and inserting himself in the space between Jeremy and Chadwick, effectively blocking Chadwick from being able to talk to Jeremy anymore.

"Thank you," Jeremy says. He uncrosses his arms, and his shoulders relax.

"Sorry, that took so long. Rose had some words for me."

Jeremy, smiling and bringing his drink to his lips, says, "I'm sure she did."

"She thinks I'm bad for you," he says while Holden starts the countdown from the stage with a "Ten!"

Jeremy leans in close. "She might be right."

"Nine!"

"Do you really believe that?"

"Eight!"

"No. Not after today."

"Seven!"

"There is hope for me yet?"

"Six!"

"Oh, there's definitely hope for you."

"Five!"

"Hope for me to get another kiss?"

"Four!"

"Come back with me tonight, and I'll give you more."

"Three!"

"Is that a promise?"

"Two!"

"It's a guarantee."

"One! Happy ..."

"Uncle Sergio! Wake up!"

"Oof ... morning, buddy."

"*Hiss* ..."

"Dad said to come get you. Breakfast is almost ready."

Sergio rubs at his eyes and sighs. The memory of Jeremy promising him more than just a kiss lingers in the forefront of his mind. Jeremy can promise that all he wants, but if Sergio can't make it past midnight, there will never be a chance for any follow-through. Frowning, he begins to sit up in bed, situating himself to sit across from Henry.

"You're a smart kid, right?"

"Dad says I'm the smartest!" Henry says with pride.

"And what about Mom? What does she say?"

"She says I'm the sweetest."

Sergio nods his head. "They're both right. Do you know what I think you are?"

Henry tilts his head to the side. "Smartest?"

"For sure," Sergio says, and ruffles his hair. "But I also think you are the sneakiest."

Henry frowns. "Mommy says it's not good to be sneaky."

"Mommy is only half right," Sergio says, hoping that today isn't the day he finds a way to free himself from this loop, as he's about to manipulate a five-year-old in a way that he doesn't want to have any lasting effects on his attitude towards his mother. But Sergio is in desperate need of an ally if he's going to garner any new and vital intel. Besides, Henry has been snitching on him for months now. Sergio may as well squeeze him like a lemon for anything useful.

He leans in close to Henry and gives him a playful, mysterious smile. "Let's talk secrets," he says. Henry's face lights up. "Tell me, what did Jeremy say when he found out I was coming?"

"He said he was excited to see you," Henry says with certainty.

"And what did your dad say?"

"He said, 'Henry! Your favorite uncles are coming!'"

"Favorite *uncles?*" Sergio questions. "I thought I was your favorite."

"Mommy says it's not nice to have favorites."

"Fair enough." Sergio shrugs; after all, trying to enshrine himself above Adrien in the hierarchy of Henry's affections isn't the point of this exercise anyway. "What did your mommy say about me coming?"

"Well, she told Daddy she couldn't wait. But she told Allison to ignore you. And she told Jeremy that if you tried anything on him this week, she was going to kick you in the nuts."

"Like mother, like son," he says, and ruffles Henry's hair again. "Do me a favor, would you, kid?"

"Sure!" Henry says, eyes shining.

"Be my eyes and ears today? It'll be our little secret," he says with an exaggerated wink.

"Okay!" Henry agrees, giving his own version of a wink that looks more like a hard blink as he squeezes both eyes closed before he reopens them.

After breakfast, Sergio, Holden, Adrien, and Henry get into Holden's Range Rover to head to the slopes for the day. Sergio nods his chin at Adrien and says, "Take shotgun."

"Are you sure?" Adrien asks before opening the door and climbing in, not waiting for an answer.

"Yeah, I'm sure." Sergio climbs in next to Henry in the backseat and waves Holden off as he starts to buckle Henry into his booster. He winks at Henry again, like he did earlier when he put this plan into motion. "I have important business to discuss with Henry."

Henry hard blinks back at him and echoes his words. "Important business."

Holden gets into the driver's seat. "Remember, Sergio, there are child labor laws for a reason. You better not be recruiting my son for work. His labor is only allowed to be exploited by me and his mother."

"A little late to be trying to explain labor laws to him, don't you think?" Adrien asks. "He's been working me like a dog for years."

Sergio, already knowing what's coming once he and Adrien are alone on the slopes, ignores his jab. *We'll see how you feel after I fire you my damn self.*

"Ignore them," Sergio says to Henry. "Our business has nothing to do with *those* two." He raises his voice for emphasis. "This is uncle/nephew business."

"Should I be worried about this?" Holden asks Adrien as he presses the ignition.

"They both read at a first-grade level. I think you're safe," Adrien says and turns on the radio, quickly finding a mellow station instead of the horrible stadium rock station Holden is prone to putting on when he has control.

As if the gods of fate are shining on him, *Wicked Game* by Chris Isaak begins playing through the car's speakers. The melody sends warmth through Sergio, as he immediately pictures Jeremy skating to the music in the forefront of his mind. He checks his watch. Hopefully, if today goes well enough, he'll be able to catch that image in real life this afternoon.

But if he wants that to happen, he needs to get to work. So with the music drowning out any extra voices in the car, Sergio turns his attention back to Henry. "Okay, here's the plan," he says softly. "I need you to do some digging for me today."

"Okay." Henry looks at him and nods. His lips are set in a hard line, and his eyes are wide as he waits for instructions. He looks as serious as a five-year-old can while being given directions.

"See if you can find out from your dad why your mom hates me—"

"Hey, Dad!" Henry yells before Sergio can finish giving him the instructions. "Why does Mommy hate Uncle Sergio?"

∞

"Uncle Sergio! Wake up!"
"Oof ... morning, buddy."
"*Hiss ...*"

"Okay, Henry, let's try this again," Sergio says to Henry while they ride in the backseat of the car with *Wicked Game* playing over the speakers and keeping Holden and Adrien from listening in to Sergio as he works to temporarily corrupt his nephew.

"Try what again?" Henry asks, confused.

"Our secret plan."

"Oh! Right!" he says with a hard blink.

"Now listen carefully. This is important. Okay?"

"Okay." Henry looks at him and nods with wide eyes and his lips pressed in a hard line.

"Once me and Uncle Adrien leave you and your dad to go skiing, you need to ask your dad why your mom hates me. Can you do that?"

"She doesn't hate you," Henry assures.

"She might not," Sergio says. "But we need to know for sure. Can you do this?"

"I can do this!" Henry says louder than necessary. He hits Sergio in the nose when he thrusts two very enthusiastic thumbs up high above his head. Sergio's vision blurs, and his eyes start to water.

"You can do what, Henry?" Holden asks from the front seat.

"Ask you why Mommy hates Uncle Sergio."

Sergio, clasping his aching nose, groans into his hands.

∞

"Uncle Sergio! Wake up!"

"Oof ... morning, buddy."

"*Hiss ...*"

After breakfast, in the car, the radio on and playing the song Sergio can't escape, Sergio looks at Henry and says slowly once again, "Alright, Henry. I need you to listen to me *very* carefully."

"Okay." Henry looks at him and nods with his most serious face.

"Once me and Uncle Adrien leave you and your dad to go skiing, you need to ask your dad why your mom hates me," he says, then adds with haste, "Not before. Alright?"

"Alright," Henry agrees.

"What are you agreeing to back there?" Holden questions.

"Nothing!" Sergio yells out before Henry can ruin the groundwork he's laying ... again.

"Well, that didn't sound suspicious at all," Adrien says.

"Yeah ..." Holden catches Sergio's eyes in the rearview mirror. "You're not turning my son against me, are you?"

"I would never," Sergio says, holding a hand over Henry's mouth.

From the top of the mountain, eager to get back down to the bottom so he can find out if Henry has anything to report, Sergio takes a deep breath and says to Adrien, "Adrien. You know I love you, but I think it's time for you to stop working for me."

"Are you firing me?" Adrien asks, his face lighting up in a genuine smile.

"Afraid so," Sergio says, gives him a salute, then skis off, taking the slope in wide swoops and curves, enjoying the momentum he builds while his day so far goes according to plan.

It's funny; now that he's found some success on the ice thanks to Jeremy's daily lessons, his skiing has improved as well. He's more balanced and more aware of the subtle movements in his legs and how they can change the trajectory of how he skis. He'd never thought the two sports would or could correlate. The only thing he ever thought they had in common was that in both sports, falling on your ass at some point was a guarantee. But even that was different, as falling on ice skates meant hitting your ass on ice laid over hard concrete as opposed to landing in fluffy piles of cushioning snow if you went down on skis.

The connection he's made makes him wonder if Jeremy ever gets on skis. He supposes not. It's likely something he's given up to maintain his broader health and to keep him able to do the things that he does love. And as much as Sergio would like to see Jeremy's wind-blown cheeks soaring down the slopes beside him, Sergio has to admit that Jeremy looks far too lovely on skates to ever give that up completely if he doesn't have to.

"Did you guys have fun?" Holden asks them once Sergio and Adrien make it to the bunny hills.

Sergio doesn't get a chance to answer as Henry is already calling his name. "Uncle Sergio! She doesn't hate you!" he shouts, then zooms down the hill in a perfect miniature replica of his father's crouched skiing stance before flipping over forward to a stop.

"Fuck," Sergio mutters and hangs his head as he comes to a stop.

Adrien skis past him and takes over Sergio's usual task of lifting Henry back up onto his feet as Holden claps Sergio on the shoulder and says, "He gave you up pretty quick."

"Yeah, I should know better than to trust a five-year-old."

Turning to face him, Holden asks, "Why do you think Rose hates you?"

"It's a pattern I've noticed over the last few days." Sergio sighs.

"Days? You only got here yesterday."

"Yesterday to you." Sergio digs the heels of his hands into his temples. Still muttering, he adds, "I think I've been here for nearly a year at this point."

"A year?" Holden asks, scratching the back of his neck. "How have you been here for nearly a year? I picked you up at the airport yesterday."

Frustrated and at his wits' end, Sergio dives into it. He shakes his hands on either side of his head and looks up at the clear blue sky as he says, "It's been a day for you, but months for me."

"Oh, yeah. I know what you mean. Like those long-ass days you just want to end, but they never do. I hate that."

"No!" Sergio shouts and stares directly at Holden. "I mean, I keep waking up on the same day! Today. New Year's Eve. And no one else seems to notice."

"I'm still not following here, Sergio. Do you want to skip lunch with us and go back to the house? We can talk about this tomorrow."

"There *is* no tomorrow. Tonight the clock will strike midnight, and I'll wake back up today, New Year's Eve. And your son will kick me in the balls and your wife will still hate me and Jeremy won't remember that I kissed him."

Holden smirks. "Oh, come on, Sergio. You can't expect every bloke you kissed four years ago to remember you."

Sergio throws his hands up. "I'm not talking about four years ago! I'm talking about yesterday and the day before that and the day before that and the weeks before that and the months before that."

"That's impossible, though." Holden shakes his head. "You seriously only got here yesterday."

"Yesterday to *you*," Sergio repeats. "For me, it's been several months!"

"You're telling me that you've been here for months and none of us has noticed?"

"Yes!" Sergio yells out.

"Wow. Sorry, mate. That sounds like a real kick in the dick."

"Funny you should say that because your son wakes me up with a literal kick in the dick every morning."

"That sucks." Holden winces. "Have you tried locking the door before you go to bed?"

Sergio looks at him and blinks, seriously debating shoving his best friend into a pile of snow.

Holden smiles at him. "I'm simply suggesting that it might help."

"What part of 'I wake up on the same day' are you not getting? Even if I lock the door tonight, it won't change the fact that I didn't lock it last night. So no matter what, Henry is going to burst into my bedroom tomorrow morning and knee me in the nuts."

"I thought you said he kicked you in the dick."

Sergio balls up his fists and lets out a groan of frustration. "I can't have this conversation with you again."

"You're right. It's the same thing." Holden concedes with his hands held up at shoulder height in defense. Quickly, he grabs Sergio by the shoulders and looks him in the eyes with intensity. "Wait a minute. Are you fucking with me? Is this some kind of prank? Because if it is, it's hilarious! You really got me on this one. I was actually concerned for a minute."

"This isn't a prank," Sergio says through gritted teeth.

"It kind of feels like a prank."

"If anyone is being pranked, it's me."

Holden lets out a slow whistle. "I wish I'd come up with this. It's a great prank."

With his head buried in between his hands, Sergio says, "Trust me, I wish you had, too."

"Okay, so let me try to get a handle on this. What you're telling me is that today feels exactly like yesterday, even though you weren't here yesterday?"

"No. I'm telling you that I have woken up here for months on end on a perpetual Mobius strip of New Year's Eves and I'm the only one who notices."

"Like a time loop?"

"Yes. Exactly like a time loop."

Holden shrugs. "Damn. That's crazy. We don't even have a hot tub."

"A hot tub!" Sergio screams, drawing the attention of everyone around them, including Jeremy, who has arrived and is waiting for Henry to finish running to him.

"Yeah, you know. Like that movie! *Hot Tub Time Machine*."

"Trust me. It doesn't equate," Sergio says, realizing once again that he's talking to a moron.

"Oh!" Holden exclaims. "Maybe this is more like *Groundhog Day*?"

"I think that's a better correlation." Sergio takes off his gloves and rubs harshly at his face.

"Yeah! Right? Like how Bill Murray had to repeat the same day over and over again to learn how to be a better person or something."

"That is my current goal," Sergio says, his eyes on Jeremy and wishing he could see what their tomorrow could look like if he could get everything he needs to get right to see it.

"Good on you, mate. I never thought of you as someone who made New Year's resolutions." He claps Sergio on the shoulder and continues to push them along towards the lodge. "I hope you're hungry. This place has a great turkey burger."

After lunch, exhausted and only halfway through this version of today, Sergio lets out a sigh in the car beside Jeremy as Jeremy pulls away from the lodge.

"What was all that about with Holden earlier?" Jeremy asks him.

Sergio takes a deep breath and lets out another sigh. He stares at the tall, snow-covered aspen trees as they speed past them. "It's hard to explain."

"Try me," Jeremy says.

He takes his eyes off the trees and turns to look at Jeremy's profile. There's a soft smile on his face, and Jeremy chances a quick glance back at him. When they make eye contact, Sergio recognizes sympathy in his eyes, as if he's the only one who sees the weight pressing down on Sergio's shoulders. The result has Sergio feeling like he can trust him despite how vulnerable he is feeling right now in his exhaustion.

"You really want to know?"

"Only if you want to tell me. But you seemed pretty frustrated back there."

Sergio takes another deep breath, and with it comes a flood of deep exhaustion. If he were in the car with anyone else, he'd open the passenger door and fling himself out of it in order to start this day over faster. But it's Jeremy here with him, and Sergio wants to savor every minute he can get with him. Even if Jeremy will never remember all that he's done for Sergio over all of these days.

"Frustration doesn't even cover it."

"So what's the problem, then? Maybe I can help."

Sergio rubs his face with his palms some more. If he keeps this up today, he'll have nothing left to rub at until tomorrow. "Fuck. I don't even know how to explain this without sounding crazy."

Jeremy looks over his shoulder and flashes him a quick smile before taking his attention back to the road. "I have an open mind. Take your best shot. Surprise me."

"Well, if you insist," Sergio says, then takes another deep breath before diving into his saga. "So here's the thing. And like I said, you're going to think that I'm crazy, but I swear to you I'm not."

"Sounds like something a crazy person would say," Jeremy jokes, but it's lighthearted.

"Fair enough. And honestly, maybe I am. I'm not sure how much more of this I can take."

"So what is it?"

"So you know that movie *Groundhog Day*?"

"Yeah, of course. Bill Murray has to keep living the same day over and over again until he fundamentally changes as a person. Going from a completely self-centered asshole to someone capable of love, selflessness, and thinking of others' needs. It's great! I love that movie."

"And what if I told you that I'm living that movie?"

"I'd tell you that you're crazy." Jeremy laughs. "It's only a movie. It's not possible."

"But what if it *is* possible?"

Jeremy's lips twist in thought as he turns into the Harings' driveway. He hits the button to open the garage door. "I guess I would need some sort of proof before I could believe you."

"What would be proof?"

"I don't know. Predict something," he says, shutting off the car and opening the driver's side door to get out.

"Hmmm ..." Sergio thinks as he gets out of the passenger seat and moves to Henry's door behind him to unbuckle him from his seat and pull him out of the car. Once he has Henry held in his arms, he says to Jeremy, "We've done this before. Several times in fact. We're gonna walk down to the barn, and when we get there, you're going to ask me if I'd like to come up."

"This sounds like less of a prediction and more like you trying to use 'The Force' on me, getting me to tell you these are not the droids you are looking for. Not gonna lie, that's not helping your case on not being crazy." Jeremy uses the keypad to close the garage door behind them.

"I haven't gotten to the prediction."

Jeremy gestures his hands forward. "Okay. Go on."

Sergio begins to lead the way to the barn. "You'll ask me if I want to come up, and I will, of course, say yes. Because that's all I ever want to do on all of these days."

"I hope you know, no matter how hard you try to convince me, I'm not going to sleep with you."

"Yes. I'm well aware." Sergio laughs.

"Okay, as long as we're clear."

"Crystal," Sergio says with playful exaggeration, even though he finds Jeremy to be nothing but endearing right now. Especially considering this conversation is going better with him than it ever does with Holden. "As I said, you'll ask me to come up, and then once upstairs after you've laid Henry down in your bed to continue his nap, you'll offer me tea."

"That does sound like something I would do," Jeremy says, tugging his left eye as they approach the barn door. "But I'm still not convinced."

"Well, what about the fact that I know the tea you'll offer me is ginger lemon."

"I have to admit, that is quite the trick. There is no reason you should know what my afternoon beverage is." He swings the door open and walks inside. Stopping, he turns to look at Sergio. "Aren't you coming?"

"God, yes," Sergio says and rushes in after him. The barn door shuts with a click, and they make their way up the stairs to Jeremy's little living space.

"Since you've apparently already been up here," Jeremy says, shrugging off his coat and hanging it on a coat hook beside the door. "Why don't you lay Henry down on my bed for me while I fix us some tea?"

"Are you sure?" Sergio asks. He's been in Jeremy's room before, but always with Jeremy and never alone. It's a small gesture, but it feels good to know he hasn't lost Jeremy's trust with his bizarre woes about a repeating day. Most people would keep someone ranting about being stuck in a time loop as far away from where they change their underwear as possible.

As if he's read Sergio's thoughts, Jeremy gives a half-smile. "Why not? If what you're saying is true, anything untoward you dare to do in there won't matter, as it will be erased by tomorrow. And if you're lying..." He pauses and looks Sergio up and down, then looks him in the eyes again as he says, "I don't think you're stupid enough to do something else that will make what you've already done worse."

"Making things worse is the last thing I want to do."

"Good." Jeremy smiles at him, then turns to head into his kitchenette. With his back to Sergio, he says, "And for the record, I don't think you meant to ruin things last night either."

A lump forms in Sergio's throat that he attempts to swallow down. For the first time since this all started, he's feeling like maybe—to Jeremy at least—he's not as big of an asshole as everyone else makes him out to be. The thought warms his heart, and he hugs Henry's sleeping body closer to his chest as he carries him into Jeremy's bedroom before he takes Henry's coat off and places him in the center of the bed.

After pulling a blanket over Henry, Sergio walks back out to the apartment's living room and hangs his own coat on the hook by the door. From there, he takes a seat on the small sofa and watches Jeremy pour two cups of tea and walk to him.

"Ginger lemon, as predicted," Jeremy says as he hands a steaming mug to Sergio before he takes a seat on the other side of the sofa.

"Thank you," Sergio says, feeling a calm wash over him with the warm mug held between his palms. The now familiar scent of lemon and ginger will forever be associated with quiet afternoons spent at Jeremy's, even if Jeremy won't feel the same.

"So ..." Jeremy stares at him with curiosity. "This time loop you're in. Is it working?"

A surge of hope courses through Sergio. "Are you saying you believe me?"

"I'm saying you've piqued my interest."

"I'll take it." Sergio smiles at him. "And yes. I do believe that it's working."

"How?" Jeremy takes a sip of his tea. "Explain it to me."

Sergio relaxes deeper into the cushions of the sofa and breathes in a curl of steam wafting from his mug. "I think it's making me become a better person."

Jeremy mimics him and relaxes more deeply as well, bringing his feet up onto the sofa and resting his mug in his hands on his bent knees. "But you're still stuck in the loop, so you're obviously not getting it right."

Sergio lifts one shoulder in a half shrug. "There's a bit of a steep learning curve."

"I bet." Jeremy laughs. "What do you think triggered it?"

"Honestly," Sergio says, feeling himself shrink. "You."

"Me?" Jeremy points at himself. "Oh no. You do not get to blame me."

"I ... I'm ... I'm not." Sergio reaches across the sofa and grabs Jeremy's hand. He lets out a breath between his lips when Jeremy doesn't yank it away from him. "I think fate wants me to make things right with you."

"Ooh, that's a smooth line, Sergio Durand. A little too smooth," he says, but still doesn't remove his hand.

"It's not a line," Sergio says, softening his gaze. "There's something about you that makes me want to be a better person."

Jeremy releases his hand to tug on his left eye, then, to Sergio's relief, immediately laces his fingers back together with Sergio's. "You're not a bad guy," he says. "You just need to grow up."

"And if I grew up, would you consider me?"

"You tell me. You're the one who's experienced this day before. What are the results?"

Sergio lets out a laugh with a weak nod of his head and an even weaker smile. He looks away from Jeremy, taking his gaze to the shelves of plants and books surrounding Jeremy's wall-mounted television. "Well, let's see. There's a one-hundred percent chance Henry wakes me up with a kick in the balls each morning."

Jeremy laughs out loud, then stops himself quickly when Sergio looks at him. He bites his lip, looking guilty.

"No. Please do laugh," Sergio says. "It's the only way that makes my wake-up call easy to deal with." He squeezes Jeremy's hand. "After that, my day has varying degrees of success. Fifty percent chance you kiss me while we're downstairs on the ice. Fifty percent chance I fall flat on my face or ass, depending on which direction I'm facing when Henry interrupts us. One-hundred percent chance I get lectured by Rose for pursuing you."

"That sounds about right. Is that all that happens?"

"No. Adrien will quit on me every day on the slopes. Though lately, I've been firing him instead. It's easier that way. And Holden will continually praise the lodge's turkey burger."

"It's a good burger."

"Not after you've eaten one every day for months."

"Try the Cobb salad next time."

"Yeah, that's been my alternative."

"That's it then? Nothing else I need to know?"

"I'm pretty sure Gus is in cahoots with Rose and tries to kill me every day by being underfoot."

Jeremy looks at him and shakes his head. "There's no way. Gus is such a sweet cat. Besides, he's usually hiding."

"Hiding, hissing, and plotting my death," Sergio says, exhaustion laced throughout his words.

"Okay, so potentially murderous cat aside, is there anyone else out to get you?"

Sergio takes a sip of his tea, then dips his head as he swallows. When he looks up, he's wearing a devilish grin. "No. But the first few times I lived this day, I punched Chadwick Levinson in the face in your defense."

Jeremy explodes into laughter, and Sergio wishes he could freeze time right here to preserve this moment of Jeremy's unfettered amusement forever. "Alright," he says, once he catches his breath. "I don't condone violence in any way, but damn it if I don't know that he deserved it with complete surety."

"You're not mad?" Sergio's forehead wrinkles.

"Why would I be mad?"

"You're always mad when I do it."

"I guess if you make a spectacle of it, I'm probably more embarrassed."

"Considering it always happens at the New Year's Eve party, moments before the clock strikes twelve, it's fair to say there's an audience."

"Yeah. That explains it." Jeremy nods his head quickly. "Let's avoid doing that tonight, please."

"You have my word. I will not lay a hand on him."

"Good," Jeremy says and places his tea down on the coffee table. With his eyes back on Sergio, he uses his now free hand to run his fingers through his own hair, pausing when he reaches the nape of his neck. "Now, how about that kiss you say happens when we're on the ice?"

Using his grip on Jeremy's hand, Sergio pulls himself out of the corner of the couch he had nestled himself into and leans in closer to Jeremy. "The tale of my woes hasn't scared you off yet?"

"Sergio." Jeremy adjusts himself to face Sergio head-on. "I have never been afraid of you."

Sergio turns and takes one last sip of his tea before he reaches and places it on the coffee table beside Jeremy's mug. He swallows. "Our history suggests otherwise."

"Did this conversation not go well before?" Jeremy asks.

With his chin dipped slightly down, Sergio looks back at Jeremy guiltily. "I meant ... before."

"Oh." Now Jeremy swallows, and Sergio watches his throat bob. "You meant four years ago."

Sergio nods.

Jeremy lets go of his hand. The sudden loss of contact causes Sergio's stomach to sink. "That was different." He places both feet on the floor and faces towards the center of the room. "It wasn't you I was afraid of. It was—"

"Everything else."

"Yeah," he says, tugging at the corner of his eye.

"And what about now?"

Jeremy drops his ear to his shoulder and turns to face Sergio again. "You still don't scare me."

"You don't scare me either."

Jeremy wets his lips with a quick roll of his tongue over them, then smiles. "Maybe I should."

"You could take lessons from Rose."

"She's not that scary," he says, shaking his head.

"To you." Sergio laughs. "I'm pretty sure she hasn't threatened your balls."

"To be honest, I'd prefer it if she'd keep yours intact."

Sergio's cheeks warm and lift as he feels genuine hope for something more for the first time in ages. "Are you saying you have use for them?"

Jeremy gives him a non-committal shrug and rises to his feet. "We can worry about their usefulness tomorrow." He holds his hand out to Sergio, and Sergio immediately takes it and lets himself be pulled to his feet. "As for now, I'm more curious about that kiss. It better be good if you keep living your days for it."

Sergio drops his head and laughs. "You have no idea."

"Then show me."

Without speaking, Sergio follows Jeremy down the stairs from his living space. Down by the rink, they both hastily lace up their skates, then step onto the ice. Jeremy takes a few glides, and Sergio presses himself against the half wall and holds his hands out, palms up, in anticipation.

Jeremy loops around and skates back towards Sergio. He gestures at Sergio's upturned palms. "What are those for?"

"For you to hold," Sergio says, presenting the answer like it should be obvious.

"And why would I do that?" Jeremy asks as he skates another loop in front of him.

Sergio drops his hands. "So I don't fall down."

Jeremy makes an abrupt stop, his blades digging into the ice, making a crisp exclamation. "I'd assume if we've kissed multiple times on this ice as you claim, then you should be able to stay on your own two feet without my assistance."

Sergio shrugs and does a tentative push-off with his left foot, causing him to glide forward on his right.

"There. See? You don't need me," Jeremy says, but grabs Sergio's right hand anyway and begins to skate at a leisurely pace around the rink, keeping the half wall nearby for Sergio to grab onto if he loses his footing.

"I will admit, you are an excellent teacher," Sergio says as they glide.

"I should hope so." Jeremy laughs. "Otherwise, this whole figure skating coach endeavor of mine will be a complete bust."

"It definitely won't be a bust; you're a natural," Sergio assures. After all, he does have first-hand experience of what it's like to learn under Jeremy's expert advice. "What's the plan after the Olympics this year?"

"Well..." Jeremy says, shifting himself so he's in front of Sergio now. He changes the hand he's holding, then guides Sergio to turn around, positioning them to skate backward with some success. Sergio still struggles a bit with the crossovers, but he's getting there. "Allison is still young enough to have another run at the Olympics in four years, regardless of how this one goes. Hopefully, she'll keep me and Rose on as her coaching team. Other than that, Rose and I will have to recruit more skaters eventually, I guess. We haven't really thought much about it, though, since Allison has been our prime focus."

"I'd imagine trying to find Olympians to coach is a competitive market."

"You've punched Chadwick. You know it's a competitive market."

"Fair enough," Sergio says. "He is trying to poach Allison by the way."

"I figured as much," Jeremy says and does another twist around, spinning Sergio to skate forward again. Now that Sergio is facing forward, he's feeling steadier. Jeremy must sense it as he lets go of Sergio's hand and does what looks to Sergio to be a complicated little twirl to position himself to skate backward-facing Sergio. "You try," he says, gesturing at Sergio. "Give yourself a little spin."

Sergio grimaces. "I don't know about that."

"Oh, come on," Jeremy encourages. "It's a little two-foot spin. You only have to go around once. You can do it."

To his surprise, Sergio does manage to make himself do an awkward twist to the left, completing a full turn and a half so that he's backward now. Jeremy grabs his hand again.

"Good job," he says, and starts to pick up their pace, skating faster than Sergio has ever gone. But he likes it. Or maybe he simply likes any reason to have skin-to-skin contact with Jeremy. It's more of a rush than the feeling of his skates moving swiftly on the ice.

"What can I say, I have an excellent teacher," Sergio says, chancing a glance at Jeremy, who, to his surprise, is looking right at him as he skates.

"Hmmm …" Jeremy hums, and a soft smile creeps across his lips. "It's funny," he says and spins them again. "As much as I love helping Allison achieve her dream, I'm not sure if that's for me in the long run."

"You could coach beginners," Sergio suggests. "Like I said. You're an excellent teacher. Look what you've done with me. And I've seen you with Henry. You're so good with him."

"He's terrible." Jeremy laughs.

"You're still good with him."

"You think?"

"Yes. He adores you."

Jeremy smiles again. "There is something about showing someone who's never skated before how much fun this is when competition isn't the goal. Especially the little ones."

"It is fun," Sergio agrees. "More fun than I ever thought it would be ... but again, maybe that's because of you."

Jeremy grabs both of Sergio's hands and spins them around again, bringing them to a stop in the center of the rink.

"Smooth," he says. There's a little twinkle in his eyes.

"So tell me, was your first coach as handsome as you are?"

"No." Jeremy laughs, causing his shoulders to bounce. "The opposite. My first coach was a very stern, older German woman named Mrs. B."

"I guess it's safe to say she's not what drew you to the sport."

"Definitely not." He shakes his head and looks up towards the ceiling.

"Then what was it?"

"That got me to want to skate?"

"Yeah."

Jeremy spins them around again and cuts a deep inside edge with his blade to give them a boost of momentum. "I'm not sure I ever necessarily did."

Sergio scrunches his face, wondering how someone like Jeremy, with all of his natural talent, could have such an answer. "What do you mean?"

"Don't get me wrong. I obviously love it, and I'm glad my dad took me to the rink, but believe me, this is not what he had in mind for me when we stepped into the pro shop to buy me gear."

"Ahh." Sergio nods his head yes in understanding. "He wanted you to be a hockey player."

Jeremy points at him with his free hand. "Got it on your first try."

"What can I say, I'm perceptive."

"Clearly." He takes a deep breath. "But yeah, let's just say my father went through a whole swirl of emotions the moment I pointed at the figure skaters on the ice instead of the hockey players and declared that's what I wanted to be."

"I'm assuming he got over his *feelings* about that at some point."

"He didn't really have much of a choice." He lets go of Sergio's hand and loops around, then spins off in the other direction, leaving Sergio no other option but to skate after him the best he can.

When he eventually catches him, clumsily employing a snowplow stop to slow himself, he asks, "What was it about the figure skaters you liked back then that made you say no to your dad's wishes?"

"Honestly?" Jeremy runs his hand through his hair. "I was a kid. I was more impressed with how high they could jump and how fast they could spin." He shrugs his shoulders, then grabs hold of Sergio's hand and begins to skate again, pulling Sergio along with him. "Although, looking back now, I may have made the wrong choice."

"I'm not sure hockey would have been any better for your situation."

"No, probably not." Jeremy laughs again. "But …" He turns to smirk at Sergio. "The thought of being chased around the ice and smashed up against the glass by a bunch of men is something young me couldn't have conceived at the time as being desirable."

Sergio's stomach drops. "Is that something you'd rather have now?"

"No." Jeremy slows them to a stop. "One man is enough for me."

"One man like me?"

"That remains to be seen." He turns to come face-to-face with Sergio. "I still haven't experienced this kiss you mentioned."

"Is that all it's going to take?"

"No." He uses his toe pick to slide himself closer. "You of all people know I'm not that easy. But it's a start."

Sergio searches his eyes, finding that his sincerity and hope are reflected back at him. "I never thought you were easy."

"And I never thought you were a total dog."

Sergio furrows his brow. "I think you're alone on that one."

"Well, if it is how you say it is, and there is no tomorrow, let's not worry about anyone else's opinion at this moment."

"I wish it were that simple."

"It can be. At least for today." He reaches and places his hand onto Sergio's shoulder, then uses his strong leg to twirl them like a pair of ice dancers. He's chewing on his bottom lip when they come to a stop. "Am I right in supposing it's around this time that you kiss me every day?"

"Just about," Sergio says, staring at Jeremy's trapped lip, the one he's come to love and crave feeling against his own each of these days. "Until Henry comes storming down the stairs from your apartment and cock blocks us."

"Oh, no." Jeremy closes the gap between them. "We can't have him do that."

"There's no stopping him."

"There's no stopping us either, is there?" he asks softly and cranes his neck the little bit he needs to bring his lips in line with Sergio's.

"No. I don't think there is," Sergio says, and kisses him like he's been kissing him for ages. Like there is no one else in the world that Sergio will ever need to kiss. Because there isn't.

"Are you two kissing?" Henry's voice echoes through the rink.

Sergio pulls away so their lips barely come apart. "Yeah, we're kissing," he says, then kisses Jeremy again.

"Mommy is gonna be so mad at you, Uncle Sergio," Henry says with a huff, and Jeremy and Sergio pull apart, laughing.

"Henry, my boy," Sergio says, this time leading Jeremy on skates to the low ledge where Henry is standing, watching them with his hands on his hips. "Perhaps now is a good time to explain to you the importance of not tattling on your Uncle Sergio to your mother."

"I don't tattle," Henry denies with balled-up fists.

Sergio bursts out laughing and sits down on the ledge, pulling Henry into his lap and tickling his sides. "You do actually," he says. "A lot. But that's okay. I love you anyway."

Jeremy puts his blade guards on and steps off the ice. He ruffles Henry's hair as he walks towards the shelves where they keep all their skates stored and grabs the smallest pair, then comes back and takes a seat beside Sergio and Henry. He taps Henry on the nose. "You want to skate?"

"Yeah!" Henry yells, shaking his fists, almost punching Sergio in the nose in his excitement.

"Alright!" Jeremy says with equal excitement. "Gimme your feet, buddy," he directs and begins to lace Henry into his skates. Once he's done, he picks Henry up from Sergio's lap and places him on the ice, then gives him a little push. Henry is clumsy on the ice, but he clearly enjoys himself. Jeremy skates to him and grabs his tiny hand, leading him around. He looks over his shoulder and smiles at Sergio. "Are you coming?"

Sergio nods and rises to his feet, making his way towards them. Once there, he grabs onto Henry's other hand. Balanced and happy, gliding together around the ice, a warmth settles over Sergio despite the barn's ice rink chill. He may want to leave this day behind, but he never wants to leave this place. He wants this life, and he wants it with Jeremy.

After another lap, when they find themselves close to the ledge, Sergio lets go of Henry and turns to face Jeremy. "Will you skate for me?"

"What do you think I've been doing?" Jeremy laughs.

"Not like this," Sergio says, slowing to a stop and placing his hand onto Jeremy's shoulder. He runs his fingertips down Jeremy's arm, then pulls his hand away and brings it to cup Jeremy's cheek. His thumb gives a gentle tug to the side of Jeremy's eye. "I want to watch you skate alone, without you having to drag us along."

"Why?" Jeremy averts his eyes, but Sergio tips his head back up to look at him. "After everything you've told me, I'm not dumb enough to think you don't find a way to watch me skate every day."

"I do," Sergio concedes. "Most days at least."

"And you're not tired of it?"

"Nope." Sergio slowly shakes his head. "Not even close."

"There you go with those smooth lines again," Jeremy says. He lets go of Henry's hand and skates away, but there's a playful lilt to his voice, and he does a series of turns on one foot that suggests he's not completely turned off by the idea.

"That wasn't a no!" Sergio yells after him.

"It's not a yes either!" Jeremy yells back, then comes to an abrupt stop before gliding back towards Sergio. "But seeing as how you've already watched me, and there supposedly is no tomorrow, I guess there's no harm in skating for you again."

Jeremy's playfulness warms Sergio from the inside. He bends down and places his hands on Henry's shoulders to help guide him to the low ledge. Once there, he sits down and places Henry on his lap to look out onto the ice.

"Is Jeremy gonna skate for us?" Henry asks.

"He is," Sergio says. "'Cause he's the best."

"The best after Mommy," Henry says in his quietest voice. It's as if even he knows there's something special lingering between Sergio and Jeremy. A bubble not to be burst. But he is five after all, so it's only natural he'd maintain an allegiance to his mother despite the tension hanging in the air around the rink.

"Of course." Sergio hugs Henry a little closer to his chest and rests his chin on top of his head. "The best after Mommy." His words are as quiet as Henry's were, and they're barely audible as *Wicked Game* begins to play through the barn's speakers.

From where Sergio sits with Henry on his lap, they watch Jeremy skate in rapt attention. Each three-turn Jeremy makes, every deep edge switch from inside to outside and then back again, all the slow spins and loops and the occasional single turn in the air has Sergio mesmerized. Jeremy makes it look effortless. Which is even more impressive given how much effort Sergio knows Jeremy needs to put into his every movement. It's not even so much the physicality that Sergio has assumed that makes it hard for Jeremy to do. It's more so the mental. These moves are ingrained in Jeremy's body. His muscles have them memorized, even if there are days when his body wants to act as if they don't. It must be terrifying to wake up each day not knowing what to expect. Not knowing what will be easy and natural, like it should be, and what will require extreme concentration. But here he is, despite all of that, skating for Sergio and Henry. Gliding across the ice to the melody of the music that encapsulates Sergio's growing desire for the man floating across the frozen water like a bird in flight.

Content and happy, Sergio lets out a low hum that is abruptly interrupted.

"Hey, guys!" Holden yells out, announcing his arrival. Jeremy puts a pause on his moves, and Henry waves so enthusiastically from his seat on Sergio's lap that he falls onto the ice, laughing. Sergio quickly picks him back up and places him back onto less slippery ground, where he runs immediately to his father, who picks him up, swinging him onto his shoulders. "Routine is looking good. Legs feeling alright today?"

"Yeah," Jeremy says, smiling at him, a slight blush on his cheeks. "It's a good day." And Sergio can't quite figure out if he's only talking about his legs, or maybe, hopefully, whatever's growing between them as well.

"Good," Holden says, and takes a look at the ice. "Looks like you guys made good use of the rink today. I'd offer to Zamboni for you, but I gotta get ready for this party. Is tomorrow morning okay?"

"Oh yeah, we're done for the day," Jeremy assures him and starts putting on his blade guards. Sergio rises to help him off the ice, taking one of his hands. Holden eyes it and grins. "Besides, I should start getting ready as well. Might do me some good to take a quick nap if I have to stay out late tonight."

"We could not go," Sergio says in a rush. The thought of leaving this barn and going to this New Year's Eve party again utterly exhausts him. "Stay in. Have a quiet New Year."

"I'm being paid to host this party," Holden says with a clap onto Sergio's shoulder. "But you don't have to come."

Sergio looks at Jeremy, asking a silent question.

Jeremy lets go of Sergio's hand, takes a seat on a nearby bench, and starts taking his skates off. He smiles at Sergio, holding his gaze as he says to Holden, "If you and Rose don't mind. I could be persuaded to sit this one out."

"Yeah. It's no problem," Holden says and smirks at them. "I'll make up some excuse."

"You can't tell her they were kissing," Henry says. "Because that would make us tattletales."

"Thanks, Henry." Sergio groans and hangs his head.

Henry gives two thumbs up. "No problem, Uncle Sergio."

Holden starts laughing and claps Sergio on the shoulder once more. "Don't worry, lovebirds," he says, walking away. "Your secret's safe with me. I'll see you both tomorrow morning for New Year's Day breakfast."

With any luck, you will.

"I'm ashamed to say I don't have anything flashy to make us to eat," Jeremy says as he rummages through his refrigerator.

"I've eaten nothing but rich and indulgent foods every time I've lived this day. Trust me when I tell you there is no need to try to impress me with something gourmet," Sergio says from where he's standing at the counter of Jeremy's small kitchenette, holding another cup of tea in his palms to warm them after his afternoon on the ice. He takes a sip and marvels at how much he enjoys this simple elixir. He's never pegged himself to be a tea guy, but now he understands the appeal. It's simple and warm and feels like home in his hands. It's also so unmistakably Jeremy that he'll never be able to drink another cup of tea without thinking fondly of him.

"That's presumptuous of you to assume I wanted to impress you," Jeremy teases as he turns around with a handful of vegetables. He shuts the refrigerator door with his shoulder, then places the vegetables down on the counter beside Sergio.

"Can I help at all?"

"Nah." Jeremy waves him off with his hand, but bumps him away with his hip. "I'm gonna throw together a stir fry."

Sergio's mouth waters. It's simple, like the tea. Taking another sip, he looks around Jeremy's place and notices, like he does most days, the lack of any displays of Jeremy's accomplishments. The absence is still striking. Lord knows Holden and Rose have an entire trophy room that doubles as their office. But in Jeremy's case, if not for the fact that Sergio has been watching him skate every day, he'd believe Jeremy had never once stepped foot on the ice. He's never had the chance to ask Jeremy about it before, but the shared vulnerability they've been experiencing all day has opened the door for Sergio to inquire.

"You keep things pretty simple around here, huh?" Sergio asks, his eyes on the functional living space. The only extras are Jeremy's collections of books and plants, neither of which overwhelms the room. Instead, they make the place feel quaint and inviting.

Jeremy shrugs and slices through a crisp onion. "I'm not really working with a lot of space."

"True," Sergio says and turns around to get a better look at Jeremy, whose eyes are watering from the onion. "But I get the feeling that even if you had the big house for yourself, you wouldn't go overboard."

"Old me may have," Jeremy says with another shrug. He slices through the onion with his knife again, releasing its sharp aroma. "But now, I honestly can't really be bothered. I don't always have the energy to keep up with daily tasks, so the solution is to simplify. Less stuff to clean, less stuff to move around, less stuff to maintain. More energy for what's important."

"And what's that?"

"Living," Jeremy says with a smile as an onion-induced tear slides down his cheek. Jeremy lifts his hand from the knife and brings it towards his face, presumably to wipe his eyes.

"Let me," Sergio says, stopping him. He reaches for Jeremy, whose eyes slowly close, releasing a stream that Sergio wipes away. "There. There. No need for all the tears. It's only dinner."

"Shut up." Jeremy laughs and goes back to his vegetables, this time to begin cutting the less-likely-to-provoke-tears red bell pepper.

"But really, I think that sounds nice."

"What? Living simply or not having energy to do regular daily tasks?"

"The simply part of course." Sergio takes another sip of his tea. "I must admit, I've had a bit of a revelation recently. That maybe simple isn't so bad."

"Huh." Jeremy slides the chopped bell pepper to the side, then slices into a head of broccoli. "I never actually saw you as someone who lived all that un-simply."

"What do you mean?"

Jeremy pauses and looks at Sergio with his bottom lip trapped between his teeth. "Well, no offense, but you tend to come across as pretty shallow, which doesn't leave a lot of room for extra."

Not sure how to feel about that statement, Sergio furrows his brow.

"I said no offense," Jeremy tries to explain, and Sergio can't help but laugh.

Jeremy's not wrong. Sergio has another revelation that before all of this, he never would have taken Jeremy's proclamation so lightly.

"You might be onto something," he says, looking at Jeremy with his lips lifted on one side. Jeremy grabs a pan and drizzles oil into it, then lights the burner. "Perhaps my shallowness is what has gotten me into this predicament."

"You think?" Jeremy asks, sarcasm and teasing thick in his voice. He may as well have hit Sergio with the frying pan to punctuate his bluntness. Thankfully, instead, he tosses the vegetables into said pan, then adds some seasoning and gives it all a good mix with a wooden spoon.

"Touché," Sergio says, laughing some more. "But it does make sense, doesn't it?"

Jeremy grabs a package of pre-cooked soba noodles out of his cabinet and opens them with a knife. "It makes sense, assuming it's working. Do you feel less shallow?"

"I'm drinking tea in a studio apartment above an ice rink-slash-barn, and it's the happiest I've been in months. What do you think?"

Jeremy mixes the vegetables again and adds a splash of soy sauce. "Then I think perhaps you're finally figuring out what's important to you in this life." Jeremy looks at him and lets his eyes rove up and down Sergio's body before they come to rest to stare directly at Sergio's face from beneath Jeremy's furrowed brow. He grins. "Or ... you're crazy and all of this is some ploy that will never work to get into my pants."

Sergio blushes at the thought of getting into Jeremy's pants. It is quite an enticing option. However, the history of this day has told him how unlikely that is to happen. "As wonderful as that sounds, the longer I live this day, the less I think getting laid is the solution to getting me out of it."

"Well, when has sex ever solved anything, anyway?" Jeremy asks and dumps the noodles into the pan, and begins to mix them in with the vegetables.

"As I've come to recently reflect, never."

"I guess it's a good thing you and I have never actually slept together then, huh?"

"Very good."

"Wait." Jeremy stands up stock straight and looks at Sergio, then tugs at his left eye. His tone and expression lose all traces of teasing and shift straight into something serious, with even a hint of concern. "We haven't ever actually slept together, have we?"

"We have not."

"Not even once in all the times you've relived this day?"

"Not a single time. All we've ever done is kiss."

"And you're not lying to me to save your own ass?"

Sergio hooks his thumb and first finger onto Jeremy's chin and directs him to look directly into his eyes. "I wouldn't lie to you," he says. "Especially about that."

"All I've ever done is kiss you?"

"Just kisses."

"Not even hand stuff?" Jeremy asks, a glimmer of a playful smirk coming back to his face.

Sergio huffs out a laugh and brushes his thumb over Jeremy's cheek. "Not even hand stuff."

"That seems unfair," Jeremy says and takes his attention back to the food.

"You're telling me."

"I'm talking about the kisses, not the lack of hand stuff, by the way."

Sergio wrinkles his nose and nods knowingly at him. "Thanks for clarifying."

"I'm just saying that it sucks that you get to remember all these kisses and all I get is the one I got today."

"Yeah," Sergio says and steps behind Jeremy at the stove. He places his hands on Jeremy's hips and hooks his head over Jeremy's shoulder. "That's what I was referring to as well."

Jeremy turns his head to look over at him, the best he can in the space Sergio has provided. "Don't think for a second that I'm sleeping with you today after I now know how unlikely it is I'll remember it."

"I guess that's a no to hand stuff then, too?" Sergio gives him a quick kiss.

"You've got your own hands." Jeremy kisses him back.

Despite the lightness of their teasing, Sergio has something important he needs to say. He spins Jeremy in his arms and looks at him with soft eyes, holding Jeremy's direct attention as he makes a promise. "I wouldn't take advantage of you. Ever. I mean it."

Jeremy nods his head at him in understanding, and Sergio takes that as his cue. He holds onto Jeremy's hips a little tighter, then kisses him with the crackle of the food cooking on the stove covering up the sound of the content sigh that escapes his lips before he kisses Jeremy more firmly.

After dinner, with *Groundhog Day* playing on the TV, Sergio and Jeremy are snuggled together on the cramped sofa. Jeremy lets out a yawn and scootches closer to Sergio, pressing himself flush against Sergio's body. Sergio holds onto him like a life raft.

The hour is late, and the clock is fast approaching midnight. All Sergio wants is more time. More time he isn't going to get into a dilemma that is giving him nothing but time for everything but this perfect version of this day that he's been reveling in.

He places a soft kiss on the top of Jeremy's head and breathes in Jeremy's ginger, lemon, barn wood, and ice smell. His eyes are focused forward on the TV screen. It was Jeremy's idea to put the movie on, claiming the irony of the situation was funny, or at the very least, it would give Sergio some clues as to what else he could do in his quest to break his loop. But Sergio has hardly been paying attention, choosing to cling to Jeremy and the idea of being able to have these near-perfect days with Jeremy again and again. Preferably, after Sergio breaks free of this torturous loop, and they both get to remember them.

"What should I expect?" Jeremy asks.

"About what?"

"About what's going to happen at midnight?"

"I'm not sure," Sergio says and runs his hand up and down Jeremy's arm. "The clock always strikes midnight at the party, and then suddenly I wake up back in my bed up at the house."

"And you've never not gone to the party?"

"Nope," Sergio says, then winces. "Except that time I pitched myself off the chairlift on the mountain."

"Yikes," Jeremy says.

"Yeah. That was not my best day," Sergio confesses. "I do not want to know how that went over."

"Well, luckily, it would seem none of us remembers it. So I think you're in the clear." Jeremy strains his neck to look at him. "But please don't do that again. Okay?"

"I won't," Sergio says, meeting Jeremy's lips to kiss him.

When Jeremy pulls away, he sighs and checks his watch. "Ten more seconds."

Nine.

"Can I get another kiss?" Sergio asks.

Eight.

"You can have as many as you want when you break this loop."

Seven.

"I'm gonna hold you to that."

Six.

"You better."

Five.

"Please don't forget about me."

Four.

"I could never."

Three.

"You will."

Two.

"Convince me again."

One.

"I think I'm falling ..."

Chapter Fifteen

"Uncle Sergio! Wake up!"

"Oof ... morning, buddy."

"*Hiss ...*"

"Dad said to come get you. Breakfast is almost ready."

"I bet it is." Sergio sighs and rolls back over in bed. At this point, after all he's been through, he's grown numb to Henry's pain-inducing wake-up. His feelings of bodily anguish have been replaced by a new form of pain. A pain he can't simply walk off, as matters of the heart have no legs.

Henry crawls over him, appearing on the other side of the bed. "What's wrong?"

"Nothing," Sergio says, pushing his face into his pillow.

"Doesn't look like nothing."

Sergio peeks out from where he's trying to hide. "You wouldn't understand."

"Do you want me to get Mommy?"

"No." Sergio pushes his face back into his pillow. Rose is the last person he wants to see right now. A lecture about how shitty he is as a prospect for Jeremy Owens isn't going to help his plight at all.

"She always makes me feel better."

"I'm sure she does," Sergio mumbles.

"I'm gonna go get her!" Henry yells and leaps off the bed before Sergio can attempt to catch him.

Sergio twists in the bed, getting caught in the sheets and blanket. He falls over the edge, landing with a thump, as he calls, "Henry! Wait! No!"

All he hears in answer is little thundering footsteps running down the hall.

"What's the matter with you?" Adrien asks from the doorway. His arms are crossed, and he's leaning against the doorframe with exaggerated casualness. "Have a little too much to drink last night?"

"Shut up," Sergio says, trying and failing to extricate himself from the knotted covers.

"Here." Adrien extends his hand. "Let me help you."

Sergio knocks his hand away and manages to get up on his own with more effort than it should have taken. "I've got it," he snaps and catches a glimpse of himself in the mirror as he rises. His hair is sticking out in all directions, he has bags under his eyes, and his eyes themselves look, well, manic. Wild. Like an animal caught in a trap, or bed sheets in this case.

"Henry wasn't kidding," Rose says, appearing in the bedroom. She picks up Sergio's fallen pillow. "Somebody is having a rough morning."

"Is that what we're calling this?" Adrien asks.

"Apparently," Rose says, pulling Sergio's blanket and top sheet apart. She hands him the latter. "So, what's the problem? Henry made it sound like you were on your deathbed."

"I'm fine." Sergio shakes the top sheet out with a snap and sloppily throws it onto the mattress. He barely even glances at the bed as he does the same with the blanket. It's not like it matters. He's going to wake up in a perfectly made bed regardless of whether he makes it or sets it on fire right now. Sergio's eyebrow quirks up. That second option sounds like a cathartic solution.

Rose and Adrien share a look. "Sergio ..." Adrien says slowly, approaching him with caution. "What's going on? I haven't seen you like this since ..."

"Since nothing!" Sergio snaps, knowing full well that the last time he was in anything that even loosely resembled distress was when their parents died. A feeling he's since designed his life to avoid ever experiencing again. Of course, Adrien would recognize his unraveling and link the two together. He grabs onto his hair and pulls, keeping himself from looking at either of them.

"Sergio." This time it's Rose. Her words are slow and even-toned. "What's going on?"

"Nothing!" he snaps again and moves to barge out of the bedroom like a football player charging through the defensive line.

"Oh, no." Adrien stops him and firmly places his hands on Sergio's shoulders. He pushes him towards the bed. Sergio tries to shake loose but fails in his exhaustion. All of his energy to fight and flee leaves him from the simple touch of his brother's hands on his shoulders. "Sit!" Adrien demands when Sergio's knees knock against the mattress. He forces him down. "Explain."

Sergio keeps his eyes focused on Adrien's socked feet. He's the one person in his life who can see right through him, and he doesn't need that level of pity right now. "I don't want to talk about it."

"Tough shit," Adrien says, still holding onto Sergio's shoulders. "Whatever this is, we're talking about it."

"Come on, Sergio," Rose says. She steps close enough that her slippers come into Sergio's view. "Don't be difficult,"

"I'm not being difficult. I just don't want to talk about it." He tries to stand, but Adrien won't let him. Slowly, he looks up at his brother, pleading, "Please let me go. You're not going to understand what I'm going through anyway."

"Oh, really?" Adrien questions with an intense and disbelieving stare. "You're my brother. I know you better than anyone. You're having a crisis of conscience."

"It's so much more than that." Sergio hangs his head. Maybe when this loop first started, that was the case. But now, his rough mornings have less to do with feeling guilty about a rude quip in Jeremy's direction and more to do with him falling in love with the man with no way of experiencing reciprocation without a possibility of tomorrow.

"Look," Rose says, sitting down beside him. "If this is about last night, all you have to do is tell Jeremy you're sorry when you see him later. He probably isn't even that mad. You pissed me off more than you did him, anyway."

"Yeah, I noticed," Sergio says, clenching his jaw.

She jabs him in the shoulder. "Don't act like you wouldn't feel the same if someone insulted Holden. Or Adrien."

"Don't be so sure about that last part," Adrien says. "He takes pleasure in insulting me."

"I do not," Sergio says, looking back at his brother.

Adrien stares at him. His lips are in a hard line.

"Okay, fine. But I won't anymore. Not after today."

"Pfft." Adrien scoffs. "The day has barely begun. You'll find a way to insult me by noon."

Sergio throws up his hands. "I thought you were keeping me trapped here to make me feel better."

"We are," Rose assures. She looks at Adrien, and his eyes flick to hers. "But I'm honestly confused as to why you are in such distress about all this."

"Because I'm in love with him!" Sergio yells out, annoyed and over this little forced therapy session he's being held against his will.

Adrien removes one hand from Sergio's shoulder and holds it to his chest, smirking. "Me?"

"Not you, asshole." Sergio huffs and rolls his eyes. This is not the time for brotherly jokes. "Jeremy."

"Jeremy?" Rose says. She leans away. He can feel her eyebrow raising in judgment at him, even though he can't see it as he's busy watching Adrien slowly let go of his shoulders, then drop his hands at his sides with a low whistle.

"Yes. Jeremy," Sergio says, staring at his brother. "Is that so hard to believe?"

"Honestly?" Adrien asks, then answers his own question. "Yeah."

"You're hopeless," Rose says. "Utterly hopeless." She rises from the bed. "Do me a favor, would you? Stay away from Jeremy. He doesn't need *your* love. Whatever that even is."

Sergio slumps further in defeat, knowing that protesting her assertion is a futile effort. In her eyes, Sergio can see why she thinks his love is not needed in Jeremy's life. But she doesn't know what Sergio knows. She doesn't know that Jeremy—on good days, at least—returns Sergio's affections. Which, if he returns Sergio's affections on good days, must mean he has some feeling of goodwill towards him even on the bad ones. Sure, he may not love Sergio like Sergio is one hundred percent sure he's feeling for Jeremy, but that's only because he hasn't experienced a second day with him yet. He doesn't wake up each repeated New Year's Day with memories of who Sergio really is. Jeremy, same as Rose, wakes up on each version of this day with Sergio's blunder from the night before fresh in his mind. Along with the memory of Sergio hitting the proverbial bricks after Jeremy had asked him to put a pin in what they were on their way to becoming four years ago. Along with only vague knowledge of who Sergio truly is, based on gossip and what he perceives him to be.

None of them knows what he really wants. Not even Adrien. Because truth be told, Sergio didn't even know what he truly wanted until recently. And what he wants is Jeremy. He wants to watch him glide across the ice. Wants to kiss him not only in the middle of the rink but also on the sofa, in his bed, in the sunshine, rain, and snow. Wants to hold his hand as they go about their days. To prepare his tea when he comes home. To watch him show the next generation of figure skaters what it means to carve edges into the ice with joy in their heart and to feel the music one skates to in their bones to make breathing, moving, gliding art.

"Rose," he says, almost in a whisper, as the air has left his lungs. "I promise I won't hurt him."

"Damn right you won't," Rose says, crossing her arms and standing above him like a disapproving mother scolding her disobedient son. "Because you're going to stay away from him."

"Rose, that's not fair."

"I don't care what you think is fair. Nothing in Jeremy's life is fair."

"Now *you're* not being fair to him!" Sergio raises his voice. He's talked to Jeremy. He doesn't want or need Rose's protection. "Have you considered what he wants?"

"Of course I have! And it's not you!"

"You're wrong," Sergio says, like it's a matter of fact.

"No. *You're* wrong."

"How about everybody's wrong?" Adrien steps in, and Rose focuses her angry gaze on him for a change. However, Sergio doesn't wish that upon his brother. It's another sign of his personal growth, because before, he would have found Adrien being on the receiving end of Rose's wrath for a change quite funny. But now, not so much. Adrien doesn't deserve it. And Rose really needs to get a handle on that.

"Knock, knock," Holden says, appearing in the door frame with Henry on his hip and Gus circling between his legs, the cat's eyes narrowed on Sergio. "Are we having breakfast, or what?"

Rose sighs and walks past him, pushing him out of the way with her shoulder. Gus follows after her with his tail held high. "I'm no longer hungry."

Holden watches her leave, his face scrunched up in confusion. "What was that about?"

"Nothing." Sergio sighs and rises to his feet, heading towards the bedroom door. "Can we please go eat some pancakes now?"

"Wow!" Holden exclaims. "How'd you know I made pancakes for breakfast?"

On the chairlift to the top of the slopes, Sergio remains sullen after his altercation with Rose and Adrien this morning. He's half tempted to pitch himself off the chair lift again to get this version of this day over quicker. However, he did promise Jeremy yesterday he wouldn't do that ever again, regardless of how desperate he feels or how little permanent consequence that is likely to have on anyone. Sergio intends to honor that request. After all, isn't that one of the things that loving someone is about? Refraining from doing anything that may hurt them, no matter how inconsequential that action may in fact be.

"I'm worried about you," Adrien says about halfway up the mountain.

"Don't be," Sergio says. "You won't even remember this tomorrow."

"I doubt that." Adrien turns to look at him. "Did you mean what you said this morning?"

Sergio sighs. "Which part?"

"The part about being in love with Jeremy."

"Yeah." Sergio nods. "I'm in love with him."

"And when exactly did you figure this out?"

"It's a long story."

"It's a long ride up the mountain."

"Not long enough." Sergio sighs again.

Adrien jostles him with his shoulder. It makes the chairlift gently swing. "Well, regardless. I'm proud of you. Confused. But proud of you."

Sergio turns to look at his brother. "Why on earth would you be proud of me about this?"

"Honestly? I never thought I'd see the day you fell in love with anyone."

"Why does everyone think I'm incapable of falling in love?"

Adrien takes a deep breath. "Truthfully? It's because you've actively shut that part of you down. You can deny it all you want, but you've avoided the possibility of love at every turn. Even four years ago with Jeremy. You could have had it then, but you took the first excuse train you could away from him and any potential of a genuine relationship."

Sergio slumps and frowns. "You're not wrong."

"I know I'm not," Adrien says and jostles him again. "You're my brother. I love you, and I know you better than you know yourself sometimes. *And* I think Jeremy could be good for you."

"Yeah, me too," Sergio says as the end of the lift comes into view. He braces himself to dismount, then glides forward on his skis once they hit the snow. Before going down, he stops and looks at his brother. It's nice to know that even after having their blowups, in the end, they always have each other's backs. This is a reminder he desperately needed. "I've been thinking."

"About what?" Adrien asks.

"All this talk about love. I think it's time we stopped working together."

A hesitant grin lights up Adrien's face. "Are you serious?"

"Yeah," Sergio says, with a sad half-smile. It's the first hint of a smile he's had all day, and he's really feeling it. "Go live your life. Follow *your* dreams now, and grab hold of Daphne like she's the most important person in your world."

"You're not joking?"

"I'm not joking."

Adrien embraces Sergio. He thumps him on the back twice. "Thank you."

"You're welcome," Sergio says, and lets go. He turns away and heads down the mountain, understanding for the first time, thanks to how he feels about Jeremy, that Adrien's love for Daphne doesn't mean he loves Sergio any less.

"Did you guys have fun?" Holden asks them once Sergio and Adrien reach the bunny hills.

Sergio gives a quick, "Yes," as Henry calls his name. "Uncle Sergio! Look!" he shouts, then zooms down the hill and comes to stop by way of a forward flip onto his rump. "Did you see?"

"I saw, Henry," Sergio says, making his way to him to help him back onto his feet. "That was very impressive. Even your flip forward."

"One day I'm gonna learn how to stop," Henry says, very determined.

Sergio ruffles his hair and bends down to unlatch Henry's skis from his boots. "Perhaps that will be tomorrow's lesson."

"Dad says it's funnier when I flip over."

"He's not wrong." Sergio picks Henry up with one arm and grabs his skis with his other before making his way towards the lodge.

"But Jeremy says it's not funny when I flip forward on the ice."

Sergio laughs. "He's also not wrong. The ice is a little harder than the snow, don't you think?"

"It's a lot harder," Henry says, nodding his head yes. "And it hurts more."

"Do you like skiing more than you like skating?"

"No," Henry says, shaking his head.

"You like them both?"

"Yes!"

"You are a man of many talents," Sergio assures him, even though he's seen him on the ice. Not that Sergio, until after a plethora of secret private lessons from Jeremy, was much better.

"I know," Henry says, smiling as bright as the sun on this clear bluebird day. He truly is his father's son.

Although it could be argued he's an awful lot like his uncle by the way he's suddenly squirming in Sergio's arms, yelling, "Jeremy!" at the top of his lungs. It's an excitement that Sergio absolutely understands. If it were socially acceptable for him to do the same, he would.

Sergio puts Henry down, and the kid takes off at a clumsy run the minute his feet hit the snow-covered ground. "Be careful!" Sergio calls out after him. But he's shifted his attention from Henry and is looking more so at Jeremy, loving the way his cheeks are flushed from the cold and wisps of his hair stray out from underneath his gray toque.

He doesn't get much time to admire the sight, though, as he can feel Rose's steel-eyed gaze upon him from where she stands beside Jeremy and Allison. Sergio offers her a little wave. She glares at him and flips him the bird.

"You hungry?" Holden claps him on the shoulder. "This place has a great turkey burger."

"I'll have to try it," Sergio says and turns to look at Holden, who's wearing a beaming smile, completely oblivious to the fact that his wife appears to be out for Sergio's blood.

"Come on," Holden urges him along. "They know we're coming and have set aside the best table."

Once inside, Sergio tries and fails not to get a seat beside Jeremy, which is his usual custom, but beside Rose. She boxes him out, and he winds up where he always does, between Holden and Allison. Though unlike all the previous lunches, even Allison is quite chilly beside him. Apparently, Rose must have been whispering in her ear during practice this morning. It's fine. Sergio isn't in the mood to engage in much small talk today anyway. All he really wants to do is prove he's not a total piece of shit and deserves at least a chance to be a part of Jeremy's life.

Once they've ordered their meals and everyone has had a chance to laugh at Sergio and his exploits in Paris, Sergio makes his move. "What's everyone's plans once these Olympics are over?"

"Elite Sports Network wants me as a correspondent," Holden answers before anyone else. Sergio nods his approval. That'll be a good gig for him. He'll crush it on camera, and his enthusiasm for all things extreme winter sports is contagious.

Allison lets out a light laugh. "Wake up and start preparing for the games four years from now."

Rose raises her glass to Allison and winks at her. "Same." They both turn to look at Jeremy.

He takes a sip of water and pales slightly. "The same," he agrees, but Rose narrows her eyes at him.

Sergio feels awful. He's inadvertently exposed Jeremy, but he supposes the truth has to come out sometime.

"You don't seem sure about that," Rose says.

Jeremy wipes his lips with his napkin, then takes a sip of water. "It's not that I'm not sure. Of course, I want to keep working with you both. But …" He pauses and rubs the back of his neck with his hand. "I like working with beginners, too. They're more my speed."

Rose looks at him, shocked. "More your speed? Jeremy, you're a world-class figure skater."

"I *used* to be a world-class figure skater," Jeremy corrects. "I'm not anymore, and I'm only going to get worse."

"But you've given me so much knowledge," Allison protests. "About feeling the music and how to make the program my own. You've given my skating so much more depth."

"And the way you describe things," Rose says. "You're much better at explaining the small technical adjustments than I'll ever be. You have patience."

Jeremy blushes slightly at the praise, and Sergio wishes he could reach across the table and brush his fingertips across his rosy cheeks. Jeremy appears not to know what to say. Especially considering that Allison, and though Sergio's loath to admit it, even Rose, are right. Jeremy, no matter his physical abilities, is invaluable to the sport. Olympians and beginners alike can learn from him.

"It's all true," Sergio says. "You're a brilliant coach, no matter who you're teaching."

Rose narrows her gaze back onto him. "And how would *you* know?"

Sergio stares back at her equally as hard. It's a good old-fashioned standoff of wills. "I saw him yesterday working with Allison, remember?" he challenges, raising one of his eyebrows before she gets a chance to level him with hers. "And Henry told me today how much he loves learning to skate from Jeremy." It's a half lie, as Henry hasn't had a chance to tell him that yet on this version of the day. But that's irrelevant. Besides, Sergio does have first-hand knowledge about how good Jeremy really is when teaching Henry how to skate. He'd like to experience it today, but it's becoming abundantly clear that spending the afternoon with Jeremy is likely going to have the kibosh put on it by Rose, no matter what he does.

"Is that true, buddy?" Jeremy gently asks a near sleeping Henry in his lap.

Henry nods his head, mumbling something along the lines of, "You're the best teacher."

"Well, I guess we could talk about expanding our coaching program," Rose concedes. She tightens her ponytail. "But that will have to wait until after the Olympics are over."

"Please, though, whatever you do," Allison says, her eyes flitting back and forth between Jeremy and Rose, "don't team up with Chadwick Levinson. That man is such a creep."

After lunch, outside the lodge, Sergio ignores every want, wish, and dream he's come to have about afternoons spent alone with Jeremy. He opts, instead, for continued time navigating the slopes. He bids his farewells, gives one last lingering glance at Jeremy, who is looking at him back with warmth, then muscles his way in between Holden and Rose, pushing his best friend to the side. "If you don't mind, Holden, I'd like to steal your wife for this first run."

"It's your funeral," Holden says, then calls out to Adrien, "Hey, Adrien! You want to go hit that double black diamond?"

"Yeah, alright!" Adrien yells back.

"I'll be on the bunny hills," Allison says, and skis off with grace.

"You're wasting your time, Sergio," Rose says as they hop onto the chairlift.

Sergio resists the urge to laugh. What does she know about wasting time? She hasn't been reliving the same day over and over again, essentially wasting days upon days upon days of time. Though that isn't entirely true of Sergio either. He is learning a little something on each of these repeated days.

"Listen," he says as their skis leave the ground and dangle off their feet in the air. "I'm sorry about this morning. We didn't start off on the right foot today." But really, have they ever started off on the right foot at all? He supposes they've come close once or twice but have never actually had success.

Rose takes a deep breath. She straightens out her legs, then bends them again, so they hang loose. "This trip didn't start off on the right foot. It wasn't only about this morning."

He slumps in his seat. "Yeah, last night wasn't a great showing for me either."

"It's not only last night." She pauses and looks over her shoulder at Sergio. "Though that didn't help," she says and turns to look away again. "I tried to get Holden to cancel this week."

"What? Why?" Sergio asks, incredulous. This is their tradition. And, furthermore, Holden is Sergio and Adrien's family. Why would she want to keep them apart?

"There's just so much going on," she says, exhaustion clouding her voice. "There's so much pressure with Jeremy and me making our coaching debut on a grand scale. And Henry is becoming a handful."

"Yeah, but Adrien and I can help. Especially, with Henry. Let him wear us out for a change. Hell, I can stay longer if you want."

Rose lets out a bitter laugh. "Have you not been paying attention? I didn't want you to come in the first place. Why would I want you here for longer?"

Sergio starts to feel anger rising in him. He swallows it down as he recognizes it isn't going to be helpful to explode. "Are you saying Adrien and I aren't welcome anymore?"

"No. Absolutely not. You two are family, and you are always welcome," Rose clarifies, twisting back to look at him. "I only wanted Holden to postpone this until after the Olympics. The pressure would be off. Allison, Jeremy, and I would be on a break. And ..." she pauses again, looking sheepish, "... maybe Jeremy wouldn't be here for you to mess around with."

"What? Are you planning on kicking him to the curb when the Olympics are over?"

"Absolutely not!" Rose defends. "Jeremy is family. I would never."

"Well, it kind of seems like you would. Especially since I'm family and you just said you didn't want me here."

"What I meant was maybe he'd go see his folks or take a vacation or do anything other than be here when you arrived."

"Right." Sergio scoffs and rolls his eyes. "Because being around me is the worst thing ever."

"Well, you do have to admit, Sergio, that you don't have the best track record."

"Excuse you, but Jeremy dumped me four years ago, not the other way around. I don't see you being all concerned about my feelings."

Rose laughs again. "Jeremy asking for you to slow things down while he needed to focus is hardly dumping."

"Alright, I'll give you that," Sergio concedes. "But I need you to know, I have nothing but the best intentions for something between me and Jeremy now. I really meant it when I said I'm in love with him."

Rose studies him. Her gaze is penetrating, looking for any clue that Sergio is full of shit. For once in their relationship, she's not going to find evidence of that. Sergio is going to make sure of it. He takes a breath and sits up taller, sets his shoulders back and stares at her with determination.

"You know," she says and presses her lips together. The top of the mountain and the end of their ride come into view. "For some reason, I think I might actually believe you."

"Really?" Sergio asks with a lift in his voice as the chairlift deposits them back on the ground.

"Yeah." She turns to look up at him at the top of the slope. Her lips twist to the side as she considers him. "You're too prideful to have been this vulnerable in front of me for you to be lying."

"Rose, I'm not lying to you."

She jabs him in the arm, and her ski pole knocks into his shin. "Did you not hear me? I said I can tell you're not lying."

He feels a rush of relief, but his conversation with her still isn't quite sitting right. His eyes soften. "Did you really mean it when you said you wished we hadn't come?"

"No." Her shoulders slump. "I am glad you and Adrien are here. It's all Holden and Henry could talk about for weeks, and you *are* helpful. Particularly with Henry." She reaches and places a hand on his shoulder. "I shouldn't have taken my nerves out on you."

"Better me than Holden," Sergio says with a half-smile and raised eyebrows.

"Believe me." She laughs. "He gets it, too."

"But he still loves you."

"He does."

"And I love Jeremy. I could be his Holden."

"Oh, God no. We do not need two of you."

"I think you mean three." Sergio waggles his eyebrows. "Have you met your son?"

Her lips pull into a tight smile, and she nods her head. She visibly swallows before she says, "They're so much alike."

Sergio gives her shoulder a slight push. "He's a lot like you, too, you know. You have stiff competition as to who's going to avenge Jeremy the hardest if I fuck this up."

"Then I guess you better not fuck it up," she says with a wink, then takes off like a bullet down the mountain, calling over her shoulder as she goes, "Race you to the bottom!"

"You're on!" Sergio yells as he pushes off to chase after her. *Okay, now we're getting somewhere.*

Rose turns around, looking over the front seat into the back, when Holden pulls the car into the garage after their afternoon of skiing. "Can you grab Henry from Jeremy?" she asks Sergio directly. There's a hint of warning in her eyes. A reminder to Sergio that he's not entirely out of the woods with her yet. He still needs to tread carefully. "I need to get cleaned up and start getting ready for tonight."

"Sure thing," Holden says.

Sergio claps Holden on the shoulder. "She was talking to me, man."

"Oh!" Holden says, surprised. "Well, this is a turn of events."

"You're telling me," Sergio says with a little laugh. He turns to look back at Rose and silently mouths, "Thank you" to her.

"You're welcome," she mouths back, then exits the car.

Sergio opens his car door. He pauses before getting out and looks at his brother. "Say hi to Daphne for me, would you? It's almost midnight in Paris."

Adrien nods his head and rushes to get out of the car. "Yeah! I will. She'll like that."

Feeling good about himself and surprisingly optimistic for a day that started off as complete shit, Sergio makes his way down to the barn. At the door, he pauses and takes a deep, steadying breath to keep himself from bursting through the door like the Kool-Aid man and interrupting Jeremy's skating. He pulls the door open as he exhales and listens to the familiar song ring through the speakers, like a siren calling him to Jeremy each day.

After the intensity of today and all the vulnerability left out in the open, which has left him feeling quite raw, a level of contentment also settled over him, the like of which he's never felt before. He pauses at the rink's half wall and watches Jeremy skate and glide through his moves. Slowly, he makes his way over to where Henry is sitting. Henry's eyes are wide as he watches Jeremy loop around the ice.

Taking care not to startle Henry or pull Jeremy's attention away from his skating, Sergio carefully sits beside Henry and pulls him into his lap. He lightly rests his chin on Henry's head.

"He's great out there, isn't he?"

"The best," Henry says, then adds, "After Mommy."

Sergio lets out a light laugh. "Yeah, after Mommy. Of course."

As Jeremy's skating brings him closer to where Sergio and Henry are sitting, he catches Sergio in his view when his choreography loops him around. Slowing in his tracks and gracefully dropping his arms to his sides, he comes to a stop a few feet away, blushing. "I thought Henry was my only audience."

"Sorry," Sergio says, taking care to hold Jeremy's gaze. "I snuck in. I didn't want to disturb you. You look good out there."

"Don't tease," Jeremy scolds.

"I wasn't teasing."

Jeremy bites his lip, looking like he doesn't believe him. "Where's Holden? I figured he'd grab Henry."

"Rose sent me instead."

"Really?" Jeremy asks, surprise plain on his face and in his voice.

"Cross my heart," Sergio says, making an X with his right hand.

"That looks a little more like cross Henry's heart." Jeremy laughs.

Sergio looks down at Henry, still in his lap, and laughs along with Jeremy. "That was me emphasizing how serious I am."

"Swearing on a five-year-old now, huh?" Jeremy grins.

"I will swear on whatever I need to if it means I get to see you skate."

Jeremy looks away from him and begins to put a blade guard on one of his blades. "I'm afraid I'm not too much to look at anymore."

"That's not true," Sergio says, shifting Henry to sit on his hip while he rises to his feet. He extends a hand for Jeremy to grab as he steps off the ice. "No matter how many times I see you skate, you never stop amazing me."

Jeremy places his other blade guard on. "You're just saying that."

"No." Sergio continues to hold Jeremy's hand even though he's back to standing on two feet. "I could watch you every day for the rest of my life and never tire of seeing you on the ice. You look ... free."

Jeremy looks up at him, his bottom lip trapped between his teeth. "I guess I am."

Letting go of his hand, Sergio brings his palm to Jeremy's cheek and uses his thumb to gently tug at the corner of Jeremy's eye. He holds him steady there, and when Jeremy doesn't pull away, Sergio dives in and places a gentle kiss onto his lips, suppressing a moan when Jeremy kisses him back.

After everything he's been through today, whatever god is in charge of this wretched loop, he silently thanks them anyway. One kiss with Jeremy was worth all the fight.

"I hate to admit it," Rose says to Sergio, surprising him as he places a tip on the bar. "He looks happy around you."

"Was it really that hard to believe?" He hands her a glass of champagne.

She takes a sip and eyes him over the rim, but instead of her usual judgmental glare, she's smirking at him. "No." She laughs. "You might piss me off sometimes, but even I have to admit there's a good guy in there somewhere."

Sergio wraps her in a hug. "Thanks, Rose. I promise. I'll be good to him."

"Yeah, yeah." Rose pushes him off and then takes another sip of her champagne. "Now go help your boy; he's being tortured by that blowhard, Chadwick Levinson."

Sergio grabs his whiskey neat and Jeremy's sparkling water with a twist of lime. "On it!" he says and walks away, weaving through the crowd as Holden jumps onto the stage and says into the microphone, "Alright, everyone, grab a glass of champagne, the countdown starts in less than a minute."

"Here you go," Sergio says, handing Jeremy his drink and inserting himself in the space between Jeremy and Chadwick.

"Thank you," Jeremy says, as his shoulders relax, and his lips lift into a smile of relief.

"Sorry, that took so long. Rose had some words for me."

Jeremy, bringing his drink to his lips, says, "All good things, I hope."

"She seems to be coming around."

"I always told her you weren't so bad."

"Is that so?" Sergio asks as Holden starts the countdown from the stage with a "Ten!"

Jeremy leans in close. "It's definitely so."

"Nine!"

"Are you saying you were hoping we could start over this week?"

"Eight!"

"I'll admit it was on my mind."

"Seven!"

"What about the hereafter?"

"Six!"

"We'll have to see what tomorrow brings."

"Five!"

"And what if there is no tomorrow?"
"Four!"
"Don't be silly. There's always a tomorrow."
"Three!"
"Well, in case there isn't. I'm going to need another kiss."
"Two!"
"I think I can give you that."
"One! Happy ..."

Chapter Sixteen

"Uncle Sergio! Wake up!"

"Oof ... morning, buddy."

"*Hiss ...*"

"Dad said to come get you. Breakfast is almost ready."

With a quick swoop of his arms, Sergio grabs Henry around the middle and starts tickling his sides. "He did, did he?"

"Yes," Henry says through his laughter.

"Did he tell you to jump on the bed as well?"

"No," Henry lies, giggling.

"I think he did." Sergio teases, tickling Henry even more before he gives him a firm squeeze and pulls him into a hug. "Did you wake up your uncle Adrien yet?"

"No," Henry pants, trying to catch his breath after Sergio's tickling onslaught.

"Do you want to?"

"Yes."

"Good." Sergio lets go of him and finally sits up in bed, rubbing his face as Henry jumps off him and goes running out of the room with as much gusto as Gus—minus the hissing—and his signature enthusiastic thumbs up raised above his head. Sergio jumps off the bed after him and pokes his head out the door. "Gently!"

Still running, Henry flicks his thumbs up even higher, then bursts into Adrien's room. Sergio pauses in his doorway and listens for Adrien's sleepily uttered, "Good morning, buddy," then goes back into his room to peek out the window. When he catches sight of Jeremy coming out of the barn holding his morning mug of tea, he presses his fingers to the glass.

"I'm gonna get it right today," he says quietly. "I promise."

After holding his view of Jeremy for a few more beats, he taps his fingers on the glass one last time, then walks away and heads towards the stairs with a slight skip in his step. Today's the day. He can feel it. He knows everything he has to do, and his plan has already been put into motion by the time he steps into Holden and Rose's office at the bottom of the stairs.

The room is filled with awards and remnants of their Olympic pasts. On the wall next to Holden's first gold medal is a picture of Holden screaming his head off in his excitement as he comes to a stop at the end of his gold medal-winning run. Sergio took that picture. It launched his career when it landed on the cover of *USA Sports*.

He gives the picture a salute, then steps behind the desk and listens for the house's usual morning sounds. Holden and Rose are in the kitchen as they should be, and Adrien and Henry are still upstairs. Quickly, he turns on the computer and gets to work booking a flight. It's the last piece of the puzzle he needs to get through today and finally wake up tomorrow. He's sure of it.

Stepping out of the office, there's a skip to his step as he's feeling quite optimistic this morning, which is saying a lot for someone who has failed all too often at the simple task of getting through a New Year's Day.

"Good morning, shithead!" Holden says as Sergio enters the kitchen.

"Good morning!" Sergio says with a bright smile on his face. He bends down to pick up Gus before the cat gets a chance to get underfoot and trip him. Gus squirms and hisses, trying to escape his arms. Sergio, wanting to avoid getting the absolute shit scratched out of him, places Gus on the couch with a little pat on his head.

From where she's pulling plates out of the cabinet, Rose looks as shocked as Gus by this turn of events.

Sergio, proud of his accomplishment with the cat, beams at her. He then turns his charm up to eleven and grabs the plates from her hands. "Lemme get that," he insists, then gestures towards the table. "Sit. Get comfortable. I'll finish this."

"Thanks," she says, looking up at him with obvious suspicion before she spins around. Sergio leans back and narrowly misses the whip of her red ponytail. Although perhaps because she's still a bit surprised by his behavior with the cat, her ponytail is not quite as whiplike as he's grown used to getting smacked in the face with day in and day out.

"So, your new skater," Sergio says, placing the plates down on the table in their designated spots. "She seems really promising. I was thinking I could take some promotional pictures of her while I'm here if you'd like. Free of charge, of course."

Rose tilts her head in thought. "That actually would be nice. Since we've moved to the barn, we haven't had the same press coverage or candid moments that we normally would. Thanks, Sergio. We'll figure something out for later in the week."

"No problem," Sergio says, then goes to grab the coffeepot and four mugs that he balances by hooking them on four of his fingers to bring back to the table. He fills one of the mugs, then hands it to Rose with a wink. "Here you go."

"Thanks ...?" she says, with confusion in her voice that makes it sound more like a question. Her ice-blue eyes are only slightly narrowed at him as she grabs it.

"Sure thing," he says and pours another cup, this time holding it out to Adrien as he appears.

"You didn't poison this, did you?" Adrien asks as he carefully flips Henry around and places him down next to his seat at the table.

Sergio laughs. "Adrien, you are the last person on this earth I would want to poison."

Adrien takes a slow sip. "Doubtful."

"Seriously. I would be lost without you," Sergio says with complete sincerity. He pours another cup of coffee and places it down in Holden's spot.

"You take that. I'll drink the sludge at the bottom of the pot."

"You sure?" Sergio asks, even though he already knows what his disgusting answer will be.

"Yeah," Holden says, grabbing the pot from Sergio and pouring himself the last remnants of the coffee. He takes an exaggerated sip from his mug and smacks his lips after he swallows. "Ahh. Delicious."

"You're disgusting," Rose, Adrien, and Sergio say in unison as everyone begins to grab food, filling up their plates.

"So …" Sergio starts once everyone is eating. He takes a forkful of pancakes and chews while he waits to have everyone's attention. "I wanted to apologize for last night … well, most of yesterday, really. It wasn't my best showing."

Holden claps him on the shoulder. "Don't worry about it. It's all water under the bridge."

"To you, maybe," Sergio says, looking over at his best friend. "But I know I hurt Jeremy last night." He takes his gaze to Rose. "And you as well. So I am sorry. I'll be sure to let Jeremy know that today first chance I get."

Rose points at him with her fork, which has a piece of pineapple hanging from it. "You better," she says. "Because I'm not smoothing this one over for you."

"I wouldn't expect you to."

"What? No apology for me?" Adrien asks, eyeing Sergio over the brim of his coffee mug.

Sergio wipes his mouth with his napkin. "I owe you more than an apology," he says, nodding in Adrien's direction. "I hope by the end of the day, I'll have managed to make that clear."

"I'll be sure not to hold my breath," Adrien says and takes a loud sip of his coffee. He eyes Sergio with suspicion—a look to which Sergio has grown accustomed. A look his brother has perfected over the years from being the younger of the two. The look that implies whatever game Sergio might be playing at, he's on board even if his words say otherwise.

Rose checks her watch and rises from her seat. "I'll take the rest of this to go," she says and kisses Holden on the cheek, then heads for the back door. "You boys have fun."

"Will do!" Holden calls out after her. "We'll see you for lunch."

Alright. So far, so good, Sergio thinks. No one is fighting. No one is glaring daggers at him. And he has a full belly of food to conquer the first half of his day.

"Take shotgun," Sergio says to Adrien, holding open the passenger side door of Holden's Range Rover for him.

"Are you sure?" Adrien asks, as he climbs in, not bothering to wait for an answer.

"Yeah, I'm sure." Sergio shuts the door behind him. He smiles and taps the door panel with his fist twice, then climbs into the back seat next to Henry. With one hand, he shuts the door, and with his other, he waves Holden off, stopping him from buckling Henry in. "I've got it," he says, then winks at Henry.

Henry hard blinks back at him and starts kicking his feet in his seat.

After getting into the driver's seat, Holden turns on the car. "Who's ready for some skiing?"

"Me!" Henry yells and throws up his hands.

"Me too," Adrien says.

"Been looking forward to it all year," Sergio says, catching Holden's eyes through the rearview mirror.

Holden puts the car in reverse and looks over his shoulder at Sergio as he backs out of the garage. "I'm thrilled you're both here," he says. "I missed my brothers."

"We missed you, too," Sergio assures him.

"Yeah," Adrien says, eyes forward as he gestures with his thumb over his shoulder in Sergio's direction. "You have no idea how hard it is to wrangle this one by myself."

Holden turns back around and hits the button to close the garage door. "Way more than a full-time job, I'm sure."

"I should be getting compensated for pain and suffering," Adrien says, reaching for the radio and turning it on, bringing forth the sound of *Wicked Game*, once again through the speakers.

Sergio smiles to himself, knowing that the next hurdle of his day ends with Adrien's freedom, making his comment inconsequential. Besides, how can he be upset when this all too familiar song is accompanying the perfect moving picture Sergio has in his head of Jeremy gliding across the ice.

On the chairlift and enjoying the gorgeous view of the mountains and the trees covered in pristine white snow, Sergio is feeling confident. Not in a Sergio of old sort of way. For the first time in his adult life, his confidence isn't coming from how many people are fawning over him. This confidence is more aligned with that of a well-practiced figure skater whose muscle memory knows their routine so thoroughly that they could never trip up.

He swings his legs, causing the chairlift to rock, and he hums a very familiar tune about falling in love at the wrong time with the wrong person. Except it's no longer the wrong time, and Jeremy has never been the wrong person.

"You're oddly chipper right now," Adrien says, eyeing him out of the corner of his eye.

"Am I?"

"Yes." Adrien laughs. "You're kicking your feet like Henry and humming along to some tune in your head."

"I am? Huh, I hadn't noticed."

"Yeah, you are. And if I didn't know better, I'd think you had a crush on someone like some junior high school kid."

"Would that be so hard to believe?"

"Yes!" Adrien laughs harder this time.

Feeling happy and with Jeremy now firmly living in his brain, Sergio shrugs. "I'll prove you wrong one of these days."

"I seriously doubt that," Adrien says with a roll of his eyes that lands them to look off into the trees. Once looking away, his features shift to his usual look for this moment of deep contemplation.

Sergio pulls out his camera and snaps a picture of his brother's forlorn yet handsome profile. "For Daphne," he says as he shows it to him.

Adrien's smile is sad as he looks at the screen. "Thanks. That's a good one."

"You miss her, don't you?" Sergio asks, wondering how Adrien does it. Maintaining a long-distance relationship can't be easy. Hell, Sergio has days when he struggles with longing for Jeremy when he's only a quick jog across the property. But then again, the situation isn't quite the same. At least Daphne and Adrien have well-established and reciprocated feelings that are ever-present, no matter how many times Sergio screws up his own day.

Adrien shrugs. "I don't know," he says with a sigh. "We spend so much time apart that I think I'm always missing her. It's kind of our standard."

"It doesn't have to be."

Adrien looks at him, his expression blank and tired. "Don't tell me you have a solution."

"I think I might," Sergio says, knowing exactly what he needs to do. He's been doing it for months at this point ,when he makes it to the slopes without some disaster before breakfast.

He braces himself for the end of the lift coming and dismounts effortlessly. Together they ski to the start of the slope. Then, high above the world with the perfect view of the Adirondacks and the lakes below, Sergio turns to look at his brother. "Adrien. You know I love you, but I think it's time for you to stop working for me."

"Are you firing me?" Adrien's face lights up with a genuine smile.

"Afraid so," Sergio says and gives his brother a firm, long hug. "It's time for you to finish your book and live your own dream. Thank you for helping me achieve mine."

"It was nothing." Adrien scoffs.

"No. It was really something," Sergio says. He thumps Adrien's back three times, then pulls away. "I couldn't have done it without you."

Adrien gives a half-smile. "You could have. But I'll take your compliment anyway. Thank you."

"You're welcome," Sergio says, then turns to look down the mountain. "Race you to the bottom?"

"You're on, brother."

"Did you guys have fun?" Holden asks them as Adrien narrowly beats Sergio to the bunny hills.

"We sure did," Sergio says, skiing past Holden. He then calls over his shoulder, "I fired my brother," right as Henry is calling out to him.

"Uncle Sergio! Look!" He zooms down the hill and comes to a stop by way of his adorable forward flip onto his rump. "Did you see?"

"I saw, Henry," Sergio says, already waiting at the bottom of the little hill to pick Henry up and place him back on his feet. "That was very impressive. You're gonna be an Olympian just like your dad someday."

"Do you think I can be?" Henry asks, looking up at Sergio with wide, hopeful eyes.

"Definitely. It's in your blood. It's what you're destined to be! If that's what you want, of course."

"It is!"

"Then you will," Sergio assures and ruffles his hair before he kneels down and starts to unclip Henry's boots from his skis. Once finished, he grabs the skis in one hand and then picks Henry up with his other arm, holding him close to his body as he heads toward the lodge. "Can I ask you something, buddy?"

"Yes," Henry says and rests his head on Sergio's shoulder.

"How would you feel if I moved here?"

Henry's head whips away from Sergio's shoulder so quickly that he almost throws Sergio off balance. "Like live with me and Mommy and Daddy and Gus?"

"Don't you think that would be a bit cramped?"

"No."

"Don't you think Gus would hate that?"

Henry throws his hands up, shrugging. His lips press together in thought, and then his eyes go wide again. "Maybe you could live with Jeremy? You could stay in the barn, too."

Now that does sound enticing. Sergio tips his head. Perhaps still a bit cramped, though. That living space above the rink is little more than a studio apartment. But he can picture himself purchasing a home here. Maybe even on the same street, in the same set of woods. He could make it perfect for Jeremy. Equip it with anything and everything Jeremy might ever need. A house they could turn into a home together. Assuming he can make it out of this day with Jeremy at least on board with rekindling their old flame.

He takes a breath. He's getting ahead of himself. He still needs to actually wake up on New Year's Day. And furthermore, he needs to wake up on New Year's Day with Jeremy in his arms for any of that to be a possibility.

"I'm not sure Jeremy would want to live with me."

"He might," Henry says, then his face turns serious as he stares intently at Sergio. "If you tell him you're sorry."

"I plan to do that," Sergio promises right as he spots Jeremy carefully walking up the icy steps leading to the lodge with Rose and Allison. He places Henry back down on the ground and points to where they are.

"Careful!" he yells out to Henry the moment he takes off running.

"I know!" Henry yells back, making it to Jeremy in record time, only to be stopped by Rose's outstretched hands, preventing a collision.

"You hungry?" Holden claps him on the shoulder. "This place has a great turkey burger."

"Starved. A turkey burger sounds perfect right now."

Holden beams as if he works in the kitchen and cooks it himself. "You're going to love it."

"I'm sure I will," Sergio says, following Holden to the lodge entrance. Once there, he opens the door for Holden, then gestures with his hand for everyone else to follow.

"Thanks, Sergio," Rose says as she strides past him with Allison by her side. They're followed by Jeremy, who's holding Henry's hand. Jeremy acknowledges Sergio with a curt nod, then keeps walking.

Sergio watches him walk away, admiring the view. It has to be said, figure skating does do wonders for one's backside.

"Shut your mouth, you're drooling," Adrien teases with a thump to the back of Sergio's head as he comes to stand beside him. He follows Sergio's gaze. "It all makes sense now. You *are* a schoolboy with a crush, aren't you?"

Sergio lifts one shoulder as if to say, 'So what?' then closes the door and starts walking towards the table. "I told you I'd prove you wrong one of these days, didn't I?"

"Yeah." Adrien laughs. "But I didn't expect it to be today."

"Well, jokes on you, little brother. I am full of surprises," he says and pulls Adrien's usual chair out for him.

"Oh no," Adrien says in his ear. "I think you should take that seat."

"Hmmm ..." Sergio happily hums. "Don't mind if I do."

"Oh, I don't know if I like the look of this?" Rose says, gesturing at Sergio as he takes his seat on the other side of Jeremy.

Sergio holds up his hands. "I promise to be on my best behavior."

"And I thought we decided last night that *your* best behavior wasn't good enough." She points at him with emphasis.

"Then I'll be on Adrien's best behavior," Sergio says back to her, staring right into her eyes.

"You can trust him," Adrien says from his other side as he sits. Sergio turns to look at him, and Adrien gives him a wink that speaks volumes in a language that only Sergio and Adrien can understand. A wink that says, 'Hey, I'm rooting for you.'

Rose narrows her eyes at the two of them, then raises her eyebrow, bringing it to a sharp point. "I don't know what you two are playing at. But I do know I don't like it."

Together, they hold up their hands in a show of innocence.

"Eh, you can trust them," Holden says. "Look at their sweet faces."

Sergio and Adrien simultaneously tilt their heads slightly down, bringing their chins towards their chests and letting their eyes go wide. They look up at Rose across the table from underneath their lashes and give her matching pouts.

"You two are worse than Henry." She laughs, shaking her head as the server comes over to take their orders.

"How long are you in town?" Allison asks Adrien once their server walks away.

Interesting, Sergio thinks. *I guess it doesn't matter who she sits next to.* Not that it matters to him at all. He doesn't feel stung, as he would have been ages ago. His interest in her doesn't go beyond wishing for her success in her figure skating career. The truth is, it never has. His interest has always lain in who's sitting on his other side. Jeremy.

Finally, with this new configuration at the lunch table, Sergio figures he can let the conversations around the table unfold. Adrien can talk Allison's ear off about Daphne and Paris and Rose and Holden can join in and Sergio can hopefully have Jeremy all to himself under the cover of their boisterous conversation.

"So," Sergio says, putting the next part of his plan into motion. He gives Henry in Jeremy's lap a quick wink, and Henry hard blinks back at him before his eyes fully close and he begins to fall asleep. Sergio smiles at the sight of Henry, takes a breath, then focuses his attention on Jeremy. "I don't want to make this awkward. But I wanted to let you know how sorry I am about what I said last night. It was insensitive, and I shouldn't have said it."

"It's fine," Jeremy says with a heavy sigh, avoiding Sergio's eye contact.

"Even if it is fine," Sergio says, knowing not to push Jeremy, but also knowing better than to take him at his word. "I didn't mean to upset you."

"Honestly," Jeremy says, positioning himself to look at Sergio more directly. "I wasn't even that upset. Everyone else made such a big deal about it, I didn't really know how to react."

Sergio considers this. So much of what unfolded that night had little to do with Jeremy's reaction to Sergio's faux pas. It doesn't excuse it. Giving Jeremy a sincere apology was the right thing to do, but there's a new level of this whole situation that he's beginning to understand. Something he's familiar with himself that will help him in the future when it comes to dealing with Jeremy. He reaches over and lightly places his hand on Jeremy's forearm.

"I think I know what you mean," he says. "When our parents died, so much of mine and Adrien's time was spent navigating other people's feelings that they were having on our behalf. We never got to actually express our own emotions about it."

"Right?" Jeremy says, sounding surprised. He flips his hands up and glows with relief. "It's so weird. Ever since I got diagnosed, I've spent the bulk of my time making everyone else feel okay about it so I've never had time to figure out how I feel about it myself."

"Yep. And because of that, all you ever really feel about it is angry and resentful."

"Because you can never have an interaction with anyone ever again that isn't tainted by it."

"Exactly," Sergio says. He places his elbow on the table, then rests his head on his hand and keeps his eyes on Jeremy, admiring his face. Relaxed and at ease, like he often is on the days when they've been alone and away from everyone else's influence. "It's always there, waiting in the shadows, haunting every interaction." Sergio pauses and realizes something. "It does get better, though. Over time," he says, thinking about how over these last however many months he's been living this same day that he hasn't thought about Jeremy in relation to his having MS. Most days he forgets about it and is only ever reminded by the way everyone else treats Jeremy in his presence. "I no longer think of you as Jeremy with MS. You're just Jeremy."

"That's impressive. It only took you, what? Thirty minutes to come to that conclusion," Jeremy says, laughing. But there is no malice behind it. Somehow Sergio has broken through.

"Oh, come on, I've spent at least a solid forty-five minutes on this."

"I bet you have." Jeremy shakes his head and laughs some more. "But really. Thank you. It's honestly nice for that to not be the center of everyone's conversation."

"I promise" —Sergio crosses his heart— "to never make that the only thing there is about you to me."

Their moment is broken by uproarious laughter around the table, with Adrien leading the charge. "And then," he wheezes out. "He had to come and find me in my room wearing nothing but a hand towel."

"Serves him right," Rose says, clapping her hands together as she leans back in her chair.

"What is happening?" Jeremy asks.

"Oh, Adrien must be telling everyone about the time I slept through my hotel room being robbed in Paris," Sergio explains, laughing lightly himself.

"Oh, my god. You didn't?" Jeremy asks. His jaw has dropped open in shock.

"He sure did," Adrien says.

"They even stole my underwear. I hope they got a good price for those."

"Yes," Adrien says, wiping laugh-induced tears from his eyes. "Everyone in Paris wanted your Versace drawers."

"Wanted them or wanted to be in them," Holden adds.

"Hey!" Sergio tries to defend. "I'm trying to turn over a new leaf here."

"Oh, come on now, Sergio," Jeremy says, smirking. "Even I'm guilty of wanting to get into your Versace drawers in the past."

"In the past?" Sergio challenges.

A faint blush creeps across Jeremy's cheeks. "Are you saying you still have some?"

"I restocked my supply later that day." Sergio smirks.

"Jeremy, no," Rose scolds from his other side. "You're better than this."

"How about you let me be the judge of that for once," Jeremy says, taking his eyes from Sergio to Rose. "I'm a big boy. I can handle myself and a man in his best Versace underwear."

After lunch and wanting nothing more than to go back to the Harings' with Jeremy, Sergio restrains himself. He'll have plenty of time for Jeremy this evening, and hopefully tomorrow and the next day and the day after that and the day after that and every day from today until forever. But he'll never get there if he doesn't make it right with Rose—who is, by far, his biggest hurdle.

So with his goal of making this his last New Year's Eve—until next year that is—he bids Jeremy goodbye, resisting the urge to kiss him on the cheek. He takes one last longing look when Jeremy walks away with Henry in his arms, then turns and grabs Rose's attention. "May I take you on this first run?" he asks, holding the crook of his elbow out for her to take. He looks over the top of Rose's head towards Holden. "You don't mind if I steal your wife for a bit, do you?"

"It's your funeral," Holden says, then clicks on his skis and calls out to Adrien, "Hey, Adrien! You want to go hit that double black diamond?"

"Yeah, alright!" Adrien yells back.

"I'll be on the bunny hills," Allison says, tucking her bundle of corkscrew curls underneath a cap before she skis away.

Sergio holds his elbow out to Rose more prominently, giving it a shake. "Shall we?"

Rose rolls her eyes. "You know you don't need to escort me," she says, but loops her arm around his elbow anyway, effectively making their skiing awkward and clumsy. They manage to make it onto the chairlift with minimal effort or separation. "What's this about?"

"It's about us."

She huffs out a laugh. "There is no us, Sergio."

"Well, sure," he relents. "There is no us like there is a you and Holden. But we do have a relationship of sorts. We're more like brother and sister."

"I guess so," she says, raising one shoulder and twisting her lips to the side. She waves her arms at the chairlift their sharing, making its slow incline up the mountain. "That still doesn't explain what *this* is about."

"Maybe not. But ..." he drags the word out and looks over his shoulder at her with a half-smile. "Siblings are interesting. Did you know I fired my brother today?"

She snaps her head to look at him. "What?" she asks, surprise clear across her face.

"Yeah," he says, raising his eyebrows and shoulders.

"Damn."

Sergio nudges her with his shoulder. "You thought he'd be the one to do it, didn't you?"

"Well, yeah." She shrugs. "I'm surprised he made it this long."

"Over the last few days, that's become obvious to me as well." He angles himself in the chairlift to face her like he's about to spill the best tea. "But here's the thing. I needed to do it. I needed to fire him. I may not have originally liked the idea, but it's what's best. He's always going to be my brother, and I will always support him and love the ever-living shit out of him. This way, we can both go our own ways with our heads held high and no hard feelings."

"Okay ..." Rose says slowly. Her face is pinched like she's trying to decipher his angle. "I'm still missing your point here."

"My point is that I've basically been controlling my brother in an effort to keep him from leaving me for the last couple of years. But I can't control him any more than he can control me, and lord knows we've *both* tried and have ended up resenting each other."

"Again, still not sure what this has to do with me."

"I'm getting there, I promise," he assures her, then looks forward, checking to see that they are about halfway up the mountain. He turns back to face her and continues, "So, here's the thing. Same as how Adrien and Holden are my brothers, you are my sister."

"Well, I don't work for you. Thank God. I don't know how Adrien did it. So you can't fire me."

"Not my intention, but thank you for the reminder. And I have nothing to fire you for. Except ... maybe I do."

She looks at him with her eyebrow raised to new incredulous heights. "What on earth for?"

"As my constant critic."

"No offense, Sergio, but you need a constant critic."

"Maybe the Sergio of before did. But I don't think I do anymore."

She lets out a mocking, bitter laugh. "You officially consider yourself to be infallible?"

"Oh, god." Sergio waves her off and laughs casually, a stark contrast to her far less jovial one. "Far from it. If anything, these last ten months or so have taught me *exactly* how fallible I am."

She lowers her raised eyebrow. "I will admit, you have seemed somewhat self-aware today. Better than last night, that's for sure."

"Fully agree," he says with all seriousness. "And I do apologize for kicking this week off so poorly. Especially since I know you wanted to cancel it."

She freezes up, and her skin pales.

"Don't worry," he assures her. "I get it. You have a lot going on right now. And I need you to know I'm rooting for you. And Allison. *And* Jeremy. I'd never do anything to derail all that you've built and worked for."

"I know you wouldn't ... at least not intentionally."

"Not even accidentally. I know I've come across as a bit of a selfish prick all these years, but I promise you that's not the case."

"Well, you do have to admit, Sergio, you don't have the best track record."

"Maybe at face value, no. But come on. Do you think your husband would have kept me in his life all these years if I were a total lost cause?"

Rose's eyebrow raises again. "I love my husband, but we all know he's a bit of a himbo."

Sergio tilts his head and points his chin towards her. "The most lovable himbo I know. But the truth is, and you and I both know this, that he's not an idiot. And he has the biggest heart out of all of us."

A smile creeps across Rose's face. "He truly does. Though Henry is giving him a run for his money."

"Yeah, he is, isn't he?" He lightly taps her side with his elbow. "He's a good kid you guys got there."

"Thanks," she says, and braces for the end of the chairlift coming soon. "And you know, you're not so bad yourself. I don't always have to give you such a hard time."

"It's not like I don't deserve it. But I'm turning over a new leaf," he says and dismounts following Rose. "And part of that new leaf involves Jeremy. I want to pick back up where I started with him. Letting him go four years ago is probably my biggest regret."

She pauses her skiing at the top of the mountain, a little out of the way of the next pair coming off the lift and turns to look at Sergio again. "He is incredible, you know? The best of them all."

"That's another thing you and I agree on. And I promise you, I have the best of intentions of never hurting him again."

Rose studies him. Her gaze is thoughtful. Finally, she smiles. "You know, for some reason, I think I might actually believe you."

"Yeah?" he asks, barely able to contain his grin.

"Yeah." She turns to face the edge of the slope that looks out over the entire town of Lake Placid below them. She gives him one last look over her shoulder. "Now, don't fuck it up," she says and takes off like a bullet down the mountain.

"I won't!" he yells out after her, then follows her at a much more leisurely and joyful pace.

As Holden pulls the car into the garage after their day spent on the slopes, Rose looks over the front seat at Sergio in the back. "Can you grab Henry from Jeremy?" she asks, giving him a little wink. "I need to get cleaned up and start getting ready for tonight."

"Sure thing," Holden says.

Sergio claps Holden on the shoulder. "She was talking to me, man."

"Oh!" Holden says, surprised. "Well, this is a turn of events."

"Maybe," Sergio says with a little laugh. Then turns to look back at Rose. "Thank you," he mouths.

"You're welcome," she mouths back and gets out of the car.

Sergio opens his car door, then pauses and looks at Adrien in the seat next to him. "Wish me luck."

"Good luck," Adrien says in a mocking tone despite the fact that he's grinning. He starts pushing Sergio out of the car. "You're gonna need it. Now don't fuck it up!"

"I won't," Sergio says, closing the car door. Besides, as he's all too aware, if he does fuck it up, there's always another chance tomorrow. But then again, the last thing he wants to do is fuck this up and wake up once again with nothing but a kick in the nuts and a hissing cat on New Year's Eve morning.

Strangely, though, this part of his day is the one he's been the least worried about. Probably, because it's been the part he's spent the most time perfecting and subsequently enjoying. Who could blame him, though? What is there not to like? It's a perfect moment on a not-so-perfect day in a not-so-perfect life. If Sergio could, he would frame the time he spends in this barn on this ice with Jeremy Owens forever in a photograph that his mind can create and keep.

Feeling good about himself and Jeremy and optimistic about their future, Sergio pauses and takes a deep, steadying breath at the barn's door. Mentally, he runs through his checklist. Everything he's set in motion is going according to plan. Taking a deep breath, he opens the barn door and listens to the music that, even after hearing it countless times, floods his heart and flows through all of his senses.

Walking in, Sergio eases into a serene smile. He pauses at the rink's half wall and watches Jeremy skate and glide through his moves. He allows himself a few extra moments and beats of the music to do nothing but admire the man he's found himself hopelessly enamored with, moving across the ice with strength and simplistic grace.

Slowly, he makes his way over to the cubbies where the skates are stored and grabs a pair for himself and the little pair for Henry, then makes his way to where Henry is sitting with his eyes wide as he watches Jeremy loop around the ice. Taking care not to startle him or pull Jeremy's attention away from his skating, Sergio carefully sits beside Henry and winks as he holds up the skates. Henry nods excitedly.

Getting to work, Sergio helps Henry into his skates and laces them up, then puts on his own pair. Once they're both laced into their boots, he directs Henry's eyes back to Jeremy. "He's great out there, isn't he?"

"The best," Henry says. "After Mommy."

Sergio feels a new warmth bubble up in his heart as he repeats the words. "Yeah, after Mommy. Of course."

Careful, still not wanting to take Jeremy by too much of a surprise, Sergio steps onto the ice and holds Henry's hand to help him get his footing. Once gliding, he looks up and sees they've caught Jeremy's attention as his own skating brings him closer to where they are on the ice.

Slowing in his tracks, he gracefully spins to a stop a few feet away. A blush blooms across his cheeks. "I thought Henry was my only audience."

"Sorry," Sergio says, taking care to hold Jeremy's gaze. "I snuck in. I didn't want to disturb you. You look so good out here. Henry and I had to join."

"I didn't know you could skate." Jeremy grabs hold of Henry's other hand and helps guide him around the ice.

"I wouldn't go as far as saying I can skate, but I do alright," Sergio says. He looks over Henry, who's wobbling between them, at Jeremy. "In fact, I'm in the market for a new instructor."

Jeremy bites his lip and eyes Sergio, looking intrigued. "Is that so?"

"Yeah. Do you know anyone who might be interested?"

"Perhaps we should ask Rose if she knows anyone."

"No, Jeremy!" Henry yells. "You can teach him!"

"That does sound like a better plan," Sergio agrees.

Jeremy smiles at him and blushes a little deeper. "I guess I could find some time to add you to my schedule while you're in town."

"I promise to make it worth your while," Sergio says, making an X across his heart with his free hand.

Jeremy spins them around so that they are skating backward. He and Sergio are doing all the work, and Henry is gliding along between them, happy as can be.

"What brought you out to the barn? I expected Holden to come and grab Henry."

"I wanted to see you skate," Sergio says, his tone of voice serious, leaving no room for misinterpretation.

"You're about four years too late," Jeremy says and looks away. "I'm afraid I'm not too much to look at anymore."

"That's not true," Sergio says, slowing them to a stop in the middle of the rink. He continues to hold Henry steady with one hand, then grabs hold of Jeremy's free hand with his other so they form a circle. "No matter how many times I see you skate, you never stop amazing me."

Jeremy lets go of Sergio's hand and tugs at his left eye. "You're only saying that."

"No." Sergio shakes his head and resists the urge to reach for Jeremy again. *Not yet*, he tells himself. *Don't rush him*. "I could watch you every day for the rest of my life and never tire of seeing you on the ice. You look ... free."

Jeremy looks at him with his bottom lip trapped between his teeth again. "I guess I am."

"I wish you could see how you look on the ice."

"That's one of the perks of this place," Jeremy says. He gestures around the rink. The inside, same as the outside, looks like a barn made entirely of wood. "There isn't a reflective surface other than the ice itself in here."

Sergio glides closer to Jeremy, working to close their circle again. "Still, I wish you could see what I see."

Jeremy swallows and moves a little bit closer. "And what's that?"

Sergio brings his palm to Jeremy's cheek and uses his thumb to gently tug at the corner of Jeremy's eye. "Strong and beautiful."

Jeremy doesn't pull away. Sergio lets go of Henry's hand, trusting Jeremy to maintain his grip, keeping Henry upright. He brings his hand to Jeremy's other cheek and cups his face. With that gentle grip, he closes the small gap between them entirely, bringing them chest to chest. He places a gentle kiss on his lips and sighs softly when Jeremy kisses him back. Chaste and simple, a reward marking an official fresh start.

Breathless, Jeremy pulls his lips slightly away from Sergio's. "I hate to do this, but I really should start getting ready for the party."

Sergio brushes his cheekbones with his thumbs. "Alright," he says and rubs their noses together. "But if you think I'm waiting until midnight for another kiss from you, you're crazy."

"I wouldn't expect you to." Jeremy kisses him again.

"So ..." Sergio lets go of his cheeks, then grabs his hand again. "Can I ask you to be my date tonight?"

"I thought that was already implied?"

"Are you two done yet?" Henry huffs, dropping his head back, which knocks him off balance and sends him laughing as he crashes onto the ice on his butt. Jeremy luckily let go of his hand in the process, keeping them both from going down.

Sergio and Jeremy share one last longing glance before Jeremy takes his attention back to Henry. "Sorry, Henry," Jeremy says, pulling him back to his feet. "I didn't realize we were holding you up."

"Grown-ups spend too much time kissing," Henry says. He lets go of Jeremy's hand and skates away from them with his arms flailing and his feet slipping on the ice like a chaotic cannonball.

"I'll argue we haven't spent nearly enough time kissing yet," Jeremy says and re-grabs Sergio's hand as they skate, following Henry. He calls after him, "Sit on the ledge, Henry!"

"I know!" Henry yells back. "Blades stay on the ice."

"I'll help him," Sergio says, quickening his pace to catch up with Henry. He sits on the low ledge and pulls Henry into his lap so he can help him out of his skates while Jeremy puts his blade guards on and steps off.

"What time are we leaving?" Jeremy asks, grabbing hold of Henry's skates one by one when Sergio hands them to him.

"Holden says we're leaving a little before eight," Sergio says by memory. He starts taking off his own skates. "We have to drop Henry off at the Weirs' on the way there."

"Okay. I'll meet you up at the house in a bit, then."

"I'll be waiting for you." Sergio rises to his feet with his skates in hand and steps into his shoes.

"Are you two gonna start kissing again?" Henry asks with an exaggerated sigh.

"Yes," Sergio says and places one last kiss on Jeremy's lips before he bends down and picks Henry up. "Okay, we're done now. Are you happy?"

Henry shrugs. "I'm always happy."

Sergio laughs and ruffles Henry's hair. "Yeah, buddy. We noticed." He takes his gaze back to Jeremy. "We'll see you in a bit," he says and walks away, leaving the barn and heading back to the main house with a lot of extra skip in his step. There are only a few more hours to go on what is shaping up to be the most perfect day of not only these New Year's Eves, but his life.

"Mommy!" Henry yells at Rose the moment they enter the main house through the back door. Rose looks over at him from where she is standing in the kitchen fully decked out in her New Year's Eve party dress. She's using the kitchen counter for stability as she steps into her stilettos. "Uncle Sergio and Jeremy were kissing!"

"Is that so?" Rose says, one perfectly sculpted eyebrow raised at Sergio. However, unlike her usual eyebrow raise, this one isn't harsh and judging. It has more of an air of knowing, as if she is officially in on a joke. Which she is. Though it is no joke.

"Yes!" Henry confirms and runs away. "I'm gonna go tell Daddy!"

"You can tell your Uncle Adrien too, if you'd like," Sergio yells out after him and receives two very enthusiastic thumbs up raised as high in the air as Henry's arms can hold them.

Rose stands and pops open a bottle of champagne. She pours a small glass for Sergio, then one for herself. "That went well today, huh?"

"More than well." Sergio holds up his glass to her.

She clinks it. "You better not screw this up."

"I wouldn't dream of it."

Sergio is beaming, shining like a star from where he stands at the far corner of the bar at the Grand Olympian Hotel, watching in reverie as the New Year's Eve party becomes effervescent and alive with the who's who of Lake Placid elites. Millionaire sports stars and businesspeople all mingle together, glad-handing and verbally promising endorsements or appearances or soliciting sponsorships with the new talent looking to make names for themselves at the upcoming Olympic Games.

But that's not what Sergio is smiling about. Though he will be doing his part to make sure that Allison lands on the right pages of the right magazines, it's her coach who has him smiling so brightly. He's barely let Jeremy out of his sight since they got here. And even now, while he orders another whiskey for himself and a sparkling water with a twist of lime for Jeremy, he keeps the man in his view. He watches Jeremy, Rose, and Allison talk with a group of sports reporters who are listening intently to what they have to say. Granted, like always, Rose is doing most of the talking, but that does allow Sergio to make eye contact with Jeremy and give him a little wink that makes Jeremy's blush glow from across the room.

"Looks like you've pulled it off," Adrien says, sliding into the space beside him.

Sergio holds up his fingers and crosses them. "I sure hope I did."

"I honestly never thought I'd see the day." Adrien gestures to the bartender to make him another gin and tonic. "But I have to admit, when you two first met years ago, I was rooting for it. I think he's good for you."

"I think so, too," Sergio says and checks his watch. It's getting quite close to midnight, and his last piece to hopeful success should be walking through the door at any moment. When he looks up, the bartender is dropping off their drinks. Sergio slides him a rather large tip, then looks at his brother. "You might want to grab a glass of champagne."

"Nah." Adrien scoffs and takes a sip of his drink. "You know that stuff gives me a headache."

"You, maybe," Sergio says, looking rather pleased with himself. "But someone else ..." he drags out the word and redirects Adrien's attention to the party's entrance. "Like Daphne, might prefer it."

Adrien's entire face lights up, and he practically chokes on his drink as Daphne, standing in the doorway, lifts her hand and gives him a demure wave. She looks like royalty in her red chiffon dress paired with a short black dress coat over her shoulders and her brown hair pulled back into a perfect chignon. Adrien waves back and grabs one of the complimentary glasses of champagne. He stops on his way to her only to ask Sergio, "Did you do this?"

Sergio nods. "I didn't want you to be alone when the clock strikes twelve."

"Thank you," he says and leans in to give Sergio the best hug he can when they're both laden with drinks in their hands.

"You're welcome. Now, go get your girl. She's had quite the day of last-minute travel to get here." Adrien practically takes off at a run to greet Daphne, and Sergio feels a rush of happiness for him.

With his brother ecstatic due to the sudden and unexpected arrival of the love of his life, Sergio balances his and Jeremy's drinks in one hand and then grabs two glasses of champagne with his other. He takes a quick look at Jeremy; he's still doing alright with Rose, Allison, and the reporters, but Chadwick Levinson is beginning to lurk around the corner trying to grab Allison's attention. Sergio is quick to make his way expertly through the crowd and across the room. He dodges all the guests with practiced ease and manages not to spill a drop of the drinks he's holding by the time he arrives at the group.

"Here," he says, starting with Jeremy, handing him his sparkling water.

"Thanks," Jeremy says, stepping out of the throng of reporters while Sergio passes a glass of champagne to Allison and then one to Rose.

"I'm not interrupting, am I?" Sergio asks, knowing full well that Jeremy is more than happy to have a reason to step away from the circus.

"No." Jeremy laughs. "Even when I was competing, talking to reporters was my least favorite part."

"Least favorite after having your picture taken."

"Well, they do tend to go hand-in-hand," Jeremy says, swirling his drink with his straw.

"You know, you've never told me. What is *your* favorite part of skating?"

Jeremy tilts his head to the side and smiles softly. "There's a moment," he says, then takes a sip of his drink. "In every skater's program, if you watch them carefully enough, you can see their faces light up in relief. It's the moment when all the major jumping elements are completed, and the music is ramping up with its final crescendo, and the skater can be free to skate in that moment like someone took their leash off. To finally enjoy the crowd and the stage and spotlight following them around. That final footwork sequence that carries a skater from one end of the rink to the other with unbridled joy is the best moment there ever is in any skater's program. It's what it's all about. It's where we all truly shine and showcase who we are as individuals with personalities that aren't tied to how well you can perform a trick. That was always my favorite part."

"It's the part you do now every time you step on the ice," Sergio says. "I saw it in you today."

"That's simply me playing around." Jeremy tugs at his left eye.

"It isn't playing around." Sergio gives Jeremy a knowing half-smile. "Whether competing in the Olympics or skating in Holden and Rose's barn, you do it because you love it. Because it's who you are. It's in your blood."

Jeremy smiles, lifts one shoulder towards his ear, and looks at Sergio thoughtfully as he says, "Maybe it is."

With their eyes locked on each other, they both take another sip of their drinks. While sharing a comfortable moment of silence, Holden jumps on the stage, grabbing everyone else's attention. "Alright, everyone," he says into the microphone. "Grab a glass of champagne, the countdown starts in less than a minute."

Holding his gaze, Jeremy steps closer to Sergio, making the world around them fall away. His lips quirk up into a smile. "When did you get so observant?"

Sergio takes a step closer and leans in to speak directly into Jeremy's ear. "When you gave me a reason to focus on someone other than myself."

"I'm kind of like your inspiration, then?" Jeremy asks right as Holden yells "Ten!" from the stage.

"Inspiration and more."

"Nine!"

"How much more?"

"Eight!"

"As much as you'll let me have."

"Seven!"

"What if I want to give you all of me?" Jeremy turns his head, so their lips are almost brushing.

"Six!"

Sergio circles his arm around Jeremy's waist. "Then I promise to grab on and never let you go."

"Five!"

"And what if I said I never wanted to let you go, either?"

"Four!"

"Then I would say we are a perfect match."

"Three!"

"Perfect enough for a New Year's kiss?"

"Two!"

"To start," Sergio says and brings their lips together as he holds on tight.

"One! Happy New Year!"

Chapter Seventeen

"Uncle Sergio! Wake up!"

Sergio's eyes open quickly. He turns and braces himself for Henry's typical morning slam into his balls. But instead, he sees Henry stopping in his tracks, skidding on his heels on the carpeted floor.

"What's Jeremy doing here?" Henry asks with huge, mind-blown eyes.

"I was trying to get some much-needed sleep," Jeremy says, reaching his hand out from under the covers to ruffle Henry's hair.

"But you sleep in the barn," Henry says. His head tilts to the side. Sergio can practically see him doing the mental math of how Jeremy ended up in Sergio's bed instead of his own above the ice rink.

"Told you we should have gone back to your place last night," Sergio mumbles against Jeremy's neck.

"At least he didn't wake us with a kick in the balls," Jeremy whispers to him.

"Thank god." They both chuckle, and Sergio lifts his head off the pillow. He takes his attention to Henry, who looks like he's still genuinely confused. "Let me guess," he says. "Breakfast is almost ready?"

"Yeah! How'd you know?"

"Just a hunch."

"Did you wake up your Uncle Adrien yet?"

"Nope. You first!"

"Because I'm your favorite?"

"No. Because I like to let Uncle Adrien sleep more."

Jeremy stifles a laugh with his hand, and Sergio lays his head back down on the pillow. "That's fair," he says, then lifts his head back up quickly, remembering that Adrien is also not alone in his bed. "Maybe knock on Uncle Adrien's door instead of bursting through."

"Okay!" Henry yells and runs out of the bedroom with two very enthusiastic thumbs up held high over his head. His footsteps thunder down the hallway.

"You were right," Jeremy says, spinning in Sergio's arms to lie face to face with him. "We should have at least locked the door last night."

"Yeah, but then we wouldn't have gotten to see his face."

"Those wide eyes. I can't with him," Jeremy says as he nestles in a little closer to Sergio.

"He is awfully cute." Sergio brings his hand to Jeremy's face and cups his cheek with his palm, letting his thumb swipe slowly across his cheekbone. "But he's not as cute as you."

Jeremy rolls his eyes. "Oh, shut up. You already got me in bed with you. No need to keep being a sap."

Sergio laughs and leans in closer. He brushes his nose against Jeremy's. "I'm afraid that might be my default now."

"I guess I can get used to it," Jeremy says and kisses him as a slight rumbling comes from the space between the pillows and the headboard.

"Jeremy? Are you purring?"

"No." Jeremy laughs against his lips. "That's Gus. He always sleeps with me when I spend the night."

Sergio's eyes shoot open again. Even larger than they were when Henry announced his morning arrival. "Gus? As in Rose's assassin cat, Gus?"

Jeremy reaches a hand above them and pets the cat lodged and resting somewhere within the mass of pillows. "He's no assassin. He's sweet."

"Easy for you to say. This is the first day I've ever woken up here where he didn't hiss at me and then fly out of the room like a bullet."

"That's hardly an assassination attempt," Jeremy points out.

"Give it time. He'll try to trip me before the day is through."

"He's checking your reflexes," Jeremy says and extricates himself from Sergio's hold to sit upright in bed. Once there, he pulls Gus into his lap and the cat immediately curls into a ball, purring even louder.

"I'll take your word for that," Sergio says, trying not to be jealous of the cat. However, since Gus isn't hissing at him or even giving him his usual cat side eye, Sergio will take that as a win.

Getting out from underneath the covers, Sergio gathers his clothes from the floor. Thankfully, Henry didn't get more of an eyeful than he needed. Not that Sergio or Jeremy fell asleep fully nude, but Sergio figures seeing your uncle and his new boyfriend—no matter how familiar Henry may already be with said boyfriend—isn't exactly the best way for a five-year-old to spend their New Year's morning. Sergio shrugs on his shirt, then digs in his bag for a clean shirt and a spare pair of sweatpants for Jeremy to put on.

"Here you go," he says, tossing them onto the bed beside Jeremy.

"Thanks," Jeremy says as he puts on the shirt then gives Gus one last scratch to the space between his ears before rising to put the pants on. He pulls the drawstring tight to cinch them to fit his slimmer frame. "What do you think Holden made for breakfast today?"

Sergio steps into a pair of sweatpants as well. "My guess, pancakes and bacon. Maybe some sliced fruit as well."

"That does seem to be his specialty." Jeremy smiles, steals a kiss, then walks out the door. Gus jumps off the bed and follows behind him before Sergio has a chance to get his feet moving. There is, after all, a part of him that is still amazed he's finally woken up here on New Year's Day. He was pinching himself all night after he finally saw the clock move past midnight. He clutched Jeremy at his side for the rest of the party, worried if he let go for even a second, the time gods—or whoever it was that reset his day every day for the last ten months—was going to snatch his future away once again. A future he desperately wants to begin today.

"Wait up!" he yells and runs to catch Jeremy at the stairs. He grabs his hand so they can walk down together.

"Be careful," Jeremy says on the first step. "I hear there's a murderous cat around here."

"He usually tries to murder me in the kitchen," Sergio explains.

"Ah, more sharp objects. I see his thought process. Though I must admit, the staircase makes for a better explanation of an"—he brings his free hand up to make one air quote—"accident."

"Well, he is a cat after all. We can't fault him for not having the best thought-out murder plots."

"Yeah. That's my job," Adrien says from the top of the stairs where he and Daphne have appeared.

"You can't still be out for my blood after yesterday, can you?" Sergio asks. "I fired you and flew your girlfriend out via private jet to spend the rest of the holidays with you. Surely I've earned a reprieve."

"You're my brother. I'll always be trying to murder you." Adrien sneaks up behind him at the bottom of the stairs and pushes himself and Daphne past. He looks over his shoulder at Sergio. "Lovingly, of course."

"Of course," Sergio agrees, laughing and glad to see that after everything, he and Adrien are back to how they should be. Brothers who tease but love each other unquestioningly, no matter what.

"Brothers are so weird," Jeremy says, shaking his head as they all step into the kitchen where Holden is toiling away at the stove with Henry watching intently from a step stool.

"Aren't they, though?" Rose agrees, then takes her attention from the coffee she's pouring to the group as they enter. She starts blindly passing out full mugs, one of which Sergio notices is full of tea instead of coffee, which she hands directly to Jeremy. "Do you have any siblings?" she asks Daphne.

"I have three sisters. All we do is share clothes," Daphne says with her thick French accent.

"I wish my sister and I were the type of sisters who share clothes," Rose says with a sigh before she takes a sip of her coffee.

"I guess those are the only sibling options then, huh?" Adrien says thoughtfully. "It's either murder siblings or clothes sharing siblings."

"Well, looking at these two," Rose pauses and gestures at Sergio and Jeremy. "Whatever Sergio may have missed by not having a clothes-sharing sibling, he's making up for now by sharing with Jeremy."

"Am I ever." Sergio smirks like the devil and pulls Jeremy into his arms for a quick kiss in front of everyone. He playfully pats Jeremy on the butt when they pull away. "Besides, he does fill them out nicely."

"You're disgusting," Rose says and gestures for everyone to take a seat at the table that she's already set. As they all sit down, she moves to where Henry is and picks him up from underneath his armpits, swings him around a bit to his glee, then places him in his seat. She goes to the fridge and grabs a bottle of champagne and a pitcher of orange juice, then stops by Holden to give him a kiss on his cheek. He beams. His smile is like sunshine as he grabs a giant, covered serving plate of what he's been cooking for breakfast and brings it to the table.

"What do you have for us today?" Sergio asks, then takes a sip of his coffee.

"I thought I'd try something new this morning." He holds the platter out in front of him, then removes the lid with a flourish. "Eggs Benedict!"

Henry pulls a face. "What's eggs bend-a-dick?"

The whole table bursts out laughing, even Daphne, who tries to hide it by bringing her hand to her mouth. Her eyes crinkle with happiness.

Holden brings another plate and places it down in front of Henry. "Don't worry, champ." He ruffles Henry's hair. "I made pancakes just for you."

"Uh, Henry," Adrien says, leaning in towards him. "Want to trade?"

"No!" Henry yells at the same time Holden yells, "Hey!"

Adrien starts laughing again.

"I'm not sure if I should be insulted or not." Holden brings his hand to his chest.

"You do make excellent pancakes," Sergio says.

"The best," Jeremy agrees.

"And I'm sure your eggs Benedict are good as well," Daphne says.

"I knew I liked her," Holden says, pointing at Daphne as he takes his seat.

Adrien leans into her and loudly places a kiss on her cheek. He's grinning as he pulls away, his eyes admiring her profile. "Damn right, you do," he says. "We all do."

As everyone begins to fill their plates with food, Rose pops open the champagne. She pours them each a mimosa, except for Jeremy. She gives him a champagne flute full of orange juice, and Henry gets his juice in a little glass. Once everyone has their drinks in hand, Sergio raises his into the air with one hand and puts his other arm around Jeremy, pulling Jeremy into his side.

"I'd like to propose a toast," he says, then looks at each of them one by one. His heart swells at the sight of all of them together around the table on this morning of new beginnings. It starts to rise into his throat, causing a lump he swallows down. He settles his gaze on Adrien first, then begins to speak again. "When our parents died, I remember thinking that that was it. That I'd never have another family because the one I'd always known was gone and couldn't be repaired. That Adrien and I were utterly alone."

"You do know toasts are supposed to be uplifting?" Adrien jokes, but he's wearing a soft smile, and his eyes portray a solemn hint of understanding.

"I'm getting there."

Holden claps Sergio on the shoulder. "I'm with you, buddy."

"Thanks," Sergio says to him, then continues. "Now, as I was saying, at the time, I never could have imagined *this*." He lifts his hand from

Jeremy's shoulder and gestures at the table. "Honestly, up until yesterday, I never thought my life could be so full. Or that Adrien and I could have so many people around us who accepted us as theirs. It's been me and Adrien against the world for so long that I missed the fact we had managed to create a whole new family. It started with Holden, and then he brought in Rose. Together they gave us all Henry." Henry beams with a mouth full of syrupy pancakes. "And for whatever reason, Daphne stuck with that one" —he points at Adrien—"despite his innumerable charms."

"He does have a lot of charms," Daphne agrees and kisses him on the cheek, causing Adrien to glow.

"He does," Sergio says, then turns his attention to Jeremy. "And then there's you. Jeremy, I should have incorporated you into this makeshift family years ago. Luckily for me, Rose and Holden brought you in instead and gave us the chance to pick up where we started." He leans in and gives Jeremy a kiss, then turns and raises his glass a little higher. "To the seven of us," he says. "May we always keep the faith in each other and never forget that a family can be remade and built stronger than ever before. Happy New Year."

"Happy New Year," everyone at the table says in unison.

Even Gus lets out a meow from somewhere underneath Sergio's feet.

Acknowledgements

I'd like to begin by apologizing to Alex, Tina, and the editing team at Rising Action. Perhaps the biggest issue with writing a time loop that no one thinks about is that if I made one error in the text, I made it 300 times. I'm sure that by Chapter 13 everyone was tired of fixing my apostrophes over and over again. Correcting my grammar and spelling turned out to be your mini loops. I owe you each a hot tub. Or at least that's what Holden recommends.

Thank you to Sarah and Jess. The two of you have been spearheading Sergio, Jeremy, and the rest of the gang since the moment I began writing this series. Both of you are amazing beta readers, and even better friends. Your continued support is greatly appreciated. Perhaps once the last book comes out, the three of us can each get a time loop as much-needed treats.

Once again, Lucy at Cover Ever After, you nailed the artwork for the cover of this book! Thank you for bringing Sergio and Jeremy to life. I can't wait to see what you do with the rest of the crew as the next two books come out.

For this next one, I'm going to go back in time a bit and give a shout-out to my old figure skating coaches. We've lost touch over the years, but I have forgotten none of you. There was JoAnne, Leslie, Cammile, Pearla, and yes, just like for Jeremy, Mrs. B. If I could go back in time, I wouldn't hesitate to go back to a day spent in the rink with all of you.

Speaking of rink time, I'd like to acknowledge my parents who gave up a lot—mostly sleep and gas money—to cart me around the Midwest whether it was for twice-daily practices or weekend competitions. I hope those years weren't as monotonous for you as Sergio's New Year's Eves.

Lastly, to the love of my life. There is nobody else in this world I'd rather spend every day with, in or out of a time loop. But also thank the gods neither of us was as much of a knucklehead as Sergio when we first met, and we could get together without either of us needing to experience a karmic lesson.

About the Author

K.C. Carmichael is an American author who writes romantic comedies. She is an ex-hairstylist who spent her time behind the chair not only styling her clients' hair but also listening to their stories and sharing her own observations about the beauty and hilarity of life and love. She lives in Chicago, where she holds two controversial opinions about her beloved city: that winter is the superior season, and the actual Chicago-style pizza is pan pizza cut into squares for easy sharing. *Boystown Heartbreakers* was her debut novel. The next in the This Is the Day series, *300 Valentine's Days*, is releasing in Autumn 2026.